~

SEAN STAMOS:
THE MANCHURIAN MARKET

~

An Epic Espionage Thriller Series

Acknowledgement

I am blessed to have had many thoughtful teachers in my life. To those that have nurtured the creativeness that I possess today, I thank you. To those who have shown me that there are narrow-minded paths in life that I should not take, I thank you as well, with hints of bitter and sweet.

I did not get here alone.

SEAN STAMOS:
THE MANCHURIAN MARKET

by

Brent W. Laartz, MD

CARIBE ID

PUBLISHING

FLORIDA ● NEW YORK ®

Publisher: CARIBE ID, LLC

ISBN-13: 978-0-9982054-3-4
Publisher: Caribe ID, LLC

For information on distribution, translations, or bulk sales, please contact Caribe ID, LLC directly:
Caribe ID, LLC
PO Box 75304
Tampa, FL 336175

Library of Congress Cataloging
Library of Congress Control Number: 2022903335
Laartz, Brent W
Sean Stamos: The Manchurian Market
ISBN 978-0-9982054-2-7 (hardback), 978-0-9982054-3-4 (paperback), 978-0-9982054-4-1 (epub), 978-0-9982054-5-8 (audio)

www.DrLaartz.com
https://www.linkedin.com/in/brent-w-laartz-md/
Ig: @brentwlaartzmd

Contents

CHAPTER 1: THE MESSAGE 1

CHAPTER 2: NATALIA .... .13

CHAPTER 3: BOOMING MARKETS .... .27

CHAPTER 4: UNCLE NIKOLAI .... .35

CHAPTER 5: DARLING OF THE OXFORD BLUE .... .43

CHAPTER 6: FOR MOTHER RUSSIA .... .51

CHAPTER 7: AC75 SAILING .... .61

CHAPTER 8: SEAN STAMOS .... .69

CHAPTER 9: NEW OPS .... .77

CHAPTER 10: THE TARGETS .... .85

CHAPTER 11: DETOUR .... .93

CHAPTER 12: THE MEETING .... .99

CHAPTER 13: DARK TRADES .... .109

CHAPTER 14: CRETE .... .117

CHAPTER 15: THE DEMANDS .... .123

CHAPTER 16: CAT AND ARTI .... .131

CHAPTER 17: GETTING TO THE POINT .... .137

CHAPTER 18: IDA .... .145

CHAPTER 19: MEANWHILE, THE SURVEILLANCE .... .151

CHAPTER 20: MUNICH .... .155

CHAPTER 21: READY .... .165

CHAPTER 22: TAKE CARE OF IT .... .169

CHAPTER 23: COORDINATED TRADES .... .175

CHAPTER 24: JIGNESH .... .181

CHAPTER 25: DOUBLED .... .191

CHAPTER 26: FIGHT AND FLIGHT .... .199

CHAPTER 27: ROAD RAGE .... .205

CHAPTER 28: SAFE .... .213

CHAPTER 29: THE PLAN .... .217

CHAPTER 30: GUINEVERE .... .225

CHAPTER 31: ROGUE .... .231

CHAPTER 32: RECORD HIGHS .... .237

CHAPTER 33: ACE IN THE HOLE .... .241

CHAPTER 34: MASSACRE .... .249

CHAPTER 35: ANOTHER ATTACK .... .255

CHAPTER 36: THE BIG ONE .... .261

CHAPTER 37: SPIRALING .... .267

CHAPTER 38: FAILURE .... .271

CHAPTER 39: REDIRECTION .... .277

CHAPTER 40: AMERICA'S CUP .... .281

*I dedicate this figment of my imagination to my children.
May they ever explore their minds to create more for the
world than they take from it.*

~

CHAPTER 1: THE MESSAGE

~

Another gusty, blustery evening began innocently enough with the usual chill in the air and the comradery of racing among these fellow Britons. But the next few minutes would change the world and every nation's economy forever with what would unfold as the most treasonous acts ever committed. Porter "Chip" Merlin had just finished devouring an overflowing dish of shepherd's pie, albeit with too much gravy and not enough peas and carrots to his liking, and a Goddard's at The Yachtsman. With tacit approval, the bartender had graciously begun to pour Chip's next pint of ale from the tap and the head looked deliciously refreshing, overflowing the lip of the glass like a beer commercial.

"Thanks, James. As always, your company and your nosh and bevvies fill the tummy and warm the soul." Chip's nightly effusive compliments of James' bartender skills were not idle banter, for the two had known each other since they were toddlers here on this tiny, British island, the Isle of Wight. Being born to quite opposite family circumstances did not inhibit their friendship over the years.

Not so unexpectedly, the text that came to Chip's phone was a delightful change to the beer and rain-soaked clientele that night. Ahh, Natalia, he mused to himself, what juicy morsel have you for me tonight? He extracted his phone from his pocket, took note of the notification on the screen, and set it face down on the bar beside his pint glass. He looked up from his phone, glancing around the room as he daydreamed about his dearest friend in the world; however, the glum atmosphere was not so conducive to the reminiscence of his oh-so-beautiful Natalia. The pub was full of salty, older sailors who were relishing the respite from the chill of the spring polar easterlies that had unexpectedly arisen overnight. That day's tempestuous practice had worn out even the hardiest sailors as they prepared for the weekend's racing. There was not much conversation among them tonight, just the usual small talk among the fiercely competitive yachtsmen.

Appreciating the break in the awkward silence, James weighed in, adding his trademark jovial input, for he had not taken part in the frigid, stormy activities. "You old salts needed a bit of warmth to ward away the chill that you undoubtedly feel deep down in the bones tonight, ole chap," exclaimed the best bartender on the island. Chip always said James had a way of pouring drinks for the soul, purging the beasts from one's life, and bringing out the best in everyone.

It was here, across the centuries-old varnished white oak bar top from James, surrounded by ancient, rough timbers and red brick sanctuary, that Chip had always come to bear his conscience with James. They had spent many an evening, often just the two of them in this cozy, dimly lit, tavern, discussing world events, Natalia, and anything else that bubbled up from the consciousness, frequently enhanced by whiskey or beer. Chip could trust James, for they were both raised on the island, best friends for the vast majority of their lives, and while James never graduated secondary school, Chip knew he possessed more intelligence than many of his Oxford classmates.

As was the norm, after one more refreshing draft, he would head home to prepare for the next day's business. Though a stereotypically gregarious Brit, he was equally at home strategizing in a corporate board room as he was traveling the world, networking for the family business empire. As a Merlin, wherever he trekked around the globe, a fairytale-like aura surrounded him about the possible magic or witchcraft he might wield on acquaintances. Entrenched in his character, he did not resist or disavow the mystical persona, often encouraging it with a few choice, perhaps exaggerated tales of adventure or those of his ancestors.

Chip was privileged to have one of the last few real houses overlooking the port entrance of Southampton. The historic house was stuffy but had been in his family for generations as the Merlins were seafaring folk long before the Viking era. It was certainly more comfortable and less isolated than the Merlin Castle on the south end of the island which he rarely visited. Besides, this location allowed him easier access to his real passion in life at the Royal Yacht Squadron. Both the house and the castle had the same mystical aura about them, and for this reason, along with family history, both were on the list of the most famous haunted houses in England.

He lived there most weekends of late spring and summer and would often commute by helicopter from his palatial accommodations in Westminster near Trafalgar Square. Luckily, the waterfront mansion was within walking distance from the club which would have come in handy on any usual Thursday night after a long week in London. However, with the weather the way it was tonight, he knew that his driver would be waiting for him for an easier means home. Most of the year, on weekdays he would remain in London preparing and editing the weekend articles at the Times, though with his status, he could take care of most of these responsibilities remotely from any of the Merlin properties around the world. But this was no ordinary weekend, and this was no ordinary time in the South of England.

After all, the Admiral's Cup was this weekend and it was only six weeks until the America's Cup World Series that would be the beginning of a world event, and the culmination in the finals of the America's Cup next year would fatefully be in his backyard. He was looking forward to bringing the race to the Channel in all its glory. The very first America's Cup, at that time named the Guinea Cup, was hosted by his family and the Royal Yacht Squadron on the Solent, a particularly windy stretch of ocean on the southern tip of England. This

Admiral's Cup would help determine the crew and which of their three seventy-five-foot prototype sailboats would be the number one entry for the America's Cup next year. He had just returned from Sardinia where his team had performed remarkably well and could very well take the whole World Series. Their campaign with these vessels was well funded with old English money, with a minority interest from foreign sponsors.

Chip's generational wealth was hidden well by his charm and nonchalant mannerisms. It was known throughout the Isle that this sole heir to Merlin Commerce, one of the world's largest shipping and logistics companies, could live anywhere and do anything he wanted, yet embraced the Isle as his only home. As a child, he was very sociable and always in the know regarding goings-on in Cowes and the Isle of Wight. His Aunt Elizabeth ran the local paper hence, as a teenager, he frequented the press offices and even helped write some articles when he was on the island. He also took a keen interest in the financial running of the Merlin empire. Thus, it was no surprise to his boarding schoolteachers that he chose to study economics and journalism in college. Like all Merlins before him, he was shipped off to boarding school at St Edward's School and then Oxford University. As was traditional, he excelled at both rowing and sailing while at Oxford, and during his younger years, crewed on multiple America's Cup challenging teams from various countries.

However, in the last several years he had been an integral part of an organizing effort to bring the Cup back to England, and he and his college racing buddies from across the Solent in Portsmouth finally had a valid challenger to win the Cup, the first time since before Chip could remember. As a matter of fact, 1964 was the last time there was an English challenger for the Cup, and an English team had never come close to winning the Cup, though it all began in the British Isles almost two hundred years ago. A few years past his world-class crewing days, for this campaign, he had been chosen as a tactician, advisor, and sometimes skipper of this AC75 class yacht from Great Britain. These ultra-fast hydrofoil yachts required a technical specialist as a skipper and Chip's beautiful J-boats in his fleet were not quite the same in the tactical sense. However, if there was one thing he was an expert at other than economics, it was the finicky wind in the Mediterranean and here on the Solent, which would decidedly be a home course for Chip's team of racers. No expense was spared in this effort, and the Merlin Commerce team had been a big sponsor of the billion-dollar effort to bring the cup back to this great island nation.

Both avid racers, Chip and Natalia Volkov were the best of friends and occasional lovers in a seesaw relationship while in college at Oxford. Neither wanted a serious relationship but their personalities were so identical it amazed their friends that they were not brother and sister. They both graduated as vale-dictorians at the famed Balliol College at Oxford, identically studied Economics and Journalism, and were equally strong in rowing and sailing. Their families were likewise intertwined for centuries in the shipping industry as fierce competitors on the open sea. Carrying on the tradition, they each represented their respective countries in the 2004 Olympics in the 470 class, which were simple yet very fast, sleek boats in any wind.

They kept in touch in a more than casual way after col-lege, and tonight was no different than any other night. Nata-lia would usually start the text conversation and Chip would dutifully ignore his phone until the middle of the evening, just after dinner. He would reluctantly remove his phone from his pocket to gauge what good bit of trouble Natalia was up to. It was difficult to keep up with each new travel adventure or interesting avenue of research she had embarked upon. If truth be told, there had always existed a twinge of jealousy in his psyche as she lived the free-spirited life of a journalist specializing in developing world economies.

Tonight, Chip had two theories rambling through his mind, as he took the last swallow of fine English ale and held the curved pint glass up to the blue light in the bar, seemingly inspecting its quality. Natalia was either going to announce another new trip to Bangkok or Vietnam on an economic development mission, or she was going to run a new finan-cial data research project by him for advice. Nonetheless, his thoughts kept returning to last summer's relaxing vacation together, and he was hoping that a third option would be for her to suggest a return trip to his family's mountain-top chalet in the Swiss Alps near Chamonix.

Chip finally set the now-empty pint glass down on the bar and again stared at his phone sitting there beckoning him from atop the bar. Placing his fingerprint on the screen, he tapped the notification to satisfy his curiosity. As expected, after the initial "Hi," that he first saw several minutes ago, it was, "Can I run some algorithms by you that are not making sense to me? Concerning..." She had dispensed with the usual small talk and got right to business tonight, but it was the dot, dot, dot that made Chip more than just curious. At the same time though, he was also more than disappointed that she was not suggesting a new summer globe-trotting exploit. It was mid-afternoon in New York. She was probably already in her office at home because she did not like to work in the hectic Journal offices. Like Chip, she had free reign to work from home or while wandering the world as long as she met deadlines for research analyses and articles. And her articles were always spot-on. She specialized in both market prediction and emerging markets. Her extensive participation in numerous economic development organizations made her one of the most knowledgeable experts in the latter.

Chip exchanged some pleasantries with the sailors in the room as he made for his final exit for the evening. It usually took several attempts toward the door before he could escape the confines of his sailing sanctuary. He had already texted his driver, who would soon be pulling the car around the corner. Before responding to this texting conversation, which would likely evolve into a video chat soon enough, Chip wanted to get home to his study where he could stoke a hot fire to warm up. He was excited to analyze the details of whatever research Natalia would be bringing to him. This one sounded serious as Natalia's light, carefree personality never described anything as concerning.

As Chip opened the door, the Northeasterly wind gusted through the opening, which faced into the harbor, and he had to bolster himself into the wind just to make it outside. Just then, the Phantom came into view, and he quickly hopped into the back seat. His second-in-command Sam set his electronic tablet down and inspected Chip's facial expression for his present mood. By the look on Chip's face, Sam had correctly guessed that Natalia had been in touch with him that night.

"Early night tonight?" Sam mused.

"Too blasted cold to do anything fun!" exclaimed Chip, half speaking to the wind and waves to his right past the harbor. Just a few seconds and they were on their way. Not more than a few blocks down Queen's Road on the right, they came to the short, gated drive with a gatehouse on the left. Following close behind them, the obligatory security detail in two black Range Rovers was usually not noticeable to Chip. They faded into the background of his consciousness because they had always been there since he was a child. The garages were beneath the house, so the drive took a steep drop below the house to the main entrance. There was already an orange glow from the fire in the study that was a very inviting sight to Chip, his driver, and his erstwhile bodyguard, Sam, who was just a few years his elder.

Sam's father had been the Merlin family butler and personal assistant on the Isle for decades, and Sam continued on after Chip's and Sam's fathers' deaths. Sam had long ago become Chip's de facto bodyguard throughout their boarding school and college years. He also attended both St. Edward's and Oxford and obtained a degree in stellar fashion from Oxford in criminology. Unlike Chip, his sporting prowess manifested in mixed martial arts expertise, leading to his unofficial bodyguard status. Moreover, through osmosis from Chip's studies, Sam also became adept at economics and journalism. As VP, he participated in Merlin board meetings, assisted in editing and analyzing articles for the Times, and was always at Chip's right side during business meetings.

Formerly Chip's bodyguard, he had advanced to Vice President of the security division of Merlin Shipping. He was also skilled nautically, driving one of Chip's chase boats anytime Chip was on the water, with tonight being the exception.

Normally, he too would be among the sailors at The Yachtsman after practice, but important security business needed urgent attention this afternoon in London, so he arrived late for the festivities.

Tonight, they hurried from the carriage house to the main house and after removing their jackets at the door, entered the warm confines of the study. There were already two chilled glasses of Blanton's Straight on the side tables and the servers were already humming with the screensaver on the large wall-mounted monitor displaying a slideshow of travel pictures from around the globe. The boys, his two Bullmastiffs, were already cozying up to each other in the warmth of the fireside rug. If there was one other love in his life, it was his faithful dogs. At every Merlin property, there were sure to be multiple dogs taking up residence, and they were always comforting him when he walked through the door.

On this evening, though, the pair of canines had barely lifted their heads off the toasty rug enough to notice Chip's entrance. "That's okay, fellas, I'll come greet you. How does that sound?" Chip asked, frisking their ears and landing a hug and a smooch on each of their enormous heads. "No, don't get up. Stay there," he commanded without actually needing to.

At first, the two friends sat opposite each other, alternately savoring the first sips from the Kentucky bourbons straight from the barrel, freshly poured by the house staff.

"Thanks for getting the servers up and running already. I have a feeling this will be a long discussion with Natalia tonight," said Chip.

Sam clapped back immediately, "I figured as much with the early call. I was about to meet you there anyway. This afternoon, we just signed another company for protection. It's another Ukrainian company. Fourth one this week. Somebody is getting nervous over there. We are sending in three more details to Ukraine with air and nautical support."

Fortuitously, the picture currently on the big screen was from the summit of the mountain at the Merlin Chalet in the Alps. It was from a few years ago in the springtime, not the time Chip was just thinking about, and both Chip and Natalia were in full white ski attire, with a light dust of powder all around them. Returning from the daydream of that vacation, he knew it was now time to settle in for a long night of serious analysis. When Natalia had questions, they were never the superficial "Why did the Dow drop by 400 points today?" questions.

Chip's study accommodated a large projection screen accompanied by two large flat-screen monitors flanking it on either side, on the wall facing his stately antique desk. To his left was the magnificent crackling fireplace with a two-story limestone chimney that heated the entire room. To his right was a spiral staircase leading to a second-floor reading room with ancient books from floor to ceiling on two sides. Mahogany bookcases, walls, and beams enveloped Chip in old-world comfort despite the modern wall of technology that faced his desk. Between the desk and the bank of monitors were two grand leather couches and chairs that he would sometimes sit at with his wireless keyboard during important meetings.

Suddenly, his phone and tablet began to vibrate simultaneously with a video call. She had skipped all of the introductory texting and manifested her impatience tonight. He clicked the green "Answer" button on his tablet first and then clicked the cast button to the large side monitor. He briefly waited as the connection established itself. "Good evening, Natalia! It is such a splendid surprise to see your smile! I hate texting anyway. So impersonal."

On the screen, her radiant smile seemed to double the glow in the room from the fire. For a moment, Chip thought her lips were dancing like flames on the screen. As he snapped out of it, Natalia cast a few slides on the right monitor and their evening discussion was off to the races. Hours later, it seemed like they had only started talking when Natalia closed the discussion with, "And I am not really sure how the numbers on the above best offer trades add up this year, it seems likely there will be a rather large fringe element if our calculations are correct. I think when our program is up and running we and the rest of the world will be in for a big surprise."

While Chip was nominally aware of the dark trades, after hearing Natalia's presentation, the realization flashed before him that the discovery of all of these trades could be earth-shattering if there was a lot of dark trading going on. "You know, I really think you are on to something. I wonder if the SEC or FBI have seen this increase in dark trades yet?"

On the screen, Natalia's green eyes sparkled with Chip's approval of her work. "But do you know what, Chip? I think that our system is going to beat them to it. My AI is probably better than theirs. It is going to analyze market timing events and cryptocurrency trades that theirs will not."

"I know you and your techies have been working on this for a long time. It's finally almost operational?" Chip queried but his mind was already wandering. He suddenly changed the subject, "Do you think the Montagnes are in the cards for this spring or summer? We could do a working trip." As he finished the sentence, his heart jumped in his throat, but he didn't notice it so much since he simultaneously brought the glass of Blanton's Straight to his lips and felt the familiar burn of the bourbon and the smoothness of the caramel.

"You know, let me think about that, there will be some downtime in the next week before my interns get the program loaded onto our servers. Maybe I could get there for a few days. What about you? Aren't you busy with the Admiral's Cup"

Surprised by the affirmative answer, Chip was caught quite off guard. He thought he could get away early in the week, but he knew after this weekend's races, exhaustion would be harsh. The anticipation was building in his mind and sleep now became secondary, but, as usual, maybe sleep could be accomplished best on the plane. "Let's tentatively think about Sunday to Thursday of next week. This is a little earlier than our usual summer trip but later than spring skiing. I am sure there will still be plenty of snow on the ground to make for a beautiful escape."

Natalia really needed to see Chip and knew she had to make this work. "Ok, I will call for the plane and I will do some work in the air as well and we will have a few hours each

10

day to relax. I've missed your calming influence on my life. Things are getting crazy here. And I miss the lads."

The lads of which she spoke were Chip's Swiss dogs - St. Bernards who lived the lavish life in the opulent chalet halfway up Le Catogne, overlooking some of his vineyards in the valley below in Sembrancher. The chalet could not be more perfectly placed. It was less than an hour to Chamonix and some of the best Swiss and French ski areas in the Alps and thirty minutes to Lac Léman, otherwise known as Lake Geneva. To make it even more spectacular, the effervescent blue River Rhône slowly meandered through his vineyards in the distance to Lac Léman.

"Nevertheless, we must make it happen. I can meet you there on Sunday night. Do you think Sunday or Monday?" Chip was hoping for Sunday...

"Yes, Sunday late afternoon," Natalia guessed. "It will probably almost be Monday morning there before we get to Le Merle d'Le Catogne."

All of Merlin's dozens of properties worldwide portrayed some sort of nom d'apres, sometimes with a play on words, since the original myths of Merlin circled around shape-shifting into birds, hence the name in English became Merlin.

"Perfect," Chip's excitement could barely be contained. "I can't wait to see you. We can work on your trading mysteries remotely. Make sure you don't tell anyone what you have found yet."

"Agreed, with the amounts I am guessing, to remain undetected, if it is one entity, it would have to be a very powerful one indeed."

Before hanging up, Chip thought twice about speaking out loud the words that his heart commanded him to say, which was that he missed her. Instead, he left her prescient statement to speak for itself and bid a simple, "Adieu."

〜

CHAPTER 2: NATALIA

〜

Natalia Volkov certainly was not obligated in any way to conduct her life in the laboring manner she did. On the contrary, she fully embraced her stressful research discourse with the New York Journal despite a meager salary. What set her apart from all her Swiss prep school friends, Oxford classmates, and fellow journalists in New York City was not just her bright and easygoing personality. Her entire ethos was driven by a steely will to succeed and help those less fortunate succeed along with her. The ultra-posh lifestyle she enjoyed from childhood through college included private jets, chauffeurs, and island and mountain getaways, yet she yearned for something more meaningful. While she had access to the best fashion in Europe and New York, she felt right at home in jeans or leggings. She could dress to the nines if the occasion required, but her casual look could easily outshine any model on the runway. Modeling recruiters tried valiantly, and at times ruthlessly, to persuade her to abandon her studies, but she consistently refused their overtures in favor of her education.

She attended an elite boarding school called École Suisse d'Élite in Switzerland, where the headmaster frequently remarked upon her as having genius status, but was careful not to single her out too much. Among her classmates were the sons and daughters of blue-blood oligarchs and billionaires, who were not accustomed to studying or worrying about a future occupation. Chinese, Malaysian, Russian, and American elite parents sought a gilded European education for their offspring at this enclave nestled on the shores of Lac Léman near Geneva. Indeed, the tuition and fees levied there were more costly than any other school on Earth. The instructors demanded more from Natalia than her peers and she expected no less from her mentors than a challenging education. Most of her classmates expected to take over their families' fortunes after they finished their studies and therefore were less than motivated. However, her dream was to be a computer scientist and journalist and she, not coincidentally due to her father's influence, had a flair for the study of economics as well.

Ofttimes, she found herself removed from Geneva though, as by the time she was a senior in preparatory school she was assisting her father and uncle with the family business affairs as an assistant in St Petersburg, which was a quick 3-hour flight. Despite her occasional absence, her grades were stellar because of her brilliance and hard work. She fell in love with sailing small two-person or double-handed 470 sailboats alongside some of the local world-class Swiss sailing squadrons. She and her mate ascended the rankings in Europe and became European Junior 470 Champions four years in a row. At sixteen, she was the youngest female crewmember ever on a winning yacht at the Bol d'Or Mirabaud sailing race on Lac Léman. To top that off, she was a junior crew member on the America's Cup-winning yacht from Switzerland, though she was not allowed to fully crew during any of the races. It was this perceived slight by the all-male crew that drove her competitive spirit at Oxford, the Olympics, and beyond.

As impressive as her drive and intellect were, her athletic abilities were even more awe-inspiring. She excelled at soccer and was recruited for the Russian national team, but she preferred sailing and rowing and favored the Swiss mountainside lakes more than Russian cities. She was almost six feet tall, with flowing slightly wavy, dark blonde hair that, in the winter trended toward brunette. By deception, her long legs created the impression that she was even a few inches taller than six feet. Never a stranger to the weight room, she was as strong as any man her age. She possessed arms of steel that could propel a single sculling boat down the water at an amazing clip. During her senior year at Oxford, only a handful of male scullers existed in the country who could beat her.

Matriculating at Oxford was such a natural fit for this free-thinker, not only from an academic standpoint but from a social one as well. Natalia relished not only the old-school rituals, traditions, and history of the centuries-old, gothic lime-stone campus but also the contrasting cosmopolitan student body and quirky social scene. She navigated the halls of those ancient buildings adeptly, with an uncanny ability to combine her academic and social pursuits into one activity. Chip and Natalia were almost inseparable every evening of the week, studying, debating, and attending swanky secret society events. The proximity of the countryside campus to London suited her international culinary needs perfectly with weekly visits to Chinatown, Camden, and the Indian Asian neighborhoods known as "Curry Corridor." Her father and uncle visited her in London quite often, with her uncle's visits perhaps too fre-quent for Natalia's preference. He had increased his presence in London so much that she felt he was overbearing, insisting that she represent the family business in London.

While Chip stayed in London after Oxford working his way up through the Times, she was recruited heavily to work for the Journal in New York. During a summer internship in their London office, she impressed them with her investiga-tional skills and connections in the business world at such a young age. There was no stopping this young woman from attaining her lofty goals, owing to her overwhelming confi-dence, grinding work ethic, and grit that the cutthroat culture of the Big Apple required to succeed. She was an intellectual giant with a take-nothing-for-granted personality that was so rare those days. The decision to move farther away from her family in Russia was difficult but necessary for her independent psyche.

Freshly graduated, she could remember that beautiful June day, as she abandoned London for her dreams in New York. Chip accompanied her across the Atlantic to assist with the move, but the distance and enormity of it all felt like she was leaving a lifetime behind. Forging ahead, she had told herself, was the right thing to do, and breaking free from her family was the logical next step. However, this was not your usual small-town whiz kid embarking on a coming-of-age story in the big city, living in a dingy, one-room apartment. She flew from London to Teterboro in her familiar private jet, her belongings were already moved into her palatial Plaza condo, and the spacious domicile was already luxuriously decorated by an interior decorator. As evidenced by its opulence, despite her self-perceived independence, her family indubitably would continue to exert their unsolicited influence on her life.

Still, back then, on her first night in the big city, as she caught a glimpse of the full moon through the floor-to-ceiling window overlooking Central Park, she shared with the moon overhead how far she had come from the shy primary school girl. Basking in the moment, she stood silently while the bright moonlight illuminated the trees and lakes of Central Park in such a splendor she had never seen before. The idyllic scene harkened to the same, yet younger moon shining over the shores of Lac Léman of her youth. Sitting on the docks, she would share her hopes and dreams with the celestial body that reciprocated in advice and spiritual guidance, that she believed was backed by her ancestors. She firmly believed her ancient, ethical, and wise Russian ancestors guided her and lent their strength and wisdom to her struggles. In retrospection, it dawned on her that she owed her present success to the formative experience of rising triumphantly through a rigorous domain of racing sailboats on that frigid, windy body of water, excelling on the world stage, and then unceremoniously being denied primary crew designation for the America's Cup.

Returning to the present-day reality, on a harsh, cold, and windy April afternoon, she was working late in her home office on the 16th floor of the Plaza. When she returned from the Journal offices, the sky was slate gray and the beautiful Central Park view should have been mesmerizing with the spring colors coming out, but a foggy haze engulfed and smothered the greens of the park below. She paused her work and stretched for the sky above, taking a breath in deeply to allow the positives to soak in. After a 10 count, with all her strength exhaled the negatives, as though to push them out the window into the gray Haze beyond. She recognized that the fates of her ancestors had always endured through harsher weather than this. She resolved to push through the work today to accomplish what she set out to do.

She was in a zone and was making so many breakthroughs, ignoring the inclement conditions outside. A standing desk perched perilously close to the window, allowing her a bird's eye view of the metaphorical world that she commanded. Focus was easy when she paid no attention to the panoramic view or any of her daydreaming episodes. Three computer monitors blocked her view of Central Park and Mozart calmed her attention deficit, allowing her hours of uninterrupted work. However, in her preoccupied state, she hadn't paid notice that the day had turned into night while she laboriously tweaked her computer program to catch transactions that stubbornly refused to show up on the usual trade monitoring programs.

Upon completing her work for the night, she drifted off into another reminiscence of that first night in New York, the distance she had traveled, and the dreams accomplished during those few short years. With persistence, she was poised at the pinnacle of her field, financial networks seeking her opinion daily, and foreign governments and corporations pursuing her for consulting positions that could have paid her a king's ransom. As the allegorical notion of staring at the same full moon jarred her out of her daydream, she suddenly realized she was already late. She was supposed to meet her best friend from childhood for dinner at the best Sushi restaurant in New York, Yoko's just down the street.

She hurriedly donned her full-length, double-breasted wool coat and made it to the elevator, and, with a stroke of luck, it was on its way up and just arrived at floor 16 at exactly the same time she pushed the down button, as though she had already summoned it. Fifteen seconds later, she was on her way down to street level. She exchanged brief banter with the doorman about his impending stock trades as she strode through the lobby, buttoning the top button of her coat and tightening her green scarf to prevent the cold from invading. Her hair was still tied in a braided ponytail, so it was clear she had no extravagant plans. Once through the open, brass-gilded door, she braced for the wind and turned quickly to her right on the most direct route to Yoko's.

Katya was already in their favorite booth at Yoko's and arose from her seat quickly to hug Natalia, pausing to allow Natalia's profuse apology for forgetting the time. After the third repetition, Katya stopped her, "It's okay. You have been busy, don't fret so much about it."

Katya explained that she had been busy that day and also almost lost track of the time. Luckily, they both resided in the same building, enabling them to schedule late sushi dinners. Even so, it felt as though they lived two blocks apart because Katya lived on the 58th Street side on the fifth floor. These two, the Geneva Twins, they were called in prep school, for a time were inseparable on the weekends and most weekdays. Katya was 4 years older, but they were teammates on sailing teams growing up and Katya's parents initially worked in the security wing of Natalia's family business in St Petersburg. Then Katya's family started their own security business which, in Russia, suddenly became a lucrative endeavor and their wealth skyrocketed. Their families would vacation together several times per year at various luxurious locales and on superyachts. Even though they were presently spending less time together, their weekly get-togethers turned into at least a few hours of catching up on the latest Manhattan social scene gossip and work accomplishments.

"I've just been so wrapped up in some idiosyncrasies of the markets that don't make sense to me yet. It's different from any other trading algorithms that I have seen. And they are coming from these aberrant accounts that I have never seen before, and it seems like there are hundreds of these peculiar algorithms."

Katya held an esteemed senior trader position at a hedge fund owned by relatives, so she was indeed curious. "But maybe it is just an automated trading program that hundreds of funds use that are operating under similar parameters. You know trading parameters are all the same."

"It just doesn't seem like the timing is right and if it is an automated trading program, the parameters and the timing are so similar for each of them. But you could be right." She hesitated for a second, as she debated the details she should reveal, or even whether she had already disclosed too much to her friend. "You know, I think I will run it by Chip when we escape to the mountains tomorrow. Let's see if he can make sense of it all. I am going to work some more on it on the plane."

"I can't believe you are going to Switzerland tomorrow. I'm so jealous. I miss it so much! Let's catch up again when you get back in town. How is Chip doing?"

"I think he is doing well. He is headlong into the America's Cup and only comes up for air a few times a year. I think this time, luckily, I am catching him during his ascent to the surface. I really need some relaxation in between my bouts of work." Natalia realized her understatement and immediately promised herself at least some sleep on the airplane in the morning.

"You know all our friends are meeting tonight at The Miami Club. It's the hottest club you know." Katya was, once again, taking her best shot at bringing Natalia out of her work shell.

"I know, but you know that scene is just not for me. How is Andrei? Do you think he is the one? He comes from a shady family though! They are not like our families." Natalia was concerned her best friend was hanging with the wrong crowd in New York. Their two families were from storied St. Petersburg pedigrees with impeccable credentials and made their wealth by legitimate means.

"He is okay, he treats me well. At least most of the time. I'm just not sure. I wish I could find some normal guys."

"I don't think you are looking in the right places," Natalia advised, knowing it fell on deaf ears.

An hour later, as Natalia tidied her scarf and navy-blue overcoat, the pair walked outside the nearly empty restaurant, and she bid her friend adieu, "Sorry we didn't have as much time as usual. Let's get together when I return next week. Je t'aime!" They exchanged hugs and parted to their respective condominiums. They walked together across the street before Katya turned the corner to the left toward the secondary Plaza entrance. Natalia continued down the sidewalk to the private entrance with her private elevator and was already back in work mode before she stepped through the door.

After working for a few more hours on the Artificial Intelligence algorithms, that night she slept well despite the excitement of her discoveries. She knew it was only a matter of time before she discovered who the offenders were. And she had a deep suspicion that it would turn out to be a criminal enterprise operating on the fringe of un-monitored trading. In her dreams, the nebulous masked perpetrators hoarded the cash they were making in canvas bags and walked out of the stock exchange under cover of night.

She had cultivated close friends at the SEC and the FBI who would be interested in what she was finding. Natalia recently acquired inside knowledge about the inner workings of two publicly known SEC AI programs called ARTI and CAT that could, if developed properly, monitor trading in real-time. The government algorithms were theoretical and nowhere near operational and the implementation kept getting kicked down the road by each administration for the past ten years. It was as though the powers that be didn't actually want to know what was going on under their noses. At this rate, she was going to beat them to the revelations.

It was a breezy early morning at Teterboro Airport as her driver slowly brought the SUV through the gate and out onto the tarmac near the sleek G-VII that would be her carriage for the quick getaway to the Swiss Alps. She stepped down into the spring chill with her ponytail bouncing as she galloped up the steps into the plane.

"Hi, Sven!" she exclaimed as the pilot and the crew who were her second family greeted her. "I have a lot of work today. Can we make sure the satellite is tuned in? I have intense server work to do." As they lifted off into the still-dark early morning sky, it would not be long before the most spectacular sunrise started to come into view to starboard over the Atlantic Ocean. Valeria, one of her family's flight hostesses, brought her some fresh squeezed orange juice and Brazilian coffee for the long day ahead. Natalia counted this kind-hearted woman as one of her favorite mother figures of her childhood and teenage years. Natalia's only company during the countless lonely flights back and forth to St Petersburg, she looked more like an aging nanny than a flight attendant, but it was only at Natalia's insistence that she remained. She was an expert in the techniques of warmth, compassion, and encouragement for her favorite passenger during her formative years.

"I will always see you in pigtails and school uniform, scared of your own shadow. My how you've grown into a fine young lady!" she exclaimed, tilting her head with an all-knowing, loving grandmother expression.

"Thank you, Valeria. I appreciate you, love you, and always look forward to your hot chocolates with marshmallows on every flight. Can you make me one?"

"Of course, my dear," Valeria said as she turned toward the galley.

Natalia pulled out her laptop for the several-hour flight and set about her work for the day, but first, stole a glance out the window at the approaching sunrise in all its glory. Closing the shade, she set her playlist to Mozart and resumed her analysis.

On the other end of the Atlantic, Chip's plane had barely touched down in Geneva, when he was alerted regarding Natalia's liftoff. He and Sam planned to take the day to visit old friends at the Société Nautique de Genève, while the advance security team set up at the chalet. They arrived in three Mercedes armored cars and the advance team separated in their Rovers to head up through the valley and into the mountains. Each of the Merlin households around the world maintained three cars and three Range Rovers for the security teams.

While Lac Léman was Natalia's home base before Oxford, Chip had a personal connection with the Commodore and was acquainted with many of the skippers here from his college racing days. Like Chip's team in England, the Swiss were busy readying some of their crew for the America's Cup challenges. While the Swiss had never regained their Cup-winning form from twenty years previous, they still embodied the best nautical seamanship, technology, and innovation of the sport. What they were missing from yesteryear was the importation of the top sailors from around the world, specifically New Zealand, who had learned from their mistakes and held their sailing talent close to the belt these days

By that evening, Natalia planned to join them for dinner at the Club House restaurant. Meanwhile, Chip was doing a bit of Cup espionage, probing the skippers for information. It wasn't true espionage, just lighthearted gamesmanship. Before everyone knew it, it would be America's Cup World Series time around the world and the real races would begin. It seemed like just a few minutes that he had been conversing with old buddies, but before long, it was already late afternoon and Natalia's plane was due to land. He sent two of the cars for the airport and continued sipping his favorite absinthe he always enjoyed here. If there was one place you must enjoy sipping on chilled absinthe, it was on the docks of Lac Léman in the Swiss spring mountain air, with the snowy foothills of the Alps in the background.

As Natalia stepped down the airstairs of the sleek jet outside the hangar of the aviation center, it was comforting to see the Merlin cars were always there to greet her. Her own security team was good, but the Merlin team was second to none. I guess that is why the Merlin team was trusted with global travel and corporate security in addition to the age-old shipping security and logistics. Sam ran a tight ship with these global operations. They had advance security teams in almost every major city of the world. It was sometimes fascinating to watch their methods of operation. Sam had arranged for two of the Range Rovers to return from the mountains to assist with

22

the extraction. He was taking no chances these days, as he just didn't feel like things were right with how the Ukrainians were tightening up security, and here he had a Russian asset in tow.

To Natalia, this brief adventure would be a welcome escape from New York for a few days. When she was a child, she knew she could relax here in the Swiss luxury while at school, representing freedom from her doting family in Russia. Even then, she had a significant security detail. Tonight, she said goodbye to Valeria, Sven, and the rest of the crew and climbed into the black Mercedes. While Valeria and Sven often accompanied her on the ground during some of Natalia's trips abroad, they knew they were not needed, nor wanted, when she was in Chip's care. Additional security and service would be unnecessary here, but they stayed in Geneva anyway. On the ground in Geneva, her father had arranged a small detail nonetheless that Natalia never noticed but always suspected.

As she arrived at the club in the usual Merlin motorcade, she could not help but notice how almost nothing had changed about this place she called home for several years. It still had old-world charm on its surface, yet from the glimpses of the foils on the catamarans and monohulls docked outside the Club House, underneath the hood was where the differences lay, with high-tech sailing written all over it. The next few hours concluded an elegant evening with old friends and mentors she had not seen in some time, and for the second time in 24 hours, she gained some realization of the distance from which she had come. At the same time, she remained the same gritty, determined teenager who began her sailing career fighting for relevance on the bow of a 40-foot racing catamaran on Lac Léman. Scanning the docks, her old boat could not be found, long replaced by newer, faster boats.

It was late when they arrived at the chalet, and Natalia was exhausted as they stepped out into the mountain chill. The dazzling night sky always amazed her out here with the stars twinkling, the Milky Way lighting up the sky, and the same full moon she knew so well. Despite her sleepiness, she was eager for the chance to talk to Chip in more detail about her discoveries and her ideas for extracting the data with the AI. As they settled in by the fire in the great room under the vaulted A-frame birchwood ceilings, Natalia and Chip snuggled under blankets on brown leather couches. At their feet, the four gargantuan St. Bernards acted like the kings of this extravagant spread. It seemed they had just started chatting about the machine learning necessary to identify the origins of trades when the sun began to peer over the Swiss Alps, revealing snow-capped peaks of the French Alps to the west. The Merlin chalet and vineyards were closer to Martigny than to Chamonix, overlooking the River Rhone, which sparkled its beautiful azur-vert currents before flowing into Lac Léman. The sky was so clear they could just make out the deep blue water of Lac Léman on the horizon. Life was always so much simpler when she was here with Chip, and she could be herself instead of explaining to Katya why she wasn't taking to the New York social scene or explaining to her father and uncle why she was in New York and not St. Petersburg.

As she drifted off to sleep in Chip's arms with her feet warmed by the lads, the soft smile did not escape her lips. They both stretched their arms as bright sunlight flooded through the grandiose triangular windows, accentuated by the white mountains that surrounded them. Sam and the rest of the crew were busying themselves in the dining room and the den, preparing for the day. As was the case when Chip and Natalia were both à bord, no matter what property it was, it would be necessary to erect a double office along with a third office for Sam.

Any trip to Le Merle d'Le Catogne would not be complete without the freshly made waffles with whipped cream, strawberries, and melted Swiss chocolate drizzled over the massive plate in front of them. She could never finish the whole plate but made a gallant attempt. It was not just Chip and Natalia eating at the long dining table as the entire crew ate together and socialized. When the breakfast feast was over, though, the grindstone needed grinding and analyses needed analyzing, so they set about the task at hand.

The study at the chalet was every bit as inviting as the one in Cowes on the Isle of Wight. The massive compound had several fireplaces, and this one was even more extravagant than the one in the great room. As Chip worked on one of the large wall-mounted monitors, Natalia toiled on her AI algorithms and programming with her laptop linked to the drop-down center screen. Every once in a while, Chip would chime in when Natalia needed some economic advice, but this advanced programming she was engaged in might as well be a foreign language to him.

Each day that week Chip and Natalia made time in the early afternoon for a snowy hike along the trail up to the ridge where there was a small wooden viewing platform that was Natalia's favorite place in the world. She was always "en paix" and everything was "en place" within seconds of reaching this summit and the breathless view. For the better part of an hour, there was only silence, and as was customary, the two would only speak French while enveloped in the beauty of this altitude. The rest of the eight-member security team kept their distance a few hundred yards down the slopes in each direction so as not to be noticed.

Each night Natalia, Chip, Sam, and the crew entertained themselves in the great room by the fire or basked in a gigantic courtyard jacuzzi nearly the size of some swimming pools. No luxury was spared in this vacation retreat, but the ability to work was also paramount. It was so easy for her to concentrate when she was in this venue, despite all the possible distractions. The fresh air cleared her mind of her family and friends, and before she knew it, it was Thursday, and they would have to return to New York. But she accomplished so much this week that Wednesday night she video-conferenced her interns to tell them she wanted to meet with them Thursday night in the lab to bring exciting news.

That night she slept incredibly well after a late-night jacuzzi break under the stars. She and Chip were made for this life. Remote work had its advantages in increased productivity for this pair. His work also seemed to fly by when he was in these confines, not only because he was in the luxury of this space, but because of with whom he was enjoying this moment under the Swiss sky. They both seemed to wonder aloud at the same time, "If only we could work remotely from here permanently…"

Perhaps soon enough their wish would be granted, but under not so auspicious terms.

Chapter 3: Booming Markets

The markets were booming that year in the United States stock indexes, while sure-fire signs of recession continued rattling everyone's cages for the last several months. The unemployment rate remained lower than it had been in over a decade, yet wages were persistently so low that the populace was getting restless. The highest real estate prices in two decades locked many in the middle class out of home ownership, and inventories increased after several months of flat sales figures, suggesting a slow-down was imminent. Most countries in Europe and Asia found themselves in the death grip of recession for the last three years, and many central banks cut interest rates to below zero to claw their way out of it. Those in the financial prediction racket forecasted the slowdown would have commenced in the US a few years ago coinciding with the rest of the world. Despite many American corporations missing earnings targets, their stock price inexplicably remained in the green through it all.

In a surprise win, Peter Zorin was elected President of the United States at what many people saw as an inopportune time. The economy had already extended its upward trajectory from the last downturn for more than eight years, and the odds were increasingly showing that the recovery was near the top of the curve. Everyone perceived up and down economic cycles as a natural thing, inseparable from reality, as certain as death and taxes. To escape the downturn eight years ago, the US government committed to buying hundreds of billions of dollars of bonds to keep interest rates artificially low. The fed also pumped hundreds of billions of dollars into a few "too big to fail" banks. However, this money had to be paid back to maintain the credit rating of the sovereign debt, keep our deficit below five percent of the gross domestic product, and prevent inflationary pressures from mounting. If inflation returned, conventional wisdom said, the economic recovery would not sustain itself, and the stimulus would disappear, creating another downturn or recession.

On top of that, this year, two world crises occurred in China and the Middle East that threatened to worsen the world's recession and feasibly further drag the US into the downturn. Iran was making waves by supporting multiple terrorist activities and multiple incidents near the Strait of Hormuz and the Suez Canal had curtailed international shipping through the area. China, with its juggernaut economy usually buoying the Asian markets, posted a less than stellar GDP statistic after several real estate debacles. However, unlike any time in modern history, each time one of these global adversities hit, world markets slowed while the US markets just seemed to shrug it off like a raindrop off the windshield. Onward and upward the market marched.

Riding on the President's coattails into the Senate, Jack Speransky was also an unlikely victor in the last election. He was seen as too conservative for New Jersey voters, and despite well-known questionable business and real estate dealings, was elected in a landslide victory. But one could only guess that a majority of New Jersey voters realized everyone from New Jersey had questionable business practices. Not only did he own a vast real estate empire, but he had also parlayed that empire into some hedge fund/real estate investment trust hybrid holdings that garnered a lot of outside investments.

28

The investment vehicles launched now-Senator Speransky from a multi-millionaire to more than a billionaire within a decade.

This get-rich scenario was not unusual for these prosperous times. It was apparent that all across the country (and the world) hundreds of billionaires sprang up from nowhere as hedge fund and real estate investors. If you could make your first ten million dollars investing in stocks or real estate, all it required was to file some regulatory paperwork, and investors from all around the globe would pour money into your fund if you promoted it the right way. The key marketing language was articulated that you started with almost nothing and made millions out of a pittance, then billions out of millions. Subsequently, every millionaire wanting a piece of the billionaire pie would buy in like it was a fad coffee everyone else was buying in a drive-through.

Both he and the President touted their business and negotiation skills as their primary means to bring continued yet even greater success to the country. However, neither of the business tycoons was accustomed to not getting their way. The last decade of real estate pursuits had jaded them due to increased environmental regulations hampering their development empires in the US. The resulting dissatisfaction with the US market caused both to start looking overseas for opportunities and consequently, their wealth skyrocketed. It was so much easier to persuade officials and influence government decisions in the developing world where the key to success was knowing and priming the right people to cater to their needs. In many third-world locales, no regulations existed to prevent foreign investments and kickbacks. It was Speransky's cousin who proved instrumental in gaining access to the Middle East, Eastern Europe, and the Mediterranean. The President was indebted to Speransky and his cousin for saving him from bankruptcy during the last two economic downturns.

Even so, the dominance of the United States economy was an amazing sight to witness. The US was riding the economic wave of prosperity while most of the world was clamoring to climb out of a hole. Or at least the top 5% of the country was, anyway. As was the case worldwide, the bottom 95% of the populace was doing worse than they were a decade before. Wages had increased less than inflation, therefore they could purchase less with their money than ever before. They subsisted on meager pay, living paycheck to paycheck, though, while not realizing it, in reality, they lived better than their parents. Moreover, they could now spend their leisure time on the weekends doing whatever they pleased, boats, motorcycles, bars, sporting events, and cruises, to name just a few of their main distractions. Sex, alcohol, and drugs dominated the youth culture, causing more strife than ever. The American way of life could be perceived as better in many ways, yet the populace perceived their life to be worse off than when they grew up.

It was this leisure life of the working class that helped President Zorin's approval rating limp through each of these crises. While his approval rating was less than stellar, it was better than expected considering the average Joe was not getting ahead in any measurable capacity. To be re-elected in the fall, President Zorin needed above all else for the economy and at a minimum the stock market to continue performing above average. Even though eighty percent of the country did not own an appreciable amount of retirement savings, at least they had the same job they had four years ago, which was more than they could say twelve years ago when the most recent catastrophe hit the markets.

President Zorin placed such a high priority on re-election that he began to ignore basic government functions in favor of strategizing over polls and deals with organizations that could promise him votes. Today, in a fit of anxiety, he paced the floor of the second-floor residence of the White House, stopping at the window to gaze out at the Washington Monument. He preferred the President's quarters over the Oval Office to entertain guests because he had fashioned a media center with multiple screens so he could take in the daily news shows. In the background he could hear the pundits from his favorite morning show as they discussed how great a job the President was doing with the economy, and by historical measures, he

30

should easily win re-election. That the economy was performing so well was no small feat, he retorted in his mind, because he was able to corral the special interests of the financial and real estate markets so that the stock market would continue to advance to greater heights.

This accomplishment could only happen with the help of the network put together by his friend and confidante, Jack Speransky, who, on today's special occasion of another stock market record, had joined the President in the living quarters. In the midst of another one of their strategy sessions about the election and the economy, the discussion had become heated as usual. Speransky, dressed in a vested designer blue suit, was sitting with legs crossed in one of the oversized leather chairs facing the bank of video monitors, each streaming news, financial tickers, or talk shows.

"Well, Peter, I have to say that all of our network is very happy right now. They continue to advance the economy, while they are rewarded with the fruits of their labor from the high earnings they are earning from this booming economy," the Senator relayed to the President, straining to glance over his right shoulder to ascertain if the President was indeed listening. Jack Speransky's voice possessed an air of self-righteousness that it was he who had built this network when it was really his cousin who should take the credit. His cousin was a Russian expat who lived an opulent life in London and whose wealth was rising exponentially alongside that of Senator Speransky and the other billionaires in their network of patriots.

"Well, let's keep them happy, shall we? Do we have any meetings with your cousin coming up any time soon? Teleconference? I want to reward him for his assistance going into election season as we desperately need the Dow to continue its upward trend through November. Everyone is saying the markets are about to tank, and we can't have that. Not at all. Do you understand? Anything he requires from us; we will do it for him. I understand your cousin also wants to re-enter the US development market. It was unconscionable what the previous administration did to him with sanctions. They dragged his name through the mud. We can rectify that. I will speak with Commerce. Then we will assist him by cutting the red tape anywhere he needs it."

"You are right. I will have a discussion with him to see what he needs next. In the meantime, the G7 meetings are coming up. Russia would really like a return to their seat at the table that they lost."

"I don't see any reason not to give it back to them. They have been well-behaved lately," the President said, tongue in cheek.

"Let's see what the focus groups think of it, then we can float it in the media and see what the prevailing opinion is." Jack had recognized that the idea might be met with some resistance since the Russians had invaded multiple countries in the name of the preservation of their people's rights in the past two decades. However, his sources demanded that he try to get this item approved by the President.

President Zorin knew exactly who submitted the request to his old friend and was determined to accomplish the desired results for the good of the country. He finally turned away from the window, expressing his approval, "Excellent idea. I will get the hosts at American News to bring the concept up to my press secretary so that it doesn't come across as our idea."

"Thank you, Peter. You're a patriot, through and through. I will set up the meeting." Jack, arose from the chair and shook the hand of the President, with his free hand grasping his shoulder tightly, ending in a side-hug, like the pair always did at the end of their sessions.

Now, if only Peter Zorin and Jack Speransky could bring about the other changes the network wished for. That fight would be for another day. This was the first step in a long process of aligning the country's interest with that of the movement. Baby steps for now. Couldn't advance these things too quickly. The resulting partnership would help keep the world economy flowing to the right people. And those people would in turn keep it flowing to the growing empire.

With that framework in place, the plan was introduced to the country that Russia, as was fitting for a major economy and superpower, should be allowed back in the G8. What was glossed over was that they were the twelfth largest economy, less than half the size of Germany. But with poverty so high in Russia, and the stranglehold that their natural gas supply had on Europe and Asia, the billionaires in that country commanded the power of Germany in terms of purchasing and exerting their influence around the world.

Over the next few days, the notion drew only a small amount of contention among the liberal, democracy-loving factions, but the media, with the bigger crises in Iran and China to cover, ignored it for the most part. And the Russian propaganda machine made sure that the anti-Russian pro-democracy voices were drowned by other voices. And that pleased Speransky's network to no end, for now anyway, because a developing disruption was about to bubble to the surface, that would need to be addressed emergently.

~

CHAPTER 4: UNCLE NIKOLAI

~

An exhausted, yet content Natalia gazed down at the hazy Manhattan skyline as the G-VII traversed the island on its descent into Teterboro.   If relaxation was the goal, then the week in Switzerland was a resounding success, but traveling, even in the luxurious jet, sapped her energy. At the same time, she had made only minimal progress on her research and coding project. With so much yet to accomplish before she launched the AI analysis program, she anxiously returned her concentration to the laptop screen before her. Just then Valeria appeared in the cabin, sitting beside her to inform her she had a phone call from her Uncle Nikolai. Valeria, better than anyone, was cognizant of Natalia's discomfort with her sinister uncle's stalking behavior

"Hi, Uncle Nikolai! What do you need?" she asked in perfect Russian. Her Uncle was a stickler for the Russian language and other formalities, including respecting Russian history. It was highly unusual for anyone to speak English in front of Nikolai Volkov, at least without consequences. In the Volkov house, he was the keeper of family traditions, a quasi-historian of the shield. Keeping the ancestral dynasty closely held was of utmost importance to him. For example, any absence of a family member from gatherings was not taken lightly and he would never approve of her befriending anyone who was not Russian, especially arch-enemy Chip Merlin. Many years had now passed, but when her father announced her attendance at the École Suisse d'Élite, it almost caused a family crisis. She and her other uncle in London were the only members of the family who dared spend any time outside of Russia. That wasn't to say they had no foreign business, but all foreign business was beneath them, handled by their underlings. However, curiously, Natalia had noticed the company was surreptitiously making more and more foreign investments these days.

Somehow, she was able to smooth over her absence by returning to St Petersburg often during prep school and college to assist with the Volkov Library which was central to keeping the family traditions alive. Within the library was a museum of sorts of St Petersburg and the Volkov family's central involvement in the leadership of this part of Russia as far back as the days of Rurik of Novgorod and Tsar Peter I who were brave enough to make Russia and St Petersburg the great land that it deserved to be. Since making the move to New York, she unintentionally slacked off on the exhibit work.

Right on cue, he admonished her, "I want to remind you to keep working on the library exhibit and avoid wasting time on silly vacations with British heathens. Soon I will expand your responsibilities, so you don't have to work with those American newspaper people." His veiled threat did not fall on deaf ears, for the timing of this ultimatum was completely intentional.

"Nikolai, he helps me a lot with my stories. And I have been working non-stop on the plane and while in Switzerland. I also have found a lead on historical artifacts discovered in Novgorod and started negotiations to return these family effects from a collection in a museum there. Can you send your assistant there to retrieve them?" She smiled first, then displayed a confident smirk, proud of the circumvention she had just pulled off. Valeria, who had eavesdropped on the conversation, reciprocated the same proud smirk.

She always did know how to smooth things over with her overbearing uncle. One monumental task accomplished each week would placate him, and it indeed WAS each week, because he called at least weekly to assure himself that she was not off the reservation. Despite his obsession with the family name and traditions, he was unfortunately unable to propagate the family name, as his only son had died in childbirth. In brooding over Natalia and her brothers, his belief that he was protecting the family name and legacy was his prime motivation.

Natalia always suspected that her father's sending her to the Swiss boarding school served to distance her from her uncle. Despite the family strife, she appreciated all that her father had sacrificed for her and her two brothers. Both of her siblings stayed behind in St Petersburg and went to secondary school at St Peter's School, the oldest school in Russia. The oldest, Aleksandr, named for greatness according to her uncle, was being groomed to take over the family business. Her youngest brother Alexei was entering the banking and investment industry in Russia and Ukraine and was gaining many connections working for the Chernov Bank. She had not seen either of them in over a month, long overdue in Nikolai's world.

Nikolai interrupted her moment of triumph with a new salvo, "Oh, I forgot to tell you Volkov is having the board meeting next week in London. Maybe we can bring up for consideration what we learn about your recent discoveries in Novgorod."

Great, another surprise meeting! They seemed to be more frequent in this year of unrest in the world. I guess that was to be expected given what was going on with trade and shipping. She wondered to herself, Why in London? They had properties all over the world and they usually held their "family" business meetings in more secret, secluded locations under Russian control. Her other uncle was becoming more powerful in London. Maybe that was it, the investment arm of the Volkov dynasty.

Just as they exchanged pleasantries and goodbyes, the plane touched down meaning she would soon be back in civilization again. She inhaled deeply to gather the negatives, exhaling them into the void, and along with them she expelled her uncle's hostility. The exercise allowed her to regain her motivation for the task at hand. She couldn't wait to start the meetings with her interns perfecting the AI, for Chip had given her several great ideas about data points to address in the formulas. If there was to be any meaningful clarity in the outcome of the data, it needed a more definitive identification of the source of the funds. From the phone conversation earlier in the week, it sounded like her interns were making strides in that regard.

Once again, she bid her farewells to Sven and Valeria and bounded down the jetway to the awaiting car. As always, her customs and passport were already checked and approved before the plane was even in the hangar and it took just a few minutes to clear with the agent. Though already late afternoon, she was eager to depart to the server lab to greet her interns and go over the plan for the next week to get the AI program ready for testing. The Volkov family meeting would delay the testing by another few days.

Less than an hour of rush hour traffic later, she walked into the lab, and at first, she couldn't find anyone. Her missing interns worried her slightly as she began to search for them, but they soon sauntered into the lab, probably from the vending machine with headphones in their ears. Natalia startled them and Sebastian dropped the spicy chips and caffeinated soda he dangled from the same hand that otherwise held the phone he was texted on. They had expected her to arrive much later tonight, as was the norm when returning from Europe. After calming down their frightened anxious selves, Jignesh and Sebastian half-fell clumsily into what could only be described as gaming chairs, those large lounge-like office chairs with neon-colored stripes and speakers surrounding the top cushion. Jignesh's chair was blue and black and looked comfortable, but Sebastian's was a red leather monstrosity that looked almost comical in the computer lab among all the servers.

Natalia, amused by the almost teenage atmosphere in her lab, let out a small chuckle before greeting her faithful workers, "How do you expect me to take you seriously when you guys look like high school gamers?"

Sebastian removed his headphones, swiveled his chair toward his boss, and stared at her with a quizzical look on his face. Meanwhile, Jignesh surreptitiously pilfered a chip from Sebastian's newly opened bag on his desk while he wasn't looking. Evidently, this pair of computer nerds were men of few words, at least spoken anyway. For the sake of her project, she hoped today they were men of a million coding words.

With a deep sigh, she tried to liven up the room, "Well, let's get back to work on this! I'm excited! Are you guys? We are almost at the finish line; I can feel it!" She pulled up a chair at her workstation and logged in, engaging their VPN with the usual passwords. The New York Journal employed state-of-the art security on all systems and that included Natalia's laptop. With the forthcoming revelations she expected, she was slowly recognizing the need for additional safety measures.

The meeting proved to be incredibly productive as she shared Chip's suggestions regarding integrating more personal information into the AI. Connecting external sources such as cryptocurrency markets to their AI via IP address would be more than ideal but obtaining full personal data from these markets could prove difficult, due to their innately secretive infrastructure. At a bare minimum, IP addresses they could obtain from the trade metadata could connect repeat trades from the same computer. Even trades in cryptocurrency included identifiable information that could be utilized to trace the seller and the buyer.

At the end of the session, it was decided they would endeavor to start beta testing a rough draft of the program within the next week. It was every programmer's nightmare - flip the switch and hear the sound of transformers blowing and the power going out, or worse yet, flip the switch, click "Run", and nothing. At least if resistors and transformers were blowing, your program might be running correctly, and your servers just needed more computing power. Late that night, they departed with a deeper understanding of the daunting challenge they faced. Yet at the same time, they were infinitely closer to the solution. The three coders felt closer to the breakthrough than they ever had.

At the end of the week, however, the results of the programming were not gaining much headway. Trying to program the collection of IP addresses from cryptocurrency coins was an undertaking in hacking that was not easy. Initially, it appeared they were not going to be successful, when the next morning, Sebastian arrived at work, strolled into the office, singing We are the Champions! at the top of his lungs, and said, "I've got it, I have the encryption keys from the coins. All you have to do is ask!"

"Okay, so how soon can you get this rolling? My family has scheduled a family meeting in London this week. Do you think we can have a better sense of how to incorporate this programming by next week?"

Natalia could not contain her excitement! She thought, What a breakthrough for the program if he can pull it off! Maybe they would be up and running sooner than she thought. For the last week, she thought they might not beat ARTI and CAT to functionality. According to news accounts each of the past several months, it was reported that ARTI and CAT would not be functional for over a year, and her inside information confirmed the same. Natalia breathed a sigh of relief and thought she could relax a little more about this project. She was just handed an important research assignment to perform for an article this week. If Sebastian could deliver on his promise, then that would lift an entire load off Natalia's shoulders during her trip to London.

Sebastian and Jignesh assured Natalia they had this well in hand and would deliver a working prototype by early next week. In no uncertain terms, Natalia warned them she would hold them to that deadline. No matter the means or the hours, they absolutely had to have this working by the time she returned. While she recognized a vague, larger picture of what was at stake for those who were about to be uncovered, she didn't fully fathom the extent of the danger at that point.

40

But soon enough, she would.

Leaving the lab in a whirlwind of goodbyes, her family awaited her mandatory appearance in London. In no time, she arrived at Teterboro to her awaiting plane. Once again, she bounded up the jet stairs to greet her travel family, Sven and Valeria. This time, however, Valeria was there at the car door to accompany her up the steps and there was a large security detail at the gate and surrounding the plane. Several of the men, who were familiar to Natalia from previous trips abroad, joined them on the plane, making for a crowded gathering for the long flight. The extra security was reminiscent of many other times of anxiety in Eastern Europe for her family for as long as she could remember. Any number of small incidents could occur anywhere in the world, and if it rattled her uncle enough, it resulted in several armed men camped outside her door at all times. Her earliest memories of her childhood in Switzerland were so eerily similar to today, down to the detail of Valeria meeting her at the car door. She paid them no mind and set about toiling on an interesting research article regarding Vietnam and the new industries sprouting up there since a new trade agreement was made with the EU.

The premise and the backbone of the piece were already provided to her by Journal interns, meaning she only needed to put the finishing touches on it, which only took an hour to complete. After perfecting the language and a few added local anecdotes from her travels, a significant amount of time remained for a refreshing sit-down dinner and much-needed sleep in the private bedroom aboard the plane. As she and her sizeable security contingent touched down in London, she awakened to greet the new day. An eventful few days in London would be in store for her which would turn her life upside down.

✦

~

CHAPTER 5:
DARLING OF THE OXFORD BLUE

~

Chip's heart skipped the usual half a beat as he caught a glimpse of Natalia rounding the corner at the pavilion at Farmoor Reservoir. For the better part of two hours, he had held court at an outdoor table at the little cafe overlooking the practice runs of the Oxford Sailing Team as they were training for their annual regatta. Chip was an advisor to the sailing club at Oxford and Natalia's visit to London seemed like a great excuse to take in a practice. It was breezy but unseasonably warm that day in early May, much different than last week's northeastern polar winds that postponed some of the practice races on the Solent that Chip's British team so badly needed to bring home the cup.

Her curly dark blonde locks dangled over the navy wool coat as though she had a mink fur lining at the neck. Natalia's rosy cheeks shone brightly in the sun, her smile was as radiant as ever, and an air of relaxation and happiness exuded from every pore. All eyes were upon every step she took along the gravel pathway that led to where all the youthful sailors were gathered. As she skipped up the stairs to the pavilion deck, there was a shout from the equipment area to her right. "Natalia!" exclaimed the excited Greek sailor who had been the long-time coach of the Oxford Sailing Club.

The two exchanged hugs as Chip arose from his chair and walked toward the edge of the deck to greet them both. Demetrius, ignoring Chip's approach, stepped back two steps, raised his arms like Moses admiring his flock, and introduced to the gathered crowd the darling of the 2004 Russian Olympic team. "Folks, gather around. Well, isn't this a special moment we can all learn from? This is Natalia Volkov, who began here as a young, timid, yet raw talent from Geneva. What she did have, though, was a chip on her shoulder, grit, and a determined look that would scare any criminal in Belmarsh Prison." He spoke with such a thick sailor accent, even Chip, who was used to it, had to crane his neck to understand. "I believe, ladies and gents, she will sign autographs!" This embarrassed Natalia to no end, as she blushed enough that it turned rosy cheeks to crimson. The effusive diatribe continued, and several minutes later, Demetrius was still glowing about her performance on the Aegean waters near his home islands as the crowd dispersed for practice and the three of them shifted to the tables on the deck of the cafe.

"How are the sailors in Blue doing this year?" Natalia asked the venerable man who looked every bit like one would imagine how the old man by the sea or some old Greek sea captain would look. He displayed a long, shaggy white beard and appeared as though there should have been a pipe in his mouth with a captain's cap over his white hair.

"Well, not a minute of practice to waste this year! These fellas are as green as you were your freshman year! But we also have two new darlings of the Oxford Blue to introduce you to!"

"Do you want to take one of the 488's out for a spin for old time's sake?" Chip queried as he embraced Natalia in a side hug.

"Oh, yes, I miss it so much. On second thought, maybe we can just go out on the committee boat since I am not dressed for it. Or should we watch from here?" Natalia began to think better of her initial agreement.

Chip and Coach Demetrius simply ignored her change of mind as they simultaneously rose to their feet. Chip looked for some of his advisees to command, "Perfect. Let's do it! We don't have much time; I think the race committee boat is leaving soon to set up the race course. I'm surprised your uncle let you free to come down here. By the way, seeing you twice in two weeks is amazing!" Chip waved down a few of the freshmen who were tending the race committee boat to hold up.

As she futilely attempted to invent any plausible excuse, none came to her, so she relented and also arose toward the docks. On her way down the steps, catching up to the other two, she explained her detour from London, "Well, we left New York early, made some time, and touched down a few hours early so it made for a perfect excuse to reminisce with my favorite senior mentor on the reservoir. I don't think he knows I am here yet. Or maybe he does since I have a small detail tagging along."

As they made their way onto the docks, Natalia changed into some neoprene sailing boots and thick, dry socks that Chip had brought for her to wear. He also handed her waterproof foul weather gear to wear in place of her wool coat. Decked out in full sailing attire, a full flashback began to take shape back to her collegiate and Olympic competition days. She imagined if she looked in a mirror, she might find her younger self staring back in disgust, asking her older self why she didn't sail anymore.

The race committee boat at Farmoor Reservoir was not much more than an oversized red inflatable dinghy, with a tiny outboard trolling motor. The two freshmen who were in charge of the boat relocated the red racecourse markers to the back, and Natalia jumped in the bow first and then assisted Chip as he ambled in as well. In the process of the dinghy leaving the dock, Natalia received a full measure of the chill in the air, as a small spray of water cast across the bow after they hit a small wave. Thankfully she had adorned the foul weather gear, as she zipped the jacket all the way over her chin and pulled the waterproof hood over her head. Now she was ready for the elements.

"Now that is the crisp Oxford breeze that I remember! How are the Cup preparations coming?" yelled Natalia, over the sound of the motor, while she felt the dinghy picking up speed toward the other side of the lake, with the bow spray blowing back into all their faces.

"Great! It's a real cooperative effort. Cowes, Portsmouth, and Brighton are all sending their best sailors, and students from Oxford and Cambridge are helping a lot! We have massive interest this year and I think we have a legitimate chance to win!" Chip knew that it was a long shot to win, but this campaign was the best set of yachts and crew that they had had in decades.

As they took their run around the racecourse, the freshmen were quietly dropping the markers in the water at their designated points for this race. Depending on the wind speed and direction, each practice race was different. Since it was windy they made the course longer and more challenging.

Chip exclaimed, "Hey, did you know two of the senior women here at Oxford are a challenger to qualify for the Olympics this year? They are in the 49er there with sail number 1422. Something like that would be monumental if we could have two women helming an Olympic Gold this year!"

As the first flags were going up, Natalia manned the air horn for the first warnings and the first starts. The 49er manned by the two female seniors was undeniably much faster than the men in the RS800s and the K8s helmed by the underclassmen. The unfair matchup was evident from the start with the two in the fast skiff maneuvering adeptly around all the other boats, keeping themselves in full wind all the way upwind. The breeze lifted the ladies upwind and they were at a perfect tack to the first mark. The committee boat was stationary with the starting line the same as the finish line so there was no need to move hence Chip and Natalia basked in the sunny breeze. A flock of ducks nonchalantly paddled by as the two old friends gazed longingly across the reservoir at the rolling hills on the other side.

"I can't believe it's been almost twenty years! Such great

times we had here with the team. Whatever happened to our trophies? Are they still up in Balliol Hall, do you suppose?" Natalia asked.

"Yes, and I think your sculling trophies are still there too. Do you want to drive by Holywell on the way back to London? Do you have a driver today? Maybe we can drive together, and your guy can follow?"

"Okay, that would be wonderful! And yes, I have a bit of a security detail!" exclaimed Natalia as she felt invigorated by the cool gusts of wind that were transforming her cheeks and nose to a color close to that of the bright red dinghy.

As the race ended, the 49er was a clear dozen or more boat lengths in front of the others, clearly beating any time the two female speedsters may owe the underclassmen. Boats in races are given ratings that allow slower boats more time to finish than faster boats, thus evening out the field. Natalia gazed at the two women and identified something in them that reminded her of herself almost twenty years ago. She proclaimed to Chip and the freshmen in the dinghy how far women's sailing had come in the past twenty-something-odd years.

"Back when I was 18, I was one of very few women in sailing and now it is becoming more common to have entire crews of women on boats challenging men for the trophies!" Natalia continued her remarks about the women who came before her in sports and those who are now carrying the torch.

Chip chimed in, "We have a long way to go, but true equality is almost at hand for women, even in this mixed-up world. Amazing that it didn't happen a long time ago. You and your mate were instrumental in encouraging the youth of yesteryear, who are now competing today. There was probably some 5-year-old girl in the audience in Athens who is sailing today because of you."

As they made their way to the dock, they helped pack up the markers and store them in the shed. As they were finishing, Demetrius, a short-haired older woman, and two young women made their way from the cafe to the dock. Chip knew exactly who it was since he was still involved with the Oxford club, but Natalia for a second didn't recognize her old mentor, who had grayed some in the interim. The two younger women were easily identified as the ladies they had just witnessed hand a drubbing to all the men on the racecourse.

"Oh, my goodness, Natalia, it has been so long! Look at you, you haven't changed a bit. Perhaps you are even stronger than in 2004!" her old coach exclaimed.

"Coach Milford, I have missed you so much, you have no idea! Are you still coaching the women here at Oxford?" Natalia asked, realizing that, in immersing herself in her work, she had not paid nearly enough attention to what was happening in England with all of her friends. It seemed the only ones she kept in touch with were Chip and Katya.

"Yes, I could never leave this place. Let me introduce you to Kate and Celine. These sailors are our best bets for gold for England this year. They did very well at the World 49er Championships in February beating, many all-male teams. Just missed the medal by a few points and one bad start. If that start had been better, they would have won gold! They are learning though. The near-perfect start they had today would have been good enough!"

The Olympic sailor in her was impressed, complementing them in superlatives, "Wow, congratulations to you both. We have come a long way since the days of merely trying to fight our way onto a boat, and you guys are going to be helming. I wish I could be there to see it for myself. We were watching you from the committee boat." Natalia was sizing up both young ladies. Both Kate and Celine were broad-shouldered and taller than Natalia. While Kate possessed red, fiery hair and an infectious smile, Celine's dark, radiant skin and black hair shimmered in the sunlight reflecting off the reservoir.

Celine nervously offered, "We have heard so much about you from Coach Milford. How did you do it? It must have been a lot of pressure!"

"Well, I also had a great teammate and great coaches in these two, that is for sure!"

Celine's deep brown eyes lit up and sparkled as she talked, and Natalia couldn't help but notice how unapologetically athletic and muscular she was. And Kate's physique was nearly the same. Natalia no doubt trained intensely when she was competing, but these girls must have been weight-training constantly. She thought to herself, This is how equality is won, with hard work and skill.

In the next hour, sitting at the cafe over a carafe of white wine, Natalia learned that Kate was originally born in Northern Ireland but came to London on scholarship for primary school and Celine got her start in her native Barbados and was the daughter of a sailing family. Celine came to London for boarding school at age 14. Identical to Natalia's Oxford pedigree, they excelled at both sculling and sailing. Natalia proudly regaled them with stories from her youth in Geneva, fighting to be a regular crew on a Formule 40 catamaran racing sailboat at age 16, and winning the Bol d'Or Mirabaud. She remarked that she had to be ten times better than the male she replaced to earn her start.

It was nearing late afternoon, and Natalia needed to depart now to return to London for her meeting, especially if she and Chip were going to pay a visit to Holywell and her old Oxford stomping grounds on the way. The schedule required her presence by 7 pm, leaving no spare time to reminisce at the Oxford campus.

It was a short drive through the English countryside to the school and the famed ancient edifices that appeared to be straight out of a Harry Potter movie. As they walked into Balliol College's Holywell Manor, with their drivers waiting at the curb, the memories came alive before them. In the foyer, in one of the numerous trophy cases, stood the trophy that Oxford seemingly won every year against Cambridge in rowing.

"Oh, Chip, we were so young and naive. What a great inspiration these walls were! We were going to conquer the world from here! Are we still going to conquer the world?" she asked rhetorically.

They didn't have long to stroll through the halls, but every step retrieved a memory and brought her full circle from where she began her career. There was a class picture on the wall that probably contained the brightest of the problem solvers all around the world this very day, remarking that she was now a Dean at Georgetown University. She needed to reconnect with some of these other people too, she thought. She was sure they were equally successful. A few were still acquaintances and communicated with Natalia and Chip due to their roles in business and government around the world. Right there, she resolved to do just that, reconnect with some of these old friends, as soon as she returned to New York.

At the end of the day, as Chip and Natalia exchanged hugs goodbye, Natalia thought seriously about getting back into sailing. Maybe she could help Chip's team win the America's Cup. After all, she had originally started her sailing career with catamarans and these foil boats were just catamarans with very thin hulls in the water on each side. But she also knew she already had too many sticks in the fire and too many family and work obligations for that to occur. Nonetheless, she could fantasize about navigating the open water and the invigorating feeling of winning once again. How did Chip manage it? She decided for that to happen, she needed more interns and more staff.

As she gazed out the window on her return trip to London, there was an unease in her psyche that yearned for the simple old days with school and her father and brothers. It dawned on her that her family life was more and more like a cutthroat business and less like a true family. Obligations and commitments existed that were no longer about family and much of that stemmed from her uncle Nikolai. It was at times like this, with all the meetings, that she felt like she had never left Russia.

~

CHAPTER 6: FOR MOTHER RUSSIA

~

For nearly a century, which was a fraction of its age of four centuries, Natalia's family owned a gothic castle in London near Trafalgar Square, complete with gargoyles and a tall tower. In a prior lifetime, the castle was the residence of a duke of some importance but had been updated through the years. The grand circle and meticulous landscaping were illuminated in an eerie way this foggy evening as Natalia's driver pulled through the gate next to the guard house. As she glanced down at her watch, she observed that she was uncharacteristically early. Unlike the last time she visited Volkov Castle, tonight, a bit more bustling activity was expected with much of the family attending the board meetings.

While she attended Oxford, Natalia would frequent these old haunts quite often to shop, watch the opera, or sometimes just to get away for an overnight stay in London. While on the surface it appeared daunting, cold, and frankly haunted, on the inside it was always very warm and welcoming to a lonely undergraduate. The long, tree-lined driveway was a trifle stark and cold with white Greek and Roman statues, which probably also led to its haunted reputation. White lights shined upward from the landscaping onto the edifice, casting shadows upon the gargoyles, which menacingly stared down upon the circle, warding away strangers.

Quite unexpectedly, Natalia spied several chauffeured cars parked beside the circle, next to the carriage house. As she exited the vehicle, she curiously walked up the well-worn limestone steps to the entrance, making a count of the number along the way. If only her father, two uncles, and two brothers were in attendance tonight, there may be four or five cars, but she counted more than a dozen cars, each with drivers waiting at the passenger door, which meant there would be more visitors than just the Volkov family. She pondered what she missed in her conversation with her uncle about this meeting that she had presumed would be just a family meeting.

As she entered the entrance hall, whatever assembly had just taken place was ending as the great hall door swung open, and from the entrance, she strained to recognize the faces of some of the participants. She knew they looked familiar, and many were expat Russians, but could not place any of their faces to a name. All except one, that is. She immediately and regrettably made eye contact with the final attendee who swaggered with her Uncle Nikolai's arm around his shoulders. This was Marcus Stefanskiy, a dubious fixture in the New York, London, and Paris social scenes, usually with model girlfriends on his arm and whose wealth had risen to billionaire status in the past decade, concurrently with her own family's rise to greatness. He was also the older cousin of Senator Jack Speransky and was rumored to have been made rich by his Russian connections. Flanking him to his left was her other uncle whom she rarely saw in London, yet supposedly he lived at this estate. He reportedly spent more time in France and Crete, often in the company of this Stefanskiy character.

It was not so unusual for her uncle to take meetings with hedge fund managers since lately her family's wealth was tied closely to the securities they marketed and not just the historical shipping and logistics business. She was pretty sure that all the participants here were also affiliated with securities of some sort. Unaware of many details of the securities division of

Volkov, she knew her Uncle Nikolai kept that part of the business close to his vest. Regardless of the details, since day one these securities had produced remarkably well for the bottom line of Volkov Industries. She was becoming suspicious, especially at this moment, that there could be some entanglement with money laundering of the Russian elite, moving money out of Russia. The mere presence of her other uncle suggested he was involved, which would make sense since he fraternized with the shadowy, underground finance circles.

Her Uncle Nikolai's eyes locked with hers in surprise, and his face contorted into something resembling a tiger's snarl but, like a cartoon character, swiftly metamorphosed into a sly smile. As shady as he appeared tonight, his demeanor was not out of the ordinary from what she remembered of him in her past. She only had a few seconds to reflect, but a thousand flashes of the same snarl played quickly through her mind. She had become accustomed to what she thought was his quirkiness, but with the passage of time and wisdom, he now seemed creepier than ever. The group of more than a dozen men entered the foyer and gave each other resounding hugs of congratulations, parting into the night - all except Stefanskiy.

Upon arrival and before the official board meeting, she and her brothers, Uncle Nikolai, and her father, would normally enter the study, providing a more informal meeting place for the five true Volkovs. Distant cousins and other relatives, while peripherally involved in the family business, were intentionally kept out of the loop by her uncle and hence not invited. True to character, the expat uncle would always arrive an hour late, finally allowing the Volkov board meeting to convene. Tonight, she thought, would be entirely different.

With the gathering disbanded, her Uncle Nikolai moved toward her, still arm-in-arm with the French-Russian playboy that he seemed to revere, based on his fawning behavior. "Natalia, have you made acquaintances with Mr. Stefanskiy?" her uncle asked, speaking in Russian, making his best attempt to make her uncomfortable.

"I have not, but I think we have some acquaintances in common. I think my friend Katya has been to your parties in

Cannes." Natalia, as was customary and required, also spoke in a perfect St. Petersburg dialect. She cringed as Stefanskiy held out his hand to her. She had lied just then but did not want to give him any satisfaction of the knowledge that she remembered him. Years ago, when she was sixteen, on a school excursion in Paris, he had made a very overt attempt upon her favor that she did not appreciate. She was utterly frightened that he was being too forceful with his advances. Escaping unscathed proved difficult, but nonetheless she managed to injure more than just his pride. After all these years, the episode continued to be a major reason she distanced herself from the expat Russian scene in Europe and the US.

"Well, why don't you join Katya next time? We always have a magnificent time! I am having a holiday party this year. I will save room for you and Katya in the guest house if you promise to be there!"

Wouldn't happen in a million years, Natalia thought to herself. She knew what happened in the "guest house" in Cannes. Never. There were few things that unnerved Natalia, but this individual was probably the only person who made her nervous. She steeled her will, clenched her jaw, and placed her hands behind her back as she curtsied politely to please her uncle while speaking through her teeth. "It seems I am entirely locked up in New York with work. I will check with Katya to see what her plans are though."

Her uncle, noticing the slight, responded, "Well, do check your calendar, Natalia, maybe you could make some time to visit our great friend for such a grand holiday, honoring Mother Russia. I have been to his estate in Cannes as well. It is magnificent!"

"Well, if you are there, Uncle Nikolai, I would definitely change my mind," Natalia corrected her supposed social faux pas with a perfect comeback only for his benefit.

Stefanskiy extended his arm toward Natalia again, this time touching her shoulder, "We would love to have you this year." He strode ever so close to her and attempted to put his arm around her.

Natalia, standing ready to defend herself, if necessary,

54

gracefully pivoted away from the vulgarity of it all, gave him a pat on the shoulder, and twisted further away to avoid the embrace. The maneuver allowed her to feign bringing herself closer to her uncle but then backed away from them both. "Thanks, shall we get to our meeting, Uncle Nikolai?"

"Why yes, let's do indeed. Thanks once again for your assistance, Marcus. We have other business to attend to and you will be the first one I notify when the agreement is executed." Not noticing his niece's discomfort, he then faced Stefanskiy and embraced him, steering his guest toward the door, where the lone remaining chauffeur awaited to whisk him away.

Natalia turned swiftly on her nimble feet and strode confidently away from the situation with all of her being clenched in a steel resolve to not look back as the foul piece of excrement exited the estate. That was the most uncomfortable situation her uncle had ever trapped her in, but from now on she would expect no less. Never again would she trust the core of his character, conceding that he exclusively worshipped wealth over integrity, and, surprisingly enough, over family as well.

She had an inkling the purpose of her uncle's gathering was to introduce a new fund or investment that either he or one of these managers had cooked up. The presence of Stefanskiy suggested a nefarious scheme was afoot and Natalia was going to find out one way or another. Her brothers were also in attendance, but from the background slipped quietly into the study almost unnoticed. Alexei, the younger one, worked closely with her uncle and, given his banking background, involved himself with the securities projects. If she had to guess, the answer to the new business dealings would run straight through him.

As Natalia entered the spacious study, she immediately melted, as that same orange flickering glow cast on the bookshelves from the roaring fire jarred her memories of the London of yesteryear. The cozy warmth stood in stark contrast to the frigid entrance hall where her uncle lingered still. Aleksandr arose from his chair to plant a big hug on his sister before sinking back into one of the comfortable chairs opposite the desk. Her father had already taken up a position on an oversized leather sofa, but also heartily embraced his daughter and pointed at the open space beside him. Natalia, finally sensing some comfort, took her place and instantly relaxed, letting out a short-lived sigh of relief. Extinguishing the warmth, her Uncle Nikolai finally entered the room and began to pace behind the large antique desk.

Preempting her uncle's impending tirade, Natalia genuinely wished she could spend some alone time with just her siblings, so she blurted out, "It is so great to see you, Alexandr! How are your studies in business school?" Natalia loved her brother's grounded attitude that could calm even the tensest situation when they were children.

"Great," he replied. "I'm going to intern for Uncle Nikolai again this summer."

Natalia's favorite studying location in Volkov Castle was deep in the comfort of this large leather sofa with its accompanying ornate iron and glass table perfectly made for a laptop. With no use for a computer tonight, she shifted and settled into the corner of the plush leather and waited for her uncle to begin. He paced a few more steps, obviously perturbed at the preemption, and it now seemed apparent there was something pressing to discuss.

Her uncle started in, again in a classic, Old Northern Russian dialect, "The next several months will be critical for the success of the Volkov family and Mother Russia. We expect to emerge in this new decade victorious against our adversaries and bring pride and victory home to Moscow and especially St. Petersburg. This will be the dawning of a new day..." Pausing for dramatic effect, he continued, "What this undertaking will require, will be unity of this family for the common good of Mother Russia. Mother Russia will emerge victorious and the pre-eminent economy in the world!"

Natalia should have expected the alarming turn of events for what was usually a low-key reporting of the upcoming family and local St Petersburg events. The customary summer lake house family get-togethers no longer existed? she asked herself. He typically did wax poetically about nationalism and

56

Mother Russia, but this was not poetic at all. She wondered what would have brought on this burst of xenocentrism but waited with bated breath to find out.

After a few more minutes of this diatribe, she soon realized that her uncle had ulterior plans afoot and she decided to feign some true nationalism so that she could ascertain what his intentions were. "What do we need to do? As you know we would all do anything to see Mother Russia in her rightful place. She will always be victorious." Her father looked at her with an inquisitive look on his face and she winked back at him surreptitiously.

Nikolai Volkov breathed in a deep breath and continued, "At this point, strategies have been laid in place for immense economic prosperity and for the West to crumble at our feet, and we will wait for Mother Russia's call for us to act accordingly!" Nikolai's voice was booming with his hand over his heart as though he was speaking in a crowded hall.

Natalia could feel her spine tingle, and the hair on her arms was standing out when a chill shook her for just a second. She sensed this Russian prosperity would require more from her than just feigned interest in Mother Russia and historical artifacts for a museum.

"Natalia, I understand you can work remotely. Do you think that this summer you could come home to St. Petersburg to assist with some financial dealings? We can renovate the summer lake house in the country, and you will be very comfortable. Your Mother Russia asks you to fulfill your duty."

She recognized the immediate, desperate occasion for her best delay tactic, thinking, This summer? It was already May. Her AI was ready to deploy, and it would take at least a month of analysis. How could she delay this until at least July? She paused to think of an excuse, ultimately deciding on the easy, "I could come home after Russia Day, soon after July 1st? As you said you wanted me to celebrate Russia Day with Katya in Cannes."

"The first of July would be fine. I will commence the renovations. Advise me now if there are any special requests."

"I shall require a workstation and video conferencing

equipment," she replied. "And can you arrange to have the summer garden and veranda renovated like it used to be when Alexei and Alexandr and I were kids?"

"Certainly. As you wish," was his terse reply. He reached for the folders he had set on the desk and cradled them in his arms as if they were nuclear secrets and made his way to the entrance hall to leave.

Now that was settled. The compromise gave her time to concoct another feasible delay in July to avoid a permanent move back to Russia. She cherished her freedom in New York and London. She felt an oppressive amount of pressure from her uncle when she was under his watchful eye in St Petersburg. The simple freedom to travel the globe, pursuing her own interests apart from Mother Russia and Uncle Nikolai, pleased her to no end.

As her uncle strode out of the study, her other uncle followed him, turning right to enter the great hall. The Volkov Family meeting adjourned with no other business than Natalia moving back to St. Petersburg. The mood of the rest of the occupants of that room could best be described as despondent, but only for a few seconds as her father slid closer to her on the couch and gently put his arm around her. After about a minute, assured that his brothers were out of range, he whispered to his children, "Not to worry, don't let his theatrics ruin a good Volkov family reunion! Let's all remember the great times we have had in London at this magnificent estate!"

He was right, for even before Oxford, at least once yearly, her father and mother would bring Natalia and her brothers here to experience the world's best opera at the Royal Opera House just a few blocks away. Her mother absolutely loved the opulence of London and the opera. They even saw the Queen for heaven's sake.

Her father sat back, staring at the roaring fire beside them, reminiscing a more innocent time, "Do you remember when Alexandr almost ran down the hall near Queen Elizabeth? Do you remember Alexei? I barely caught your arm before you escaped, running full speed."

Alexei laughed, and sputtered, "No, I don't. But I do

remember the opera. The best part of London!"

With the mood lightened, Natalia knew she had better return to New York before any further family developments happened. "Let's come back this fall to attend the premiere of the season! Can we?" she asked her father.

"Yes, let's plan it. Don't mention it to your uncle though. You know how he gets about Russian opera being the best on the planet. We may be obliged to make an appearance at the St Petersburg opera to assuage him."

"You have a point about that. Is it possible to turn around the plane tonight to go back to New York? I have so much work to do this week."

"But you just arrived! Can't you stay for just one night? I think between Sven and the copilot it could be done, but..."

"I think I will take my leave now before Uncle Nikolai tries to bring me back to Russia on your plane," Natalia said with a frown.

"Don't you worry, Nikolai is not going to force anyone to go anywhere they don't want to go. It won't happen while I am still here to prevent it. Let's collect your bags and I will summon Sven and Valeria."

In less than an hour she was half-way to the airport, wistfully wishing she could stay in London with Chip instead, but her future lay in New York. She managed to hold it together for her father, but she knew something was dreadfully wrong about her uncle's plans. The only person she could confide in was Chip. She wished he could fly to New York with her. Maybe she could trust Katya but for the first time in her life she sensed that may not be a good idea. What about Valeria? And the Wi-Fi on the plane? Good thing she used a VPN for connection. She thought about texting him regarding the developments, but it was slowly becoming apparent that she should only send encrypted texts from now on.

As she boarded the plane, she remarked to Valeria that she would like to get some rest. "Could you make up the bedroom?" This would remove herself from the watchful eye of her detail. With all that was on her mind, she would not sleep a wink tonight, but she needed silence to consider her options. How would she delay what would surely be an inevitable confrontation with her uncle?

~

CHAPTER 7: AC75 SAILING

~

Within an hour after Chip said goodbye to Natalia on the Oxford campus, he headed by helicopter directly to Portsmouth for meetings and then on to the Isle of Wight to prepare for the Admiral's Cup. The race pitting various British sailing teams against each other was the first in several years. With the hosting of the America's Cup coming up, the Royal Ocean Racing Club had set about reorganizing the annual race to increase the number of practice runs on the Solent. He arrived late in the evening on the helipad at the waterfront house, and as he and Sam hopped down under the now barely spinning blades of the rotors, he knew why he so loved this island home of his. The chill in the air granted him new-found energy as he deeply inhaled the crisp, salty ocean air through his nostrils. The excitement in the air on this island for sailing was palpable and electric.

Tomorrow promised to be a big day, and the weather was predicted to be perfectly breezy for a long-distance practice race. A good rest tonight would be essential because he would be rousted out of bed by Sam and the staff by 5 am to be at the docks for team preparation by 6 am. The rest of the crew had been busy getting the boat provisioned and checking all the gear. On Saturday, the Admiral's Cup would be a shorter race, but tomorrow's practice race would be 35 miles, from Cowes to the mouth of the Lymington River, then past Portsmouth and back. Practicing with the last of the polar easterlies of the season would be crucial to their success, by simulating what it would be like next March for the America's Cup. One more race Sunday would again have a more eastern bent past Portsmouth and back to finish out the last of the practice runs before the easterlies would die down for the summer. These would be tough upwind close reaches with the wind just off the bow followed by downwind speed trials.

The spectator views during the America's Cup and indeed every race on the Solent would be spectacular, from Queen Victoria's Castle on the Isle of Wight to the forts and castles of Portsmouth. The backdrops of the historical HMS Victory and the Portsmouth Dockyard were sure to bring the history of sailing into close contact with the future of foil sailing. Portsmouth and the Solent had been famous for first building and then hiding the Allied submarines during World War II. The German Luftwaffe could not penetrate the Solent with the close proximity of the batteries along the shores. And now the British would hope to defeat the Kiwis to bring the Cup back home.

As they arrived at the Royal Sailing Squadron base early Friday morning, the boats, large and small, were lined up like sardines on the many docks toward town. They arrived more than thirty minutes early, so it was still dark as they followed the many sailors to grab their only sustenance of the day from the hospitality tents set up on the boardwalk.

They were both decked out in yellow waterproof foul-weather gear, ready to take whatever punishment this small piece of the English Channel had to dish out. Chip's excitement couldn't be contained as he almost skipped down the boardwalk. "Are you ready, Sam? Today marks a huge swing in momentum for English sailing! By this time next year, we will be so ready for those New Zealanders! They won't know what hit them when they taste their first Easterly across their jaw!"

"You've got that right! Experience will win the cup for us next year!" Sam replied, receiving his hot breakfast sandwich on a paper plate from the breakfast vendor who was bundled up, complete with knitted mittens. Today, Sam would be captaining the pursuit boat, a fast 44-foot center-console powerboat to monitor the racers for safety reasons.

The skipper's meeting was slated for 8 am and the approach to racing began at 10 am. As the first hint of daylight crept into the Eastern night sky, he met the crew at his boat, a beautiful brand new J45 with pristine teak and an impeccable waterline. She was maintained well by the vessel maintenance crew of Merlin Commerce, who were based in Portsmouth and were just as adept at repairing a 300-meter cargo ship as they were at keeping a 45-foot racing sailboat in tip-top shape.

The morning was a crisp 8 degrees Celsius, the visibility clear, and a nice easterly breeze was beginning to brew as the rising sun outlined Fort Gilkicker at the inlet to Portsmouth Harbour. The sunny, yet chilly weather would provide the sailors with a magnificent weekend of racing. As the fading night changed to morning light, at the end of the municipal dock, Chip could now identify one of three new AC75s each with her team ready to be tested in the winds and chop of the Solent. Much of the remaining America's Cup backup crew was racing on the local boats today to be sure they had three full teams of backups.

He saw his job today to keep a clean race, to evaluate the AC75s as their start was before his, and to monitor the tactics of the foiling yachts as they passed Chip and his J45 on the way back to Cowes, probably finishing before his class even rounded the first mark. He was happy to be given a small part of this revolution of sailing which was the AC75 class. The America's Cup likely would never return to the one-design monohull concept of yesteryear. Speed and tech were the name of the game in the future of sailing.

It had not been long since Chip's last America's Cup sailing experience, and the sport had changed so much in those few years. As the boats motored out to their starting line where the committee boat awaited, the slower yachts steered completely clear of the first start because these AC75s were astoundingly fast and needed a lot of room to jockey for a starting position. Seconds before the start, the sails filled, the boats lifted up onto the foils and literally began to fly through the air just aloft of the water. Like a rocket, they were off and running toward the first mark, and then after rounding that first mark, the boats were traveling so close to head to the wind that it amazed all who were within sight of the inspiring display.

After the two starts, the distance made the race long and arduous, but they accomplished what they held this race for, which was great practice in a tough wind. The sleek AC75s performed flawlessly in this wind, in both directions, upwind and downwind. Undoubtedly, the British team would be hard to beat in this iteration of the America's Cup. If Chip and Sam were betting men, they would have placed their bets within minutes of coming ashore that day.

As they were wrapping up the day, Sam docked the pursuit boat behind the J-boat, with the wind dying down and the sun slowly escaping to the west. This time of year, even the storm worthy boat he was driving could prove to be a wet one because of the rough weather, often necessitating a change of clothes. He removed the wet foul-weather jacket and laid it over the seat to dry in the sun. On the J45, Chip busied himself securing the lines and closing hatches. Stepping down onto the dock, he checked his phone and curiously noticed that he had received a text from Natalia. However, this time she sent her message via an encrypted app, which piqued his interest. Nevertheless, he decided to wait to read it after he made it into the warm comfort of the Yachtsman.

Sam quipped, "What magnificent speed they displayed out there today!" He had just finished tying the lines on the pursuit boat and set about helping the crew of Chip's boat as they tightened her lines and stowed the sails.

Chip, ready to enjoy the warmth, started up the dock a few steps to hurry Sam, before turning around, remarking, "Amazing, I think they held an absolutely incredible line upwind!

Should be fun to see if down in New Zealand the crew can perform this well consistently."

As he and Sam wandered up the wooden dock to the promenade, they commented to each other how much better prepared the AC75 team seemed to be than they were a year ago. The race was a stunning display of how swift and nimble they were on the water at the marks. When they finally ascended to the promenade, they shouted to the AC75 crew-members, who were walking up the main harbour dock after buttoning up their boats for the night. Security was tight on the promenade as each of these boats was valued at more than twenty million pounds.

As Chip entered his favorite pub, he removed his phone from his pocket to glance at Natalia's text and then stopped abruptly. As Sam turned around to ask what he would like to order for dinner, Sam observed the eyes-wide-open surprise on his face. Chip read the concerning text out loud to Sam, "My uncle is requiring me to work from Russia this summer. Am trying to delay it." The next text, "I flew back to New York late last night to get away from the family. Something is up with my uncle and his business dealings. Can't place my thumb on it. Sorry, I didn't text you. I didn't want to text on the plane."

At first thought, the move didn't seem ominous, but it suddenly dawned on Chip exactly what her controlling uncle had in mind with this requirement. By keeping her close to the family estate in St Petersburg, he would be able to more closely monitor her movements and activities. Deep down, Chip also thought there could be something even more sinister at play. What was his motive for this sudden change? he thought. And now it seemed, with her early departure, Natalia was fearfully running away from her uncle, and she must have some of the same thoughts that he was having.

After Chip showed the physical text to Sam so he could read it himself, it set off a cascade of thoughts in Sam's security-conscious mind. He rattled them off one by one to an incredulous listener, "First, she took the family jet, once she departed, she didn't want to text on the plane due to her family spying on her. Second, let's activate some basic security measures for both ourselves and more importantly, for Natalia. Don't let her know that simple fact. We don't want to scare her any further than she already is. Third, let's track her tail number and all her family's other planes. And fourth, and I am not done, I will secure all our teams, and let's not take on any other security contracts. Any of these Ukrainians I told you about that want our security services will have to wait."

Chip shot back, "Agreed. Let's get back to the house and call in Torey for some help in the US. It should be early afternoon there now. There is something not right about this Nikolai Volkov. I've thought he was shady ever since I met him when Natalia and I were in college." When Chip had gut feelings about bad people, they were never wrong.

Torey was Sam's go-to guy for these situations in the US. He was a former Army Ranger and now retired FBI agent who had perfected personal protection in the most dangerous areas of the world. This soldier was precisely the solution Sam always counted on in New York. "Agreed, Torey is the guy. I can have him in New York tonight. Calling him now. Why wait? Just to be ready and get the lay of the land, so to speak,"

A few minutes later, a brief phone call was placed to Torey, and the arrangements were made for Natalia's security. Sam spoke a little more calmly now that Torey was involved. "He will keep a close eye on her for the time being. Let's get back to the house and weigh all of our options."

Tonight, the Goddard's and the shepherd's pie would be put on hold until another night. The phantom was parked close by, and they did not waste time turning up Queen's Road and darting down the driveway into the underground garage. Sam and Chip spent the next few hours working on logistics and security with their several advance teams. Torey's team would be in place by tonight while Natalia was fast asleep. They called in two additional security teams for their own purposes.

They could not anticipate in a million years how many teams they would ultimately need just to survive the next several weeks.

~

Chapter 8: Sean Stamos

~

An epic crush of activity waited impatiently for Sean Stamos to arrive early this morning at the Washington offices of the Federal Bureau of Investigation. The sun would not rise for another two hours, and the night watch in the war room was rocking with Europe and Asia's daytime crises. The J. Edgar Hoover FBI Building was the epicenter of protecting American citizens from global threats to the security of the United States of America. The aging, monolithic building belied the technological powerhouse housed within it that protected its fellow citizens. It was still three months before the G7 meeting of the ministers from the seven largest economies in the world, and the Counterintelligence Division was actively assessing ominous warnings from terrorist organizations and had set about the work of meticulously vetting each country's guest list.

In addition, the daily threat list compiled by all the clandestine activities organizations, including the CIA, FBI, and National Intelligence was growing longer each day as loose chatter from terrorists and credible intelligence was closely monitored. Sean Stamos was fresh off assignment in the Eurasia Section where he had investigated, uncovered, and then negotiated the prosecution/settlement of multiple cases of Russian money laundering through a major European bank and in the process unearthed staggering corruption in our own country linked to a major election.

Sean Stamos' specialty was national security law and technology. The team he was an integral part of was especially adept at uncovering transactions such as mirror trades and following shadow cryptocurrency transactions. How they monitored this clandestine, illegal activity was highly classified. It was so classified that the information they had uncovered for the most recent settlement wasn't even brought forth into the case. It was withheld so that they could continue to trace the monetary transfers. Once they became aware of the mirror trades, all they had to do was subpoena the accounts from which the trades came. FISA warrants and the classified material never came to light, and it never surfaced in the election interference investigation, because it was classified.

The secrecy was not ideal, for the American people deserved the truth about their leaders' involvement in this episode. However, Stamos also recognized that the methods that were used to uncover this episode of American history needed to survive to see another day. The malware and surveillance techniques being used on our enemies could and would save countless American lives in the future, but only if they remained hidden. He was comfortable with that fact, for he appreciated they would be utilizing those same tools today and day after day after that.

The well-worn trail was dark this morning with the new moon, and Stamos and Chelsvig were not alone, with probably about a dozen cadets sharing the training grounds. Built next to a wooded reservoir, most of these lands were completely overgrown for training but a single four-mile trail along the shore was a popular pre-dawn ritual. Headlights were a prerequisite here for all, because, despite the marked trail, there was not a single light near the trail. Even on full moon nights, the tall trees provided cover that blocked out all light.

"Welcome back, son! Shall we get started? I'm not in the shape I used to be in. Run at your own pace; don't wait

70

for me." Chelsvig, a few decades older than Stamos, was being modest. His idea of being out of shape, even with his beat-up body, would compete with most of the cadets on the trail.

"Alright, old man. Let's see what you've got. I'm pretty beat up too. Just getting back into it. Still have a slight limp. Whatever. So, what do you think of my new temporary assignment?" asked Stamos, already a yard behind his mentor.

"I think you will get bored really quick. I give it about a week before your adrenaline junkie brain begs you to get back out into the field." Chelsvig rounded a young sapling at a bend in the trail and jumped over the same old log these two had been jumping over for the past decade.

The younger agent, hurdling the log with his headlamp illuminating the hazard, retorted with a question, "How do you think I am going to even need fieldwork for the next few months in this position?"

"Don't worry it will happen," Chelsvig was surprised Stamos still clung to the notion that he was not addicted to the action, especially after dozens of injuries had briefly sidelined him and the same Jonesing occurred time after time.

"You're probably right. That's not what happens though. I can quit any time I want. I just don't have a reason to hang it up yet." Stamos was sure of that. There was only one reason he would give up fieldwork.

The sprint to the end of the trail would challenge their abused joints, but Stamos pulled ahead at the last minute, besting his mentor again. There were times like these when he thought his elder allowed him to win every time just for psychological reasons. Regardless, he was running late and only had enough time for a few circuits in the gym if he wanted to arrive early at 6.

Having finished weight training at the gym on the fourth floor of the FBI training facility in Quantico, he casually skipped down the steps toward the parking lot, taking note of all the cadets and Marine recruits also getting their starts to the day. Most of his fellow Counterintelligence Cybersecurity division team members were computer hackers, not the gym rat types. Stamos mused they were more likely to be found living in their parent's basement. Stamos certainly was not your usual FBI Counterintelligence agent either but for a different reason. Most of his comrades had risen through the ranks of the Criminal division, however, Stamos had arrived at the FBI as a hybrid CIA and National Intelligence appointment. He possessed a coveted law degree from Georgetown University and was recruited heavily by the CIA. After joining as an attorney, he was initially assigned as part of the inspector general's office, the legal watchdog for the CIA.

After only a month on the job as the junior attorney at the CIA, he became acquainted with a man who would eventually become his mentor, the infamous Bret Chelsvig. As Stamos tells the story, he was actually investigating Mr. Chelsvig for possible wrongdoing but found far from it in his estimation. Afterward, the pair began to work out together since Chelsvig, the clandestine CIA agent, also lived near Quantico. Subsequently, Stamos was gradually drawn into the field as an undercover attorney for the CIA and DNI because of his expertise in monitoring financial transactions in real-time.

No longer an office job, cybersecurity and technology counterintelligence at the CIA required more and more field-work to get close to those under surveillance. Agents were not only tracing account activity that occurred last month, last week, or even yesterday, but they were also tracing up-to-the-minute transactions. These transactions in cryptocurrency could not be monitored from afar unless you had access to a keystroke program embedded in the trader's computer or the crypto-exchange computer. In today's world, financial surveillance was waged like a drone strike in a war room, with immediate consequences. The FBI and CIA's targets had developed sophisticated means of operating undetected, at least until Sean Stamos came on board with not only legal expertise of subpoenas but also the experience of using more modern surveillance techniques. For Stamos, more effective surveillance now involved capturing the cellular, satellite, Wi-Fi, or Bluetooth signal directly from the computer to hack into the transactions. He functioned as the electronic drone pilot, taking out financial and cybercriminals.

Due in no small part to Stamos' tactics, which brought to bear the largest money-laundering settlement with the German bank, money-laundering banks and criminals had begun to change their schemes for these mirror trades, and the monitored activity slowly began to disappear. However, with the FBI, CIA, and National Intelligence surveillance directly on the signals of the bad actors themselves, the spigot of information could be turned on again. Installing keystroke programs on these computers helped initially, but the Russians and Chinese had begun utilizing brand new computers out of the box called virgins for each set of transactions, so it became difficult surveillance to tackle. Investigators monitored the IP address location of the computers and servers on a daily basis in addition to all electronic communications entering and leaving whatever building they were watching.

Constantly ahead of their pursuers, bad actors had begun to trade in the stock markets in dark trades that were not able to be monitored. Again, the only way to recognize and capture these traders was to know that they existed in the first place and directly surveil them in real-time. That was where the state-of-the-art modern surveillance by our Cybersecurity division came in. Because this surveillance by necessity was in the field, the division required new recruits to be more like field agents but with computer science training, and not just hackers eating Doritos in their parents' basements. This line of work could be dangerous; therefore, it was crucial for these agents to be athletic and lethal if they had to be. The ideal agent was a military-trained, but well-educated, hacker.

Coincidentally, growing up in Maine, there were two local sports that Stamos liked and those were sailing and rugby. He was a mediocre sailor but just good enough to keep him in good standing with the family, particularly his father who built boats for a living. What he really loved and excelled at was rugby and Aussie Rules Football. He was also extremely proficient at gaming of all kinds. He was mediocre in school subjects during middle school and woke up academically when he was finally able to take mostly science and computer classes in high school. In fact, between his rugby prowess, test scores, and his grades he earned full-ride scholarship offers from almost everywhere that had both rugby and computer science. That meant most of the Ivy League, but also some English schools including Oxford and Cambridge. He chose the latter because of its association with Stephen Hawking and the Physics and Computer Science departments there.

Fast forward a few years and here he was, the secret star of the intelligence community, fresh off this victory against one of the largest German banks which was now licking its wounds and had learned its lesson. It was now under various consent orders to monitor money laundering activity under KYC (Know Your Customer) procedures, which became standard banking practice. But in no time flat, the money laundering had moved to smaller privately held banks in more difficult locations such as Cyprus, Crete, and Tanzania.

Not the city type, he consciously avoided living in Washington, DC, maintaining a small house near the Quantico, Virginia FBI Academy where he could train and be close to the fresh law enforcement officers and new Marine recruits at Marine Base Quantico. He preferred this residence far away from the politics of the District. He was so rarely home anyway, so why spend the big dollars to buy anything in the city? This meant a long drive through traffic to his offices in DC, but Stamos didn't mind as he took the back roads in one of his two babies, his vintage Porsche 911 or his Ducati Superleggera muscle bike.

Today, he chose the 1968 V6 fully restored, flashy, red German supercar and as the whine of the engine expressed his control over the road on this stretch of backwoods Virginia highway, he was excited for this new assignment. He was probably the most publicly facing secret agent in all of the CIA, National Intelligence, and the FBI. The timing of this position change could not be any better, with the new investigative tools coming online later this year.

The radio was blasting classic John Mellencamp as he finally reached the Hoover Building parking garage. As he downshifted, the whine increased in both pitch and volume, but Stamos paid no notice to the engine, as the speakers continued to burst forth with the classic song, "Hurts So Good". He played two drum beats to the music on the steering wheel while he backed into the parking spot. The noise of the engine dissipated, but the radio played on for a minute, while Stamos removed his mirrored sunglasses, which were unnecessary since the sun had not even risen yet. Now that was relaxing, he thought, as he sat in his car, changing his mindset into the analytical mind he needed for this mission. So, this was how the change would begin, he thought. Now he would begin the next chapter of his legal career, and it would test every mental and physical element of his being. He was happy for the moment to be out of the field since he thought the last assignment was so rough with the resultant loss of agents' lives.

It would be easy for Stamos to think that all new assignments would be easier than that one, but he also knew that he had only scratched the surface of the underbelly of cybercrimes and money laundering. Money launderers were not exceptionally pleased to be discovered and often eliminated their pursuers. Luckily for Stamos, no bad actors from this most recent stint who knew his face or name lived to tell about it. Not even our intelligence counterparts in Germany knew of Stamos' clandestine roles.

He took off his flight jacket, placed it over the leather seat, pulled a suit jacket out of the back seat, and shut the door. He was dressed sharply in a thin tie and blue collared shirt. As he nonchalantly pulled the suit jacket over his shoulders, he strolled through the parking garage and into the Hoover building. Ready for next.

§

$$\sim$$

CHAPTER 9: NEW OPS

$$\sim$$

On its surface, the thought of less fieldwork and proximity to home working here at FBI headquarters would be a welcome temporary change for Stamos. At the very least, it would allow his injuries to heal before Chelsvig's prediction would likely come true and the lure of the action would draw him out of this cocoon. Until then, he envisioned the light duty forced upon him by the government would allow him to perform an advisory role for a month or two. What kind of trouble could he get into supervising these agents? After all, the targeted money launderers were not exceptional and the banks they used were small and surely would not possess the deep legal pockets that the previous case had carried. Even so, his mentors and indeed all of his antecedent experience had taught him never to underestimate his adversary.

The morning kicked off with a flurry of financial intelligence dispatches that could not be ignored, complete with flashy titles such as "Critical" and "Time Sensitive" attached to them. Multiple overseas field offices of the CIA had noticed an increase in financial activity by known criminal organizations at a few smaller European banks with an unknown extent and nature of these transactions. During that morning's meetings with his team, Stamos had developed a plan to first obtain the warrants needed for surveillance and then subpoena the necessary documents from two of them, the Bayerngeld Bank and the Chernov Bank. The accounts of these Russian oligarchs that might be laundering money would be difficult to trace. It was painfully obvious that the Chernov Bank was not going to comply in a meaningful way with up-front subpoenas. Therefore, it might be necessary to obtain these documents by other means and then follow up with subpoenas related to the information to find out how truthful they were. This meant the involvement of the DNI, NSA, and CIA. This is precisely why Stamos and Chelsvig were placed in leadership of this FBI division. The pair had a track record of success and previous experience as CIA cybersecurity operatives. They also cultivated high-level contacts and trust within the Office of DNI and the NSA that would prove useful for intelligence gathering.

The entire basis of Stamos' career was laid down before he graduated from law school. It was more than a decade ago when he first set his sights on national security and technology law at Georgetown. Those few classes taught by an aging professor and retired CIA agent named Theodore Kremer exposed him to the vital importance of protecting America's interests abroad. When he graduated, he was first invited to interview with the FBI but at that interview, in attendance, were all four of the clandestine three-letter agencies. Even though he was to be trained in the FBI academy and officially would be an FBI attorney in the inspector general's office, his duties extended to all clandestine activities. It was then that he first met Bret Chelsvig, who at the time was the star of the CIA, having bested their Russian and Chinese counterparts in dozens of classified and never-reported cyber battles. Soon enough, his true clandestine duties would fall under both the FBI and CIA. After a rigorous year of training in cybersecurity and espionage at Langley, his official office was in the Cybersecurity Division in the J. Edgar Hoover Building, but his clandestine activities would take him around the world, first to Japan, then China, followed by the Eastern European countries of the former Soviet Union.

Today, lost in thoughts of lessons learned from his former exploits, he strolled from his offices down the halls, and into the final planning meeting in the sensitive compartmented information facility (SCIF) room, he could remember walking these same halls to the same meeting room as the rookie on the team and vividly envisioned Chelsvig beaming with all the confidence in the world. At the time, and still today and always until his dying breath, the je ne sais quoi about Chelsvig was indelibly imprinted upon everyone he touched. Put simply into words, at least part of le quoi was the notion that each and every day, through ups and downs, America and its ideals of justice and freedom would always win the day.

At that first meeting ten years ago, he raised his out-stretched hand to shake Chelsvig's, and there was no hesitation as Chelsvig stretched his arm around Stamos' shoulders and brought him to the front of the room. At that time, Chels-vig was not in any leadership position on these teams yet, but you would think he was by the way he commanded the room. "Come up here, Mr. Sean Stamos, and tell us how we are going to win today," Chelsvig projected. As they were studying what was a dossier on a Russian money laundering operation, Chels-vig rattled off the entire list of forty Russians who were under active surveillance and the daily reports of all conversations, electronic or otherwise, were flashing in real-time on the 10 screens on the long wall of the room. Notably, there were a few Americans on this list who would eventually become famous and infamous.

At first loathe to comment, Stamos remarked, "We are already winning, just by the fact they have no idea we are here."

Chelsvig threw his arms up in the air, bellowing in a deep baritone voice, "Exactly! This is where you and I are going to show these mafia guys that, even in the safety of their mother-land, they will not truly be safe from the long arm of the FBI. We are going to use their own weapon of anonymity against them today." The entire room of investigators was standing at this point and suddenly felt the electricity of a lightning storm through their spines.

"Yes, sir. I am all in one hundred fifty percent! Let's turn the tables on these guys," Stamos proclaimed as everyone prepared to perfect the action plan for that eventful week in 2010. Russia had just invaded Georgia a few years before, while the Russian President and Premier were cementing their power over Russia and their Russian billionaire henchmen were wreaking havoc all over Eastern Europe and Northern Asia. And America had run into its worst economic downturn in history. Little did they know how important the groundwork that was accomplished that day would eventually become for their future missions over ten years later. And how the economic events of 2008 in America would tie into their work in Russia.

As part of his clandestine duties, whenever there was an official joint meeting between China or Russia and the US, he was sent under diplomatic cover as either an inspector general or a state department attorney under a pseudonym created by the FBI or CIA. He operated frequently in both bureau offices and set up surveillance out of these embassies concentrating on financial surveillance. In full disguise at all times, he became a master of physical feature and dental enhancement. He would be assigned the title of Legal Assistant to the Ambassador for either the East Asian Bureau for China or the Eurasian Bureau in the case of Russia, but in reality, he was cultivating intelligence through surveillance of the computer systems of the Chinese or Russian criminal investigative agencies.

Following the money trail, this venture ultimately led him to focus on Russian money laundering activities. The Chinese government certainly had its fair share of nefarious operations but paled in comparison to the Russians in scope and size. Chinese state corporations were wholly occupied with increasing their manufacturing capabilities which required technological corporate espionage, the subject of an entirely different team in the FBI. Most of their investments internationally involved bribing local officials to allow these investments for natural resources. The Chinese tech and bribery espionage was handed over to a different team and henceforth Stamos was assigned to monitor the Russians and Eastern bloc countries, especially Ukraine and Belarus.

Today, eerily similar to a decade ago, Chelsvig held the same confident swagger, greeting his men, "Gentlemen, this is Operation Genghis Khan. How do we defeat our adversaries? With no mercy! By the time we are finished, we will know every detail of their money laundering enterprise. That knowledge is the first step to ending the Russian influence campaigns in Europe and Kyiv. Let me tell you how we will win!"

Several experts from the Eastern Europe office of the CIA offered descriptions of the Russian intelligence agencies and their officers who might be involved. With that information, Chelsvig led a discussion to identify the targets of the investigation, with emphasis on known Russian criminal targets and intelligence already gleaned on them. Four hours of pouring over the details with these experts resulted in the official birth of Operation Genghis Khan.

The ambitious program involved compiling and monitoring transactions tied to these oligarchs to trace the money laundering and funneling of money out of Russia through certain suspected banks. The Chernov Bank, based in Kyiv, and Bayerngeld Bank, officially domiciled in Germany, were both under Russian influence via various oligarchs. The Russians always utilized planted individuals at the banks who implemented the money laundering activities. Once they identified these planted officials, specific accounts could be targeted for surveillance. When he exited the final planning meeting, Stamos could envision two ways this was going to go down. Either they would encounter an exceedingly difficult wall of defenses, and they would come away with nothing, or they would find limited paths to discovery. In any event, those limited paths could be explored with whatever means necessary. The final thirty minutes of the meeting discussed the plans for just that, what "whatever means necessary" meant operationally. Especially in Kyiv, if events unfolded in an unsavory way, there was a real danger to everyone. So much for staying out of the field.

As always, he and Chelsvig were the last ones to leave the room, allowing them to commiserate about the pitfalls expected along the way and how to defeat their enemy despite the odds. That ever-present mindset of confidence and winning at all costs pervaded their psyche, but there was also an air of caution. Chelsvig instructed, "When you are there running the surveillance, I want you to secure multiple routes of egress. I also want to pre-stage multiple cars, agents, and aircraft. I want security to be tight on egress. These guys almost had us four years ago with Hurricane. I don't want another loss of life this time."

"Okay, we will operate this almost like a strike force with a rescue contingency at all turns. I don't think we will have as much of an issue in Germany as we will in Kyiv. In Kyiv, even protecting the security will be difficult."

"Are we clear? I do not want a repeat of 2016," said Chelsvig, and he could not be more clear.

Stamos also did not want a replay of the events of 2016 as he had a brief flashback to the moment both Chelsvig and Stamos almost lost their lives in what could only be described as sheer luck. After several years of undetected electronic surveillance on multiple key players in the Russian money laundering schemes, the method of their undoing, to this day, was unknown. Regardless, somehow the whole operation snowballed into an ambush of the entire team en route to meet an informant. On the positive side, before the tragedy struck, they scored all the information from the informant and their surveillance, resulting in a bittersweet victory. Chelsvig would be rewarded and promoted soon afterward due to his bravery. The promotion was just what he deserved, for he was a born leader.

Prior to go-time, Chelsvig would seek approvals for the operation, the FISA warrants, and the surveillance. The subpoenas would not be filed until after the information started flowing. He explained to Stamos the painful process that would encompass the next several hours of his day. Gaining approval entailed arranging a meeting with both directors of the CIA and FBI. Operational approval meetings were quite difficult with the FBI but far easier with the CIA. Chelsvig learned long ago to present little classified evidence during meetings with the

FBI director as these officials were often political appointees who might not have true security clearance. The process of security clearances in the White House was not exactly sound these days. The CIA director was a career intelligence officer who lived and breathed security clearances. Even the deputy director of the FBI suggested as much that they should prioritize CIA approval. The less the FBI knew of the surveillance the better as far as he was concerned.

Stamos smiled a wry, confident smile back at Chelsvig as they parted ways down the long corridors and through the inner security of the operation rooms and SCIFs. As he exited into the parking garage, he decided to return to Quantico for last-minute training before this mission. He slipped into the gently-worn leather seat of his driving machine and immediately he was surrounded by a classic Eagles tune, "Take It Easy", as it started with the initial guitar riffs from both acoustic and electric guitars. As he alighted from the parking garage and onto the streets of DC, he was in another world with his music and became one with the asphalt for the hour-long drive to the training facilities.

There was no other place he enjoyed more than Quantico with its elite training facilities and attitude of youthful vigor. As predicted, he would be returning to the field sooner than expected, and he wanted to be at the top of his game. Preparation and training were his strongest suits, and they were likely the only reasons he was alive today. If there was one thing he never did, it was to leave the success of a mission or his life to chance.

∾

CHAPTER 10: THE TARGETS

∾

After nearly a week of remote surveillance on accounts associated with Bayerngeld and Chernov banks, the FBI investigators had already uncovered mirror trading that could not be incidental to the normal course of business. The trade was bought by Chernov and sold to Bayerngeld, but then immediately bought again by Bayerngeld and transferred to an unknown entity. They could not discern the money trail after it left Bayerngeld. Both Chernov and Bayerngeld were heavily involved in cryptocurrency trades, so it was entirely possible that the cash moved immediately to a cryptocurrency which would be harder to track. To add to the difficulty, Bayerngeld's security was lock-tight in public-facing architecture, therefore surveillance of email and other communications would be impossible.

That day Stamos and Chelsvig held a meeting with their corresponding teams from the Office of National Intelligence and CIA, which was tense as some of the individuals were already overworked with information gathering for the G7 meeting. Due to the political ramifications of investigations that could implicate US targets, all warrants were vetted by senior DOJ and DNI officials, namely the directors of FBI, CIA, or the DNI. The agents were all seated in one of the SCIF rooms and the thick, soundproof door had just vacuum-sealed a minute before and the humming of the sound-canceling apparatus was in full swing. Stamos had just begun to speak when the tell-tale sign of either a late attendee or an interruption occurred in the form of a series of beeps followed by a gush of air through the heavy white door. Through the opening door walked the most unusual attendee for a mid-level subpoena and warrant session, none other than Director, National Intelligence. Her last-minute interest in these two banks could point to potential bigger fish in this net they were casting. All information gathered had to be brought to bear for the warrant application they were soon considering. Stamos sat straight up in his chair, his mind racing with the ramifications of who could show up in the net with these two small bait fish.

Chelsvig, also at attention, took over the introductions and salutations of what just became an even more official meeting. "Good morning, Director. We were just beginning to go over these FISA warrants and subpoenas that we plan to utilize. As per protocol, I will seek approval from DFBI, the DCI, or you, of course. Let me know if there is any information you need, and feel free to interrupt."

"Thank you. Proceed. I will try not to interrupt too often. Just information gathering regarding this operation." The Director took up a position at the head of the table, displacing Chelsvig, who took his place closer to Stamos, facing the CIA and DNI agents

Stamos began by explaining that one of the most challenging aspects of mirror trade and money laundering investigations is proving intent to launder and documenting direct communications of that intent. Difficult to intercept were direct telephone calls using encrypted VPN cellular technology applications. Even harder to intercept were keystroke messaging programs. Essentially these are encrypted VPN system pairs that ping back and forth with two lines of input. There is no actual data exchanged except video signal sent back and forth as each computer gets to see what the other is entering in real-time, everything is encrypted and then erased. As long as neither the computer itself nor the VPN was compromised, then the communication could not be intercepted

Stamos thought but did not disclose to the DNI, as he did not know her clearance status, all his knowledge of prior similar communications they had intercepted. The DNI was more of a political appointee in this iteration of the Office, which he was not accustomed to. Nevertheless, this was the same type of communication Stamos had uncovered during surveillance and used by the Russians to communicate with their American counterparts in 2016. To prove that the Russians were behind the money laundering and election meddling back then, Operation Hurricane had computer-level malware installed to spy on senior Russian officials and bank officials. But this never came out in the prosecutions because it was source-level classification, and its discovery would compromise future espionage of Russian and Chinese government communication. Nonetheless, somehow it was disclosed to the Russians, and their source was quickly extinguished after that surveillance was revealed to them by an unknown individual.

"Is there any more information we can gather, and how will we obtain this intel," the DNI interjected.

"I would bet there is info locked into the cryptocurrency trades at Bayerngeld. To obtain that information would require another local surveillance job. There is another offline computer at Bayerngeld that has this information and is sending it directly to Chernov Bank via an encrypted VPN tunnel or a keystroke program," Stamos was unsure how much to divulge to the DNI so he did not mention that a keystroke logging program was already installed on that computer long ago in 2016, but because it was offline, only physical interception was possible. Moreover, the team would require local surveillance to capture the communications and IP addresses of trades. Stamos had another idea. "Is there any more information coming out of ARTI yet? We need it to match these trades." Stamos asked the DNI.

"Not that we know of. I think it is still months off," stated the DNI tersely.

That's not what Stamos had heard recently from his counterparts at Treasury. The operational security of ARTI was intact even at the highest levels Stamos thought as they shifted to the operation approvals. The fact that this deputy was unaware of ARTI suggested her clearance was not as high as she thought. At least the approvals were easy, full approval granted and the operation was a go for local surveillance.

"Great. Anything else?" she asked.

"This is the present status, ready for surveillance after approval."

"You have my approval. Full green light." she curtly replied, while rising from the table to push the button for the exit. Upon leaving she did express the usual godspeed and good luck verbalizations, from the side of her lips.

Stamos let out a deep breath when the vacuum was re-established. "Well, that was unexpected. Are all agreed we need to proceed with Operation Genghis Khan? If so, we will obtain new schematics of these banks just in case they've changed. Also, let's try to obtain crypto trading information from both banks from publicly facing computers."

"Great thinking....Alright, let's get that information from the appropriate computer at Bayerngeld. What can we match from these trades? We need to solidify who these actors are and why they are mirroring these trades. Is it for money laundering? But something does not match up. It is double the money moving westward. Where is the money going, who is it going to?" Chelsvig was more thinking aloud than actually asking the questions.

The rest of the meeting was spent updating the teams on the targets and the methods they would deploy, but now that they knew the DNI had no knowledge of ARTI, they intentionally withheld information about ARTI from her office and were vague regarding details. Stamos cut the session off with a feigned excuse as he was eager to get this operation underway. There was no time to lose because every day without this surveillance was a day their targets could cover their tracks.

88

A few key players remained behind to finalize operational needs and security protocols. When they were alone, Stamos asked Chelsvig, "Do you think she is legit? She didn't even know about ARTI. On another note, you know there is direct surveillance of this computer at Bayerngeld already, and we can use that to our advantage. We need to find out who is on the other end and get that IP address so we can target them. I suspect that it is either a Russian Bank or maybe even Chernov Bank. We know from Operation Hurricane that Russian banks are keen to use keystroke messaging programs. This will be our preliminary foray into this. I just hope we weren't compromised by this DNI this early in the operation before we even get our feet wet."

"Right. I heard we are developing intel on some high-value targets already. Let's go meet with the analysts to see what they have."

What they would discover next were heretofore unknown targets from the surveillance who were heavily involved with the Chernov Bank in Kyiv. Two targets in particular were interesting as they were under FISA surveillance, which would prove convenient. One had powerful friends in Russia, and another had a powerful friend in America.

"This could get interesting, for sure. Her involvement suggests that similar to 2016, we are going to net some high-level Americans in this operation." Stamos could not be more right, and with the information that he already personally experienced from Operation Hurricane, he was certain his prediction would turn out to be spot on.

Chelsvig retorted, "This is going to be a bumpy ride. The captain has turned on the fasten seat belt sign. Time to fasten our seat belts. I'll see you bright and early in the morning."

"Great, I'd better heal myself quickly," Stamos joked.

Next up on the schedule was the fun part, Stamos thought as he exited the situation room and headed for the elevator. While he enjoyed the legal aspects of the assignments to try cases in court, the most exhilarating was accessing the information their adversaries would not reveal willingly, which meant taking risks in the field. Plans were made to do just that, starting with traveling to Europe for the initial foray tomorrow.   Tonight, his team hurriedly assembled the required surveillance equipment to transport to Germany and Ukraine, though most of it was already in-country.

What seemed like minutes later, amid the excitement, he tried to calm himself by flattening the hills and straightening the curves of the back roads toward Quantico. With more Eagles tunes blasting, Stamos experienced flashbacks of every close call and operational failure of his past, and unfortunately, the reasons behind them were not always obvious. The possibility of a breakdown was always real, and they were not always catastrophic or fatal. To prevent the worst outcomes, he promised his more sensible side that in the future he would be less risk-taking and keener to recognize the collapse before it happened. That was the key to avoiding lethal failures - detecting the probability of discovery before being fully exposed and escaping those situations early or avoiding them altogether.

As he was analyzing those failures, suddenly he flashed back to 2016, lying flat on his back in a Kyiv alleyway outside their safe house. He vividly pictured Chelsvig staggering toward him, collapsing onto his chest before rolling off to the side. Chelsvig had said something to him about being exposed, just before he became unconscious. But the flashback ended, and he could not recall the details. What was it? All this time he had forgotten to ask. Tomorrow he would be sure to inquire if Chelsvig knew what he had voiced. For the first time since that fateful day, he realized it was important advice or knowledge that he was missing. Perhaps Chelsvig didn't even remember, otherwise, certainly, he would have revealed it in the intervening years.

One more training session and tonight, his anticipation of the mission would surely deprive him of sleep. That expectation was a welcome one, as it meant he was alive, and his adrenal glands were still the strongest part of his body. At any rate, he would sleep on the plane tomorrow, for it was something about jet engines that had a way of calming his soul and lulling him to sleep.

~

CHAPTER 11: DETOUR

~

The fact that no one knew that Stamos was even in the Counterintelligence Division had been an overwhelming resource to the agency. With his official title as an attorney in the Criminal Division, he would operate as though he was conducting investigations of known criminals. While he disguised himself perfectly when under diplomatic cover, this method unquestionably would be short-lived after the last operation with Russia's ubiquitous use of facial recognition software. Regardless, every time he stepped out into the public realm, he risked adding to his facial recognition by foreign governments.

On the last sting of the large European bank, Stamos first went in under diplomatic cover and set up the surveillance. With complete physical feature and dental enhancement, he was unrecognizable, or so he thought. In that initial surveillance, they uncovered money laundering by a Russian mid-level mafia member, followed by systemic money laundering activity at the bank, including an American, who was previously under investigation, committing bank fraud. With that discovery, the FBI was able to attach Stamos as an attorney to the ongoing investigation of that individual. Because he funneled money through this bank, Stamos obtained warrants to access this information, allowing him to hack the bank's computers, then also obtained warrants against the bank revealing the pervasive money laundering. What resulted was massive amounts of information regarding money laundering on an enormous scale from Eastern Europe to the West. To keep Stamos' identity protected, the warrants were filed under the names of lower-level attorneys in the FBI, Europol, and Interpol.

In this fashion, Stamos was able to function as an attorney and as an undercover agent in the FBI/DNI/CIA. With their usefulness drying up with increasing notoriety, Stamos planned to drop his diplomatic cover and the disguises in the future, but the FBI attorney and interagency spy roles, for now, would continue. As Stamos worked out and prepared early that morning for the operation, he mused that he may soon require a dedicated disguise artist if he anticipated continuing fieldwork. Field agents normally performed their own physical enhancement but for critical operations, the artistry was performed by professionals. Bypassing facial recognition software required more skill these days to alter the facial architecture enough. For those other agents along for the ride, traveling with the enhanced Stamos was always comical as he would attempt to change his character for the role also.

Stamos' team normally included eight CIA paramilitary officers but for this mission, they added sixteen more Force Recon members to assist with extraction if necessary. Early that morning, the team assembled at Quantico Marine Base in the joint command hangar. The tactical team was preparing and stowing all the surveillance into the transport plane, including the fleet of armored G63 SUVs that would be utilized. As they watched the C-17 take off in the night sky, the anticipation of this week's events was unfathomable. In a heartbeat after landing, these teams would be deployed and armed by the time Stamos and the rest of the agents arrived. It would take them a week to set up and Stamos and Chelsvig would be working the rest of the week on logistics and would arrive in Munich in a few days to begin the real surveillance.

Before embarking on this mission, though, these two had

to make an unscheduled trip. As Chelsvig was ascending the stairs into one of the two Gulfstream jets for the agents, he and Stamos were talking about a new development they learned about only this morning, namely one of their targets was undertaking some of his own nefarious surveillance. It seemed that the target was becoming more paranoid about his own family discovering their money laundering. They would fly to Teterboro and pay a quick visit to Manhattan to assess a source that could help them break through some of the background information. But they would remain clandestine so as not to be caught up in the foreign surveillance of this source.

"Here is a long shot. How about we just interview her under the subterfuge of asking for information on a case? It could backfire but these targets seem to be all abuzz with something this person is doing here in New York." Stamos detected Chelsvig's concerned look as he asked this question and half-expected a rejection from his elder.

Remarkably their potential source was someone who had crossed Stamos' radar years before as one of the most intelligent and capable rowers and sailors he had come across. While at Cambridge, from afar, and on opposite sailing and crew teams, he had admired her reputation as a fierce competitor. He was but a freshman and she was a senior, but he and his teammates would never forget her due to the resounding defeats she would hand them. With some quick research, he discovered she was stateside in New York and was in market research with the New York Journal. Her specialty wasn't just market research; she was heavy into predictive market surveillance and was developing analytical programs that nobody else possessed.

Immediately, and with incredible foresight, Stamos felt compelled to get to know this rising journalist, who had crossed their intelligence flash bulletins as "Critical" intercepts. The coming introduction Stamos envisioned could prove to be a valuable professional symbiotic relationship. No matter what mission or unit he would come to command in the future, a research journalist might even be better at turning up financial crimes than their undercover sources. She probably possessed better sources than the FBI or the CIA, who would be more willing to tell a journalist their secrets than a fed.

"What are your thoughts about this ascending star of the financial arena?" Stamos asked his superior, probing for the approval he sought in cultivating his old acquaintance.

"When you first told me about her, I thought she could be a risk given her family background, but I changed my mind. Now, I think she could be a real asset. She does not seem to be of the same ilk as the rest. From her articles, there seems to be a proclivity for the truth, rather than an abnormal appetite for money or power." Chelsvig was being particularly philosophical at this moment, while they taxied for takeoff. "I agree, let's go see her."

"You hit the nail on the head. I think she came to America to escape her family, rather than as the conduit for money laundering like other expats," mused Stamos.

"What did the team find out from her financial and personal dealings," Chelsvig asked pointedly.

"Well, she definitely has family support for her condo that was purchased with family money, and she has exclusive use of one of the family's jets. Other than that, all her money is her own. She has not appeared in any Suspicious Activity Reports in the past decade. She has one friend in New York who is an expat with mid-level Russian mafia family ties. This friend is a suspicious person, especially for someone so young, appearing in multiple Suspicious Activity Reports, without the capability to do so. Owns a condo way over her family's financial means. She has two interns at the Journal who are unremarkable. She has a college romance that has been off and on for years, a guy who is a billionaire of his own right, old English money. He has a shipping and security company. If anything, he protects her from her family. The only one that concerns me is the Russian friend."

Stamos continued, "For now let's ascertain the target's surveillance methods and investigate the team that is monitoring her movements. Place this Katya under surveillance, she could be a mole in her sphere here in New York. But then let's get to Munich as soon as possible." Stamos looked forward to this foray into the source's life, a chance to covertly monitor his target's activities here in the US and abroad.

"I agree. Let's explore this avenue. Call her now, let's see if we can meet her now," Chelsvig concurred.

"I will get on it. File the flight plan for New York," Stamos commanded the pilots to follow the flight plan he had given them hours ago. On the way, they would proffer the invite for the reconnaissance.

"Should we place her under protection?" Stamos asked, trying to disguise his conflict.

"Maybe. She will prove useful. I can tell. Let's decide after we meet her today. Make sure we can meet her today. I want this wrapped up before we head east."

"Okay, wheels up! It's go-time!" Stamos exclaimed using two of his patented sayings in one statement.

As they once again pointed the Gulfstream towards the sky, Stamos' gaze over the skyline of the Capitol and Washington Monument was interrupted by his flashbacks to Kyiv in 2016. His flashback began at the point of being discovered in the building next to the target bank's Kyiv offices. Ukrainian officers were questioning the female CIA agents who were disguised as front office secretaries. Their answers appeared to be inadequate, and they were asked to summon their managers.

The officers, who Stamos recognized as Russian agents, were certainly tipped off to the operation because the questions they asked of Stamos when they walked into his office were pointedly demanding to know what he was doing with equipment that they had not yet discovered. The equipment they were being asked about was behind false walls and would not have been able to be detected with routine surveillance of their activities. Bret Chelsvig eavesdropped from the office next door and immediately signaled for a lockdown. Their fellow agents behind the false walls were as quiet as mice yet worked to shut down computers and any other active electronics.

The officers spoke with Russian accents and their line of questioning became more and more intimidating. The two officers were speaking to each other but were also appearing to listen to hidden earpieces. Chelsvig appeared in the doorway and asked the officers if there was a problem. There appeared to be a recognition among the two officers and whoever their handler was and that is when things went haywire.

The flashback flickered and suddenly he was back in present-day on the Gulfstream, and they were rapidly approaching the Manhattan skyline on the right as they approached Teterboro. How did the Russians uncover their operation? he asked himself as he attempted to regain his composure for the present operation.

"Get your game face on. Have you reached her yet?" Chelsvig asked, noticing his partner's distraction.

"Not yet," Stamos replied as he dialed Natalia's number again. While waiting for an answer, he asked, "Hey, do you remember what you told me when you were shot in Kyiv?" Stamos wondered why he hadn't remembered the question before now.

"No, I don't have any recollection after the shots started. Did I say something important?"

"I'm not sure. After all these years I am getting some flashbacks of some importance of something you had just discovered that was not in our official surveillance logs. You said it just before I became unconscious during the extraction. I can't quite put my finger on how the Russians blew open our investigation, and I have this gut feeling you knew the key at the time, but amnesia is keeping it from us."

CHAPTER 12: THE MEETING

Natalia caught an aggressive early morning workout at the Plaza gym after a late night of tinkering with the AI program and was feeling exceptionally present this morning. After returning from London, her focus morphed into increasing her awareness of the present and the concept of immersing herself in the present. Easier said than done, that focus allowed her to recognize any negativity in her world that she needed to eschew and emphasize all the positives that surrounded her. Past negatives such as her family could only harm her if she did not embrace the positives of her future, for example, Chip and her burgeoning career. With sunrise still a few minutes away, her looming massive accomplishment took center stage as her main positive this morning.

The cool, overcast morning bared all that was typical of Manhattan, dirty, wet sidewalks and trash on the street, which could have brought anyone with seasonal affect disorder down in the dumps. However, Natalia chose to walk five feet off the ground as she made her usual detour to The Java Life NYC coffee shop. There was the expected drivel that was barely audible from the early morning foot traffic on 58th Street, and as she was waiting for her order, she gazed at her surroundings. To her right in the corner of the room, there was the usual bad news displayed on the television. Dire economic indicators were rolling in, Asian stock markets were down, but US stock market futures were still increasing. How could that make sense, Natalia thought to herself. All across the world, economies suffered losses, but the three lone US markets, the bellwether for the US economy, were booming.

As she stepped out of the shop and onto the wide sidewalk, her cell phone buzzed in her pocket. Who could be calling at such an early hour? She half-expected it to be Chip, or less likely her father or her Uncle Nikolai since their time difference made them call at weird hours. But no, the number was unknown, and it was a Virginia number. At once, she thought it might be a spam caller and hesitated before answering.

"Hello," Natalia answered, not giving away her name in her greeting.

"Hi, Natalia Volkov?"

"Yes, this is she."

"Hi, Natalia, I'm glad I reached you. So sorry for the early phone call, but my name is Sean Stamos, an attorney with the Federal Bureau of Investigations. Do you have some time later today so that we can talk? Off the record. First, let me say you are not under any investigation. We are hoping you can help us with an outside inquiry. It is of utmost national importance."

"I suppose so. Completely off the record? I don't need my attorney or the Journal attorney present?" Natalia was suspicious of a scam.

"Not necessary unless you wish. I am in New York today only, so that is why I was hoping to catch you today. By the way, I was a novice on Cambridge's rowing and sailing teams while you were a senior at Oxford. I think we met briefly at a mixer once."

"Really? That brings back memories. I was just at Farmoor Reservoir last week. And all of England is abuzz for the America's Cup next year."

"Yes, you guys bested us quite frequently that year. The

Blue had quite a run for several years between you and that guy Merlin. Well, can I send you the location and time through encrypted text? It will be a secure location."

"Okay, it would have to be later in the afternoon." She couldn't wait to see what this was about. She had a hunch that it was regarding the market investigations.

"Thank you, Natalia, we will definitely appreciate your assistance." Stamos finished by relaying the phone number from which the location and time text would be coming.

Natalia's Uncle Nikolai would be furious if he knew that she had met with an FBI attorney without the family attorney, but the circumstances of the past several weeks suggested she should not inform her uncle about this meeting. She was becoming more and more distrustful of her family business dealings as the week went on. A midlife rebellion perhaps, or were there deeper issues? It seemed her independence and stubbornness were growing the farther she strayed from St Petersburg and her uncle's grasp.

Today was probably the only day she could fit the meeting in this week, as she would be working from home later today and would be working on the server all week at the Journal offices. All these interruptions were not very amenable to completing this project. She received the encrypted text displaying a time 6 pm and a location one block from Central Park. That would be a convenient walking distance from her home.

Stamos and Chelsvig and the rest of the teams in both planes landed in Teterboro less than an hour later and, as they descended the stairs of their airplane and silently headed to the awaiting cars, the other plane taxied to a stop a hundred meters ahead. Stamos shared an insecure look with Chelsvig about the potential consequences of the plan they were about to embark upon, which could compromise their cover and put this young lady in danger. They needed to execute it under clandestine cover without divulging to this source why they were asking for her assistance, while extracting information she may know about money laundering contacts of their target in the US.

Stamos and Chelsvig borrowed secure cars from the DNI office in New York for this miniature side operation. All the armored cars this team used were surveillance-proof and were akin to the Secure Compartmented Information Facilities (SCIF) found in government buildings, utilizing secure communications and specialized vibration and electromagnetic inhibitors to prevent anyone outside from listening or photographing inside. As Stamos and Chelsvig pulled up early to scout the Upper East Side location, it was perfect for the pickup. They parked near the Indian Consulate to blend in with the diplomatic cars that were often near the consulate buildings and waited.

They were beginning to worry that Natalia would be a no-show, but then they saw the striking figure in a black knee-length dress and beautiful flowing dark blonde curls walking toward them. Not the ponytail that Stamos remembered from the Thames River of yesteryear. Stamos immediately dialed her from his cell phone.

"Hello," Natalia answered when she recognized the same Virginia number. She looked around to see if anyone was watching her. She felt a deep and sudden distrust of the whole situation.

"Hi, Natalia. This is Stamos, do you see the black SUV in front of you about 20 meters ahead?"

The black SUV made Natalia nervous as people of her stature were at risk of kidnapping all over the world, including in New York. "You know I will need to see some identification. Who is with you?"

"I am with my boss Ben Chatfield, as I told you we are attorneys with the FBI, just researching for a case I have for securities fraud. I have heard you are doing market research for the Journal." He had to use a pseudonym for Chelsvig because he did not have the FBI attorney cover like Stamos and the call was not on a secure line. It hadn't crossed his mind until then, What if she asked for his ID too?

"Alright, I will be there in a few seconds," Natalia answered as she crossed the street.

"I think she is in play," Stamos reported to Chelsvig as

they anxiously waited.

As she approached the bulky Chevy Suburban, she saw the back window was down and the face she saw, she thought she recognized but could not be completely sure. As she noticed the familiar armored door, she trustingly climbed through the overly thick door that Stamos held open for her, and he immediately handed her his FBI identification. She examined it, finding an authentic-looking hologram and a picture that looked a few years old. She knew better than to base her trust on looks alone, but this new acquaintance seemed innocent enough.

Feeling comfortable now, she settled down into the seat and Chelsvig motioned for the driver to drive around the corner for a few minutes.

"Thanks for meeting with us, we are only in town for a few hours and wanted to meet with you regarding your market research and analytical programs. How is that going?" Stamos asked.

"I kind of figured that might be what this was about. I know that my analytical programs are gaining some rumored notoriety. We have an Artificial Intelligence component primed and ready to monitor all market activity. The algorithms will take into account cryptocurrency exchanges also." She suddenly realized she had revealed too much.

Stamos and Chelsvig were taken aback. This AI program was almost identical to the ARTI programs that were also almost operational, run by the Securities and Exchange Commission. ARTI, or Artificial Reconnaissance of Transactions Intelligence, would forever revolutionize financial crime monitoring. Maybe this was why every move she made was being monitored by their targets. She may soon have the capability to discover all mirror trades and fringe market trading. Depending on how far she was in the development stages and how sophisticated her techniques were, she may also be in danger from those who wished to stop her.

"Wow! We hadn't heard that this was that advanced. Kind of like ARTI at the SEC. Tell me more," Stamos' voice cracked a little in incredulity.

"It's pretty simple really. We have invested in a lot of computing power and have AI monitoring trades just like ARTI can. At the Journal we have access to the trade streams from all world indexes. It is almost complete as a matter of fact. Honestly, I am meeting with my interns today to finalize the specifications." Natalia realized she was starting to sound too proud of her work before it was finished, stopped there, and paused.

"So, what case do you need information for?" Natalia added.

"Ahh, well we are investigating a few companies from Ukraine," Stamos began giving her the names of two companies that were unrelated to this target. "They may be involved in some money laundering or mirror trading."

"I don't know about either of those companies, but when I gain operational integrity of the AI, I can do some research for you that you might not otherwise be able to accomplish on your own." Natalia could not believe she just offered to help the FBI, but this Stamos just seemed very trustworthy. You would think they could just access the same information with ARTI even if it was only partially operational, she thought.

"We would really appreciate that," Stamos squeezed in promptly when he saw her confused look.

"Let's drop you off around the corner from here. You will have to walk an extra block."

As they made their way through traffic and around the corner, Stamos nervously closed with, "Well, it was great to finally meet you again. It's been more than a decade. Let me know if you find out anything. This is my encrypted cell phone number. Don't hesitate to call if you need me." Stamos offered as he again wondered if she was in danger. She may need help sooner rather than later if their target was placing her under surveillance.

"By the way, how is your family and that Merlin guy who was always around Farmoor?" Stamos asked, feigning casual curiosity.

"They are fine! Actually, I was just there in London last week and saw Chip and some of the old coaches. You know

Oxford has a pair of women who are challenging the all-male 49er teams in the Olympics this year."

"That is great. If they are half as skilled as you were, they will pull off another gold for the Oxford Blue women!"

As she left the vehicle, she glanced back at Stamos, and as he smiled at her, she realized she did remember him. What was it that she remembered about him? It would come to her. She walked two blocks back to 59th and turned the corner, and as she turned toward Central Park, she was standing on the corner of 59th waiting at a crosswalk. Walking toward her as the walk sign illuminated was Katya. Natalia called out to her, "Hey, Katya!"

"Oh, hi! I've been hoping to run into you. I think your father and your uncle have been trying to get in touch with you. Do you want to grab some sushi tonight?"

"Yes, let's do that. I don't have much time, though." Natalia had so little time to give to anyone, let alone herself.

"Where are you coming from?" Katya asked, nonchalantly.

"I had started to go for a walk, but just realized what time it was, so I am headed back to the office," Natalia ad-libbed.

"Oh, okay. Let me know about tonight. If you are headed to the office now, you may need to eat later, right?" Katya persisted.

As she walked down 5th Avenue, she thought, There is so much to be accomplished before Monday. Just then, her phone rang, and she recognized the number as her uncle's phone. It is evening in St Petersburg, she thought.

"Hi, Uncle Nikolai! How are you doing?" Natalia, of course, spoke in perfect Russian.

"I just wanted to check on the work for the benefit of the St. Peter's School. Did you check with your friends at the newspapers?" he queried, quite annoyingly.

"Yes, I did. I have at least three commitments so far. Thanks for involving me in this. I think that it is going to be a great event this year. I have some connections with the Moscow Times through my boarding school classmates."

"Ok, perfect. Have you thought more about when it

would be best for you to make the transition to St Petersburg and work here for the rest of the summer?"

"I have a few deadlines for the next month here with research that is required to be local, but after that, I think it can work." she fibbed.

"What kind of local research? Everybody is available by phone now." Her uncle could be too logical sometimes.

"I will let you know."

"Ok, I will check with your father," her uncle declared in a brusque voice, sounding like a mother informing her daughter that she was unleashing the father threat.

That afternoon she had brief conversations with Jignesh and Sebastian to keep them on track to complete everything by Monday. She could tell from the loads of snacks on the desks that they had been and would be living in the server room for the next week. They were well tucked in, and plans were on course for a Monday go-live date. Indeed, loads of work on her part should be completed tomorrow in order for the AI to be ready.

Meanwhile, Stamos and Chelsvig hastily returned to the airport to fly back to DC. As they climbed up the jet stairs, Stamos finally blurted out his valid concern, "She needs a protective unit. She is in real danger, you know. Her uncle probably knows what she has and what will happen to him and his cronies if she is successful in getting this off the ground."

"Yes, I will get a full team on it now. She is going to find the dirty laundry before ARTI does. This thirty-something-year-old reporter is going to bring down her family and an entire country. If she is alive to see it, that is."

The next few days would run smoothly and uneventfully for the advance team in Munich, moving surveillance equipment into the building next to Bayerngeld Bank to initiate the surveillance. Some of the team was already in Kyiv for the Chernov Bank surveillance, which would be more difficult under the watchful eyes of Russian sympathizers. The Kyiv team posed as a German investing company and traveled by land through Poland to position the different team members throughout the city.

The FBI and CIA in Munich choreographed the operation in both cities being completed in the next few weeks, coinciding with a self-administered deadline before the G7 conference.

～

CHAPTER 13: DARK TRADES

～

That creep, she thought, there he is again. Natalia had sprung to life at 5 am, which was all too early for a Friday, and descended the elevator on a mission to start her day even more present than usual, for an early spin and weight session. She found these sessions liberating and refreshing, establishing a beachhead to the day with an adrenaline pump. Today, in the Plaza gym on the fourth floor, she encountered the usual sleepy early morning crew. Most of the trust fund babies that resided in the Plaza were never in the gym this early, though they may be cruising in at 5 am from whatever cash-fueled binge they were on. Only the true working rich would be awake this early. Among the early risers that she had the good fortune to share the gym with on almost a daily basis were a local billionaire real estate investor, a local news celebrity with her plastic surgeon-sculpted face, and the impetuous son of a venture capitalist who had recently secured the initial institutional round of investments to start his own fund, all of whom she superficially was acquainted with because of the New York philanthropy scene.

But today, and every day this week, it was that creepy venture capitalist - the father, not the son. He was a Ukrainian out-of-shape sixty-something-year-old who definitely had no business being here at 5 am. He spent more time texting on his phone than working out on the machines and his form was atrocious. Who is on their phone at 5 am? Her skin crawled every time she saw that he was there. It was not that he stared at her, but he definitely glanced over at her each time she neared the exit door. A few times she suspected he could have been feigning texting, while surreptitiously snapping photos of her. When she finished her workout and grabbed a clean towel, she spied in the mirror on the way out that he was watching closely her every move as she prepared to exit and again began typing on his phone. What a creeper! I'm most certainly too old for his tastes, she thought.

She arrived back at her condo by 6:30, hurriedly threw her key fob on the counter and, after a quick shower, started prepping for a day of data gathering. Today she would head to the server room at the Journal for intense hands-on work with her interns on the servers and the AI programs. She made her habitual detour to the corner cafe, and as she waited, she was glancing at the morning business talk shows on the TV screens in the corner. Yesterday, the Dow Jones had dropped by 642 points with dismal manufacturing news, but in the afternoon, there was a slight rebound due to the usual trading programs buying bargains, but it all stopped when the prices started to increase, and by the end of the day the markets had recovered to positive territory. While it is not unusual for a buying response to coincide with dips in the market, these days of positive market responses to bad news were becoming more frequent and the indexes continued to be buoyed by the late trades. The market rebounded late in the day, and the after-hours trading continued in the same vein. All eyes were on the market this morning to predict what would happen today because important earnings calls were occurring later this morning that were expected to be negative.

Healthy skepticism raised its threat level again, but she shrugged it off as she picked up the latte with her usual pseud-onym written on it. Her instincts loudly whispered in her ear that here was another conspicuous hint begging her to redouble her efforts on this breakthrough endeavor. The predictive utility alone would be remarkable, the market-calming effect noteworthy, and most of all, the criminal deterrence earth-shattering. For a few decades now, the markets have been performing admirably for the rich and not so much for the little people. And these dark trades, if discovered, would likely reveal why and who was behind it. She caught herself staring blindly at the television, so she took another sip of her latte, so it was not so full, and she was out the door with a flash. This momentous day would be a productive, pivotal one she told herself, noticing for the first time that the weather had finally made a turn for the better, and spring perhaps was springing, The rain had made a noticeable impact, wiping the grime from the sidewalk, and the blue sky above was a welcome change as the approaching sunrise began to brighten the Manhattan streets

When she arrived at the office, her interns, Jignesh and Sebastian, were busily engaged in the programming chores of the day. She audibly noticed the servers actively capturing data as it was input live from a preset data stream of all world markets. During this testing phase, the data was not live but from a date in the past so they could verify the accuracy. They always used the same day to verify the calculations - September 29, 2008, the most recent stock market crash. However, the data was incomplete, so they could not identify most of the traders, only the amounts and sources. The next step would be to go live as soon as possible to input live, raw data for analysis. These servers were the most powerful available outside of the government and the data storage industry. At close to a million dollars its cost proved beyond a reasonable doubt the best indicator of what the Journal thought of her work and its importance to their reputation.

Their workspace was on a special below-ground floor of the Journal building for research where there was little foot traffic, which made it easier to concentrate than in her staff office upstairs on the 46th floor. Her editor, secretary, and intern journalists knew to find her in this office most days if she was not working from home or abroad. By 10 am she had finished her work on the programming files and from the snack foraging activities of her interns, they seemed to be finished with what was hopefully final testing on the market crash of 2008.

"Jignesh and Sebastian, when do you think we can start testing the program on live, raw data? Do you think by Monday you will be ready? I think testing on the old data has ceased being useful. You know, we have already uncovered some anomalies with the trading that day, possibly suspicious activity, but we can't identify all of the actors on these short trades on the securities outside of the mainstream trades. If we go live, we can begin testing our ability to capture all information, security, price, location, IP address, buyer, seller, broker, intermediary, it goes on and on."

Jignesh replied with a pressured speech, "I think we can be ready by early next week. I am finishing the programming today for the bitcoin market data and once we do that we will be ready." He leaned back in his chair, folding his hands behind his head, and smiled that cocky smile he always had when he was about to attempt sophomoric humor. It turned out not to be humor at all, as he was just boasting, "When it is ready it will rival ARTI and CAT as the best trading analysis system ever. Retrospectively, I think we can capture data from 2008 forward with more data inputs. I am also working this weekend on the manipulations investigation tool and that will give us more information. I will test that later today on the 2008 crash date."

"Great! What are you working on, Sebastian?" she asked hesitantly, also expecting a wisecrack out of her other intern.

"I should have all the pinpoint query interfaces finished this week. As we planned, we will be able to query any trade or sequence of trades by any variable, pattern, actor, or IP address. I think if our suspicion is correct regarding certain market manipulators at the fringe, this will help us identify and locate those actors. Let's attempt a go-live by Monday, which will enable us to tweak the programming using up-to-date data. Can I show you something I just found that is amazing for 2008?"

112

"Yes, let's see it." Natalia's curiosity was piqued because Sebastian never described anything as amazing. The serious demeanor of her interns today was indeed amazing. This sudden change of attitude spoke volumes about the program's nearness to completion.

"Okay, look at what the AI already parsed out from the data from that date in September 2008. These trades here appear to come from one IP address, and then this series of trades comes from another, and then there are twenty others. These similar trades account for about 40% of all the shorts on the Dow that day. They were all outside the mainstream, so never tracked by the SEC and all were from similar, yet different IP addresses. My pet theory is they are all from the same VPN. They are not from any known IP address of the big players of VPN software that traders usually use. It also appears to me to be spoofed to this US IP address. I wonder if we can also program into the AI an IP address and VPN search protocol that can narrow this down. One would need to geo-locate the intermediary IP addresses that each trade is pinged through. The AI can accomplish this from live data, but not on test data."

"Wow! The AI is really starting to learn to uncover anomalies and to parse the data for unusual patterns. I didn't think we would glean anything from the old data, especially since the AI isn't even complete," Natalia nervously blurted out, bursting with excitement.

Jignesh also chimed in with his excitement, "I can quickly program a VPN investigation interface tool that will identify the VPN and its location. With that, we can narrow down the location of the trades to defeat the VPN utilization."

Sebastian, his chest puffed out, added, "I just realized we will need to use our own VPN proxy that uses spoofed IP addresses, so they won't be able to detect our queries. The last thing we need to do is notify them that we are knocking on their door, right?" Sebastian was an expert in VPN and IP spoofing, which would allow them to work anonymously, under a different identity. They could display an IP address that to other computers would make it seem like they were operating from inside that offending organization.

Neither Jignesh nor Sebastian would be suspected of being online hackers in their real lives. Both came from relatively wealthy families and were undergraduates at NYU in computer engineering majors. Despite being awkward college kids, they were not exceptionally nerdy, nor did they exhibit anarchist behavior in their social media posts. They had a normal social media presence just like almost everyone else. Most online hackers had little public social media presence outside of hacker channels. And her interns did not use any of these channels. The Journal had vetted them well, neither of them were into exceedingly illegal activities.

"Alright, let's get to it and start live on Monday. Jignesh, after this launch, let's tweak the AI a little bit to think outside the box, as it were." Natalia could not be more delighted at the progress her interns had made. Could it be that they were this close, and live by Monday? She could not have fathomed one year ago that her dream idea would come to fruition this quickly. She had a premonition, complete with spine-shuddering goosebumps, that her program would enlighten the entire world. If only they could uncover who the September 2008 crash perpetrators were. It very well could have been a concerted effort by many actors to short the market and cause the crash. Then buy up the market with the proceeds. If they could find out who, the discovery would be earth-shattering. Was there a historical source to look up the IP addresses of VPNs from that far in the past? Maybe her hacking interns could hack the VPN to find out, but that was over a decade ago.

By the time Natalia left the office it was almost nine in the evening, and she suddenly remembered she was supposed to eat sushi with Katya. As she was about to reach into her pocket for her phone to call her, the phone buzzed with the ringtone she had set for her father. It had been since London that she had spoken to him. She placed her headphones in her ears, before answering in English, "Hello, Father!" Her father didn't force her to speak Russian like her uncle did.

"How are you, my darling?" her father asked.

"I am great, Father! What is happening with you?" she

also felt comfortable speaking informally with him.

"Just worried about you being halfway around the world. By the way, we received the Volkov artifact for the great hall antiquities. It looks great! Nikolai says you will be coming back to St Petersburg in July. Is that right?" he queried.

"Yes, Father, I am working on it. Not sure of the timing though. What I actually told him was that it would likely be after July. I am really busy with this project. It is taking up all my time. Uncle Nikolai is becoming more and more overbearing by the minute. He is almost as creepy as that Stefanskiy guy I told you about."

"I know, I know. He is stressed out with all the changes around here. He is under pressure to bring Ukraine back into the fold. Well, let me know if there is anything I can do to help." he always found a way to ask her if she needed anything. "I do have a favor to ask, though."

That was a change. Her father never asked for favors. She suspected her uncle immediately. Why did he always interrupt her work?

~

CHAPTER 14: CRETE

~

She didn't blame her father. Her uncle was insisting, he said. She sometimes wished she didn't have an uncle with so much power, Natalia thought, as she packed her overnight bag. The request to join him and Uncle Nikolai was a last-minute, but necessary weekend retreat on the island of Crete where the family had a villa. They were meeting with some bankers and fund managers there and would like Natalia to show her face for a public show of support. Her father had added his reasoning that he had not seen her since last month in England. The jet would be ready for her by tonight at 11 pm. Luckily, she did not have a new article until next week and her editor was giving her some leeway with the programming the last few weeks. After this weekend, she could take the months of May and June to concentrate on her research and support this program.

She was supposed to meet the interns before going live on Monday but now that would not happen. She texted them regarding the change of plans and that she would return Monday night and discuss over a conference call on the plane regarding preparing for Tuesday's opening bell. She would meet them Tuesday morning early for Go-Time!

As she was packing, Katya called. Natalia answered the phone quickly with an apology, "I'm sorry Katya, I've been ignoring you."

"No, don't worry about it!" Katya exclaimed.

"Do you want to come with me to Crete for the weekend to see my family?"

"I guess so. I don't have any boyfriend plans to cancel. I think my father may be there too," said Katya.

"Okay, we don't have much time. Quickly pack a bag and Dimitri will be ready downstairs in about 15 minutes."

Natalia met Katya in the lobby, exchanging hugs and clothing and hair complements, then the pair located Dimitri, her long-time driver and bodyguard, who also had a small apartment at the Plaza on the same floor as Natalia. Sure enough, he was waiting at the door to the 58th Street entrance. "How is the programming going?" Katya asked as Dimitri took their bags.

"Amazingly well!" Natalia proclaimed. "We are going to have a breakthrough next week!"

This absolutely had to be the last trip she could take for the next several weeks! The G-wagon was only a half-block down the street, and after the two climbed in, Dimitri sped off toward Teterboro. They would be flying all night, and Natalia was exhausted from all the excitement and the long hours she had been putting in. She brought some dumbbells for the flight so she could work out before getting some much-needed sleep.

As they descended into the Lincoln Tunnel, Katya turned to Natalia and said, "I just booked my trip to Cannes for the Russia Day celebration, then I'm going to spend the summer in St Petersburg. Do you want to come with? It's going to be a great party!"

What a coincidence, Natalia thought, and now knew it wasn't. Why did she just tell Katya about the breakthrough? Her instincts detected the need to lie again, "The breakthrough we are making is with a program to predict African commodities shortages. I have an intern working on it now." Then she reframed the next lie into some truths, "Katya, I have so much work to do. But I can spend some time back home with you this summer. My uncle also wants me to spend the summer there. Are your parents making you return for the summer too?" Not waiting for the answer, Natalia checked her phone for voicemails and emails.

Katya didn't answer, just stared out the window at the passing lights of the tunnel. She looked up at Dmitri and then back at Natalia. Natalia wasn't really expecting a response but interpreted her silence as the affirmative. And she then questioned herself, Hopefully, Katya's only directive was to convince Natalia and assure her family that she would do the same. Right? What were Katya's motives?

As the black SUV made its way to the airport and passed through security at the hangar, they made plans for the summer and Natalia played along with the suspected charade. She wasn't sure she would comply with her uncle's demands, but she figured she needed to play along for Katya's and her family's benefit. She still had plenty of time to back out of the arrangements.

The chariot awaiting them to fly them over the Atlantic sat lonely on the tarmac feet away from their arrival. Valeria eagerly awaited her adopted daughter to climb up the steps. She sensed Natalia's disappointment with the last-minute plans and offered comfort snacks to soothe her mood. Every one of Natalia's favorite foods was always stocked in the gallery of the plane, at all times. It didn't matter if Natalia had not flown with them for two weeks, Valeria simply threw out the spoils and bought new snacks and meals to replace them. It was such a waste, but there was not much Natalia could do about it. Natalia declined but ordered a fruit spread and avocado toast for the morning.

With smooth skies and the soothing sounds of the jet engine, Natalia slept most of the flight, leaving Katya to sleep on the sofa in the main cabin. Though it was midday on the island nation of Crete, they sleepily made their way to the villa which overlooked the Aegean Sea with whitewashed natural stone buildings. The two girls collapsed on the guest house beds as jet lag set in. Only a few minutes later, as they were drifting off, Natalia regained energy and leaped off the bed. Her psyche and seasonal affective disorder desperately craved bright sunlight so she and Katya headed for the pool for an hour before they ate lunch in the sprawling kitchen overlooking the few yachts anchored in the bay.

Her uncle, father, and brothers were working in the great room as they munched on the spread of pitas, olives, and souvlaki with tzatziki sauce. As Natalia joined the group, they greeted her and brought her up to speed on the investments they had with various hedge fund managers with whom they were meeting this week. A few were arriving this weekend for their pitches and would be staying in the guest houses. She found it strange that the various, supposedly competing, hedge fund managers would be at the villa at the same time during the week.

Over the weekend, she dared not work on her programming due to the lack of a secure connection and her new-found suspicions. Even her VPN would not be effective in this locale. Natalia recognized this would put her behind by a few days, but she had faith that her interns were doubling down on their endeavors by toiling non-stop over the weekend. She grinned as she thought of them camping out in the server room for the last few days. There was an overwhelming sense those two genius goofballs were on the cusp of more breakthroughs that would bring them up to fully operational status sooner than expected.

While the weekend was quite relaxing, there was also a sense of unease with her family that she could not escape. The forty-eight hours went by quickly as she and Katya read by the pool and enjoyed the privacy of the whitewashed guesthouse to escape the families. Katya's father was in attendance in a separate area of the compound but was rarely seen. He was busy with security arrangements and also had meetings of his own, according to Katya. Sunday morning ultimately arrived, and the time neared for goodbyes and the long flight back to New York. The pair of New Yorkers joined the rest of her family for a late breakfast and the conversation was surprisingly lighthearted and pleasant.

Natalia and Katya took their plates into the open-air kitchen and her father followed them in after the brunch concluded.

"Have a safe flight, my dear. It was great to see you again. You know, we will have a great time this summer. You will see," her father whispered to her encouragingly.

"I know we will, Father," Natalia responded with a smile her father loved to have just a glimpse of every once in a while.

"And," he paused, "...You know, I would like for you and your uncle to get along. Just listen to him and give him a chance, he has the best interest of the family at heart." Now she knew her father must not know one iota of any nefarious dealings his brother may be getting the family and the family name into, because she knew he couldn't lie to his daughter.

She couldn't wait for Sunday night's departure from this arid island and Monday's arrival back to civilization and her impending work. Natalia was relieved when Katya suggested they leave early and drive through the coastal town of Chania on the way to the airport. The two had joyously spent several weekends of their childhood running up and down the concrete boardwalk while her father sipped his Mediterranean coffee and met with various bankers in the seaside cafés.

As they strolled down the ancient city boardwalk, they reminisced about their childhood and entertained themselves by watching the tourists taking pictures of the magnificent views. It was a relaxing end to the weekend, but now Natalia was really ready to return to the task at hand. One chauffeured car ride to the airport was all that separated her from another plane ride nap and a welcome return to the quantum leaps she fully expected this week. New ground rule, no family commitments until this AI program goes live.

The next few weeks would be a blur of excitement, but she would never in a million years have been able to anticipate exactly what lay in store for her.

Chapter 15: The Demands

For President Zorin, the elections would live on in perpetuity as the defining moment of his legacy. He would either win a come-from-behind victory or he was going to be forever known as the divisive one-term President. The economy stood on a precipice that for now was buoyed by the stock markets. Most businesses in the country were posting losses but their stock prices were increasing because of what was theorized at the time to be a proliferation of stock buybacks. Each time there was bad news in the economy, everyone expected the markets to take the hit with significant losses. The markets themselves would take a small dip and invariably and miraculously bounced back within 1 or 2 days. He was not a popular President but with the markets continuing to climb, he was climbing in the polls, and there was still a good possibility he would be re-elected in November.

Today, a moody Monday market prevailed early but was no exception to the rule of the past three years. The opening bell brought with it devastating news on the economic front, and these large-cap companies found their stock at a bargain price and in years past would have spent the cash they had hoarded buying back stock. Conventional wisdom held that the markets were bolstered by these buybacks. At least that was the prevailing theory expounded upon every day by the morning business channel talking heads. These were the same shows that President Zorin and his Treasury Secretary Tom Stanton watched every morning to start the day. Stanton had vaulted to fame and fortune as a hedge fund manager in the past decade and before becoming a cabinet member, was also on occasion one of these talking heads.

It was mid-morning in the personal residence of the White House, and President Zorin was still poised in front of the television watching the business channel like it was a tense football game, as the stocks started falling into negative territory. All three market indexes were down by one percent when the trend plateaued and began to reverse. And so, it had played out, day after day, with markets increasing by a steady ten percent over the past year. Peter Zorin had the utmost confidence in HIS markets, and it was SO important to him that they remain in record territory. If there was ONE thing he could count on, it was his friends who were working on stabilizing these markets.

With the tenuous state of his markets, surely, he would miss the beginning of today's meeting of the Council on Economic Advisors, but he also knew that Secretary Stanton would work the preliminary introductions and briefings. He had scheduled various interviews with every financial news show to help boost the markets before the elections. Earlier, he had been on the phone for an hour with the host of one of the most popular cult news shows discussing everything from political strategy to economic theory. Interest rates were well below zero for a few months, and he continued to press for further cuts.

Secretary Stanton turned to the President on his way out of the room, "Don't fret about this, I got this. All we have to do is keep our message positive about the economy."

"I know you are right, but if we make any wrong turns, it is going to go South, and hard. You know how to handle the fed; I want another quarter cut and now."

"I understand. Leave it to me and Jack. As you know, we do have to have a united front though. And Jack has a network of leaders ensuring the markets won't tank. All we have to do is keep the message clear. They have the same straightforward requirements as they always have."

"I know, Jack has done a great job." the President sadly lamented.

"You met his cousin at your inauguration. He needs continued support when you talk to President Prokachev later today. As per usual, your continued code is that you support Jack in all his endeavors for US-Russian relations," the secretary reminded the President.

"Right, make sure Jack is here for that teleconference like usual. I like having him there during these meetings so that he can help placate this guy. We don't need another December surprise like last time I didn't fully understand his suggestions."

"No need to worry. Jack and I have this handled, and pay less attention to these talk shows," he advised gently as he closed the door, accompanied by Secret Service. That was easier said than done. Tom Stanton could only do so much with the President of the free world absconded in his bedroom watching television.

Despite a hectic schedule that was otherwise pre-empted by his obsession with the markets today, he was scheduled for a teleconference later that day with the President of the Russian Federation, Mikhail Prokachev, who had been a thorn in the side of the United States for over a decade, invading neighbors, supporting right-wing dictators around the world, and aiding and abetting terrorists against the West. But for the first time ever, there was cooperation between the two countries, in effect bestowing an outward appearance of peace in the world.

In December there was a drop in all of the major US markets that was thought to be due to computerized automatic trading. It proved to be short-lived and rebounded by the first week of January and continued its climb from there. The market ascent was credited to the stock buy-backs resulting from the previous year's tax cuts, which were paid for with cuts to a multitude of programs.

As the preceding two years of his presidency proved, the stock markets would be this President's legacy if nothing else. America under this business-centric President had enjoyed relative peace in the world according to the prevailing news currents. There was precious little reporting about the increasing poverty and ruthless dictators continuing to cement control over their countries around the world with Russia's assistance. His handlers had taught him, and President Prokachev had set him straight, with a lesson in consequences, that the winds of public opinion were just as important as facts in these digital times. Mother Russia could be a master of disinformation and from December onward, President Zorin came to realize the power of Jack Speransky's cousin

That November and December, the markets were up despite job losses with the past year's world political upheavals. Amid the turmoil, the Administration's foreign policy missteps were numerous but not widely reported, and if they were, would not play well for the nervous populace. No one wanted to report on the negative and be the one who ruined the decade-long financial party. Thus far, his supporters in the media had controlled the conversation quite nicely. With his popularity dwindling among moderates, there was no room for error in the news cycle, and the economy and the stock market were key.

A phone call had arrived to his switchboard secretary the day after Pearl Harbor Day, and President Zorin had barely unpacked from his Hawaiian political appearance. The President of Russia would like to take his call whenever it would be convenient for him. This meant now, in Russian parlance. That day, Zorin had meetings scheduled with two business talk show hosts who were very important to his re-election bid and overall keeping the peace within his party. As was the norm, these informal meetings were also held in the residence, all while watching the evening news. Spirited conversations led to ultimatums regarding access to the White House, which then led to promised exclusive content for each of these two hosts in return for favorable coverage. It stood to reason that these meetings would eventually stretch over their allotted time.

126

Nevertheless, by the time the President reached Prokachev, the latter was quite perturbed. The first words spoken from Moscow were mostly unintelligible Russian curse words, which subsequently calmed down to the effect of, "You were so close to Mother Russia, after Hawaii, you should have continued westward to Moscow. We could have more private talk, without these others on the line."

President Zorin had grown accustomed to the rudeness often displayed by the former KGB agent turned President. He sought to assuage him once again, "Yes, but here we are. To what do I owe the pleasure of your company today, Mr. President?"

"Well, here is concern. You have been President two years and as part of your elevation to Presidency, your platform was Russia in G8. We would like to call in chips to make this happen. How do we make this happen and now?" The urgency could not have been displayed more clearly, even more apparent than the rudeness.

Russia had been dismissed from the G8 due to violent actions toward other countries and President Zorin couldn't just force the other six countries to allow them back in. But he also knew he was under a mandate from more than just President Prokachev. He had senators and many important business leaders pushing him to do the same. Their voices had become louder in the past week.

"Yes, Mr. President. I will call a meeting of our cabinet this week and then each of the G7 ministers to accomplish just that. We will push for it, but the other six have not been so keen..."

President Prokachev interrupted deftly, "Do what it takes, extract this from them, force them, threaten them with tariffs or sanctions. You can do it."

"Agreed," the American President paused, thinking of the maneuvers and favors this would require, before he continued, "You will have your G8, Mr. President. Are there any other concerns?"

"That is concern. We appreciate your consideration. Good day." The line disconnected before President Zorin could take leave from the call.

The next two weeks passed, and while a cabinet meeting was called and a proclamation requesting a G8 return for Russia, the efforts stalled in upper-level talks with the other ministers. With a subsequent full week of market tumult and losses for friends of the Administration, those talks suddenly progressed, with at least three other ministers voicing support for the ascension.

Calm was finally restored, and thus far six more months of record market returns also came to be, and President Zorin could thank those friends of his Administration for their support. The President delayed his attendance at the economic advisor meeting, instead thoughtful soul-searching continued alone in his residence, with the muted television continuously displaying the ticker that he turned and took note of every few minutes.

The gatherings that day went well enough, and Senator Speransky and Tom Stanton would help him through the rough call with President Prokachev. It was clear there were some expectations from the Russians that made all of them uncomfortable but were not impossible to accomplish. And to make President Zorin really uneasy, the Russian President cryptically let President Zorin know he was more than aware of the existence of potential monitoring of Speransky's network.

"Now Mr. Prokachev, you have nothing to worry about regarding the financial markets here in the US. They will continue to operate as they always have and will continue to march upward like they have the past four years."

"I understand," the Russian President confided, "we have a great peace and partnership with the US now and on into the future. I am looking forward to the G8 summit so that we can continue that partnership."

"We will welcome you with open arms when you are ready," Zorin remarked. This was a tall order to float by the rest of the six largest economies and thus far they had backed it, but only with severe repercussions threatened. But the rest would have to fall in line with him if they wanted Zorin's support for any of their initiatives. As they ended the call, Zorin looked up at his two biggest supporters. "Well?"

"Perfect Mr. President," Jack declared. "I think that will go over very well."

"Yes, Peter," Tom Stanton was one of the only to still call him by his first name. "Let's get to work next week on smoothing this over with first Britain, then Germany. The French will have to go along if we have the support of those two. Italy we can count on. I can get that accomplished easily."

∼

CHAPTER 16: CAT AND ARTI

∼

They had been waiting for the reveal for months, and even years. The FBI, the Secret Service, and the SEC finally possessed the means to monitor in real-time all market activity in US stock exchanges. For the past twenty years, through the Financial Industry Regulatory Authority (FINRA), almost 100 billion market events could be analyzed daily through a program called MIDAS (Market Information Data Analytic System), however, this was just a fraction of the daily trades that should be analyzed if you wanted to track all trades.

Because of the lack of monitoring of the markets in totality, the financial watchdogs could easily miss money laundering events. The new CAT (Consolidated Audit Trail) would attach new personalized data to each trade and would analyze all trades in the US stock markets, which would bring the monitored market events to 10 trillion market events daily. Furthermore, most of the rest of the world's stock markets were also already connected to this new analysis algorithm, and once these events were included, the total would be 30 trillion trades per day.

It had not been announced yet that the system was live or even close to going live. As a matter of fact, the go-live date was still officially not set until September 1st. Almost all brokerage houses, fund managers, banks, and insurance companies had long ago signed onto and were connected to the data stream. Even though they were aware the connection was present, these entities were unaware that the stream was live. As far as they knew that connection was present but no monitoring of the outflow of data was occurring. Even if a bank or brokerage house had disconnected their end of the feed, the program could, through other means, immediately trace a trade to that entity and log the trade.

For years, but especially the past few months, there was a lot of pushback against a system that was due to be operational a few years earlier. Multiple brokerage houses and fund managers were concerned about the privacy of their investors. The system implementation was delayed so many times over the past year that once again it was very likely that there would be another delay to the commencement of the analysis. The administration had successfully delayed the debut from the year before due to security issues. But unbeknownst to everyone, even the Secretary of the Treasury, Tom Stanton, the actual go-live date was this week. It was being billed internally by the lower-level administrators of FINRA as testing of processes and therefore did not need upper-level approval.

But to the aggressive officers of the FBI, DNI, SEC, and Secret Service in this hybrid unit, it did not matter whether it was just testing that was occurring, there was data to be analyzed and lots of it. These guys were itching to start the artificial intelligence portion of their programs, which was called ARTI. In the Secret Service offices in New York, on this extraordinary Monday, the investigative officers were there bright and early in a planning meeting when it was announced they would be moving that day into the SEC offices in Manhattan to test the AI for investigative purposes. The officers included all of the bright stars of the electronic and financial crimes unit.

All the officers who were called in today were required to sign new non-disclosure agreements and new security clearance checks as this week's mission would require higher security clearance than the usual clandestine operation. As he was preparing the team that day, the newest member and leader of the unit, who had just moved over from the FBI's Criminal

132

Division, had the adrenaline pumping in his veins. This was why his old boss had recommended him for this post. He was made for this position as leader of the most radical unit of the Department of Treasury. With his Computation and Cognition degree from MIT, he had revolutionized the facial recognition and investigative capabilities of the FBI. With the AI needing a facelift at the SEC and the CAT program getting off the ground, this was his time to shine.

Steven Point was born behind a computer screen, and he had been building computers since he was 8 years old. He was a brilliant scholar, and it was a shock to his college and graduate school mentors that he was going into law enforcement at the FBI. He had helped usher in a new era in the Criminal Division and for the past six months had refashioned what was previously designed as a remarkable computational analysis program that was CAT into an interface with an artificial intelligence-enabled program that could find the patterns among trillions of data points.

As Steven left the Secret Service building with the rest of the unit, they seemed like an army of agents on their way into battle. They traveled in a convoy of black Suburbans that, when they arrived at the SEC offices, took over a whole section of the parking garage. The security on the floor that the servers occupied in the SEC was extremely tight with redundant power backup and designed for secure communications. The windows, walls, floors, and ceilings all had electromagnetic shielding to prevent disruption, interference, or surveillance by outside forces. The SEC normally wasn't an agency with any need for such advanced surveillance defense, but this new operation was different.

"This is our Super Bowl fellas!" exclaimed Agent Point as he looked down on the 9/11 Memorial from their offices.

"The world cannot go back now. And the world will not be able to hide from this point forward," remarked one of his fellow teammates from behind one of the sixty workstations set up outside the server room.

Testing of the programs today would culminate in a secretive go-live that would analyze data from every market in the

US and soon every market in the world. What the FBI and SEC wanted to avoid was driving the illicit trading away from US markets to foreign markets to avoid detection. Hence the widespread notifications that eventually CAT would include most foreign markets, and since criminals worldwide mistakenly thought cryptocurrency exchanges were safer, that missing link would also soon be corrected. For Steven Point, the verifications of the testing were going well that day and it was decided that the launch was ready.

"Alright, let's run the final testing sequences." Point watched the connections for each of the major US markets on one of the large video monitors as they glowed green, while the world markets remained red for now. On the other monitor, the indicators for ARTI and CAT also displayed red for now as they ran the testing scripts.

"Both CAT and ARTI are ready. Shall we go live, Steven?" one of the team asked.

Point straightened his thin black tie, making sure it was tight to the collar of his pressed cotton shirt, for any go-live needed the appropriate attire and respect that it deserved. "Remember, folks, it's all ones and zeroes, and ones and zeroes never lie." He glanced around at the group to observe who in the room shared the same humor. Seeing very little reaction, he continued, "Yes, flip the proverbial switch."

It took a few seconds, but first CAT started up and glowed green, and for what seemed an eternity, but was perhaps only thirty seconds, ARTI remained red and finally flickered to green. At the same time, the servers in the server room next door were humming louder, suggesting their computational abilities were being stretched. Agent Point was ecstatic, though it would be difficult to tell from the outside, other than an assertive smile. He was so confident the launch would be a success that he would have bet the proverbial farm on it.

Notwithstanding the initial results, green lights and all, he recognized the results would not be immediate as ARTI could not search all twelve years within minutes. The process would take at least a week or two by Steven's calculations. There were many thousands of petabytes or many exabytes of data to digest. The so-called testing had begun in earnest, and they would uncover more trades than they wanted soon enough.

Once they were finished with this initial testing, the plan was to slowly add foreign markets with live inputs as well as cryptocurrency markets. It might take a few weeks, but they had decades of lost time to make up. ARTI was going to learn all the usual patterns and hopefully make sense of them. It would soon ascertain all the automatic trading algorithms of all investors. For instance, that one certain bank or investor, each time a certain index or combination of indexes changed by X percent, that change would trigger a market action, and ARTI would recognize every time they implemented that strategy.

That learning would be valuable for market analysts and predictions for each event. However, ARTI could also be used by anyone who wanted to use that information for illicit gains hence why the data would be safeguarded. How much more of the data and patterns this AI would provide was still unknown but Steven Point was confident that its capabilities were not limited to the knowledge of him or his whole team. The AI had already proven very useful in the field in the high-stakes game of mafia activity and now would help catch other criminals.

Steven Point commanded an army of engineers now and this was his baby. Testing would continue on into the night and indeed on into the week. His army would toil day and night to assure operational integrity for world markets within two weeks. He would not leave the building until early the next morning, even though no new developments were expected. His adrenaline just did not allow him to leave the brightly lit command room. At 2 am, he descended the elevator, with his heart still positioned high in his chest, to the exit, only to return before the sun rose in the morning. Only now could he loosen his tie, though he would not unbutton the top button of his shirt until he was home. What a day.

∾

CHAPTER 17:
GETTING TO THE POINT

∾

With the initial surveillance officially commenced in Europe, Stamos and Chelsvig returned to DC from New York to plan the legal framework of their subpoenas and warrants. There would be long meetings in the few days ahead with lower-level FBI lawyers to craft these so as not to tip their hand regarding the full nature of the inquiry. Then the real surveillance could begin as Stamos, posing as one of the attorneys, could gain access to the inside of the bank to serve the subpoenas on the banks, planting monitoring devices. They would ultimately utilize some of the equipment that Steven Point, the IT guru from Criminal, had developed for them on their last mission.

Stamos and his boss had been instrumental in allowing Point the latitude to work on and finally bring to life what was probably the fastest and most versatile AI in the world, Guardian Artificial Intelligence or GAI. Specifically built for the FBI, DNI, CIA, and Secret Service, the set of programs was altered and tailored to the needs of the SEC and was now renamed Artificial Reconnaissance of Transactions Intelligence or

ARTI. Its artificial intelligence programs, which would soon help analyze CAT and its trillions of trading events, also tied them to news events, earnings announcements, bank accounts, and personalized data of everyone from investors, traders, and corporate personnel.

A few years ago, when Point first developed GAI, it was used to monitor facial recognition, news events, and telecommunications such as cell tower surveillance and underwater communications cable intercepts. Data from thousands if not millions of sources from around the world were fed into this AI analysis program and housed at a data facility at Langley. Each day, this information led to meaningful investigations which then resulted in prosecutions by the FBI and DOJ. Particularly on this mission, the teams in Germany and Ukraine would be feeding all of their data into GAI for analysis.

GAI was still being tweaked to add financial information, and at some point, GAI and ARTI could be merged so that communications surveillance would add to the data. Since there were very few who knew of this AI analysis of the trading world, there would be perhaps a year of really good intelligence information on the nefarious world of fringe trading and money laundering. No doubt, this would push money laundering even further into the world of cryptocurrency.

What even fewer knew was that counter-intelligence information that was gathered directly from the major cryptocurrency exchanges and the brokers themselves would also soon be tied into ARTI. Even FINRA was not aware this aspect was even possible. And as of six months ago, it wasn't conceivable. Well, that was true until Steven Point joined the SEC data analysis team. One of the ways money launderers and fringe traders had evaded MIDAS in the past, was by putting trades in one of two zones called "above best offer" or "below best bid" trades and then doing so using offshore cash in the past or, in the present day, using cryptocurrency. These trades were not searched by MIDAS. Now ARTI and CAT would catch all trades in these zones for the past dozen years.

And now with the help of the DNI and the CIA, Guardian and ARTI would have clandestine access to the cryptocurrency information including IP addresses and likely owners and crypto trades that occurred for the past decade. IP address data, which could be spoofed or hidden behind a VPN, was not foolproof for identification purposes but often led to the perpetrators after surveillance of those IP addresses if they were subsequently used for identifiable web traffic.

What prompted this extensive intelligence gathering of the trading world? Events such as the dot.com bubble, the Flash Crash in May 2010, and most recently the 2018 crash. The earlier sudden crashes of the markets prompted the SEC to fund the MIDAS project which gave some insight into what may have caused the crash. But the real reason for the bottoming out of the major stock indexes had eluded investigators. The Flash Crash was the reason for the retroactive look-back from ARTI, which was going to retrospectively search transactions back to January 2010.

Now the publicly known go-live date was still a few months away, but there was a team of fifty FBI and Secret Service computer specialists that were already linking the systems together, and that top secret go-live date was earlier today. For Point and his team, this would be a live look-in on trading with a computer database and artificial intelligence that would change the face of financial regulation and investigations for the next decade.

There was a chill in the air early that next morning in the Virginia countryside as the insane Ducati Superleggera motorcycle propelled Stamos through the fog on the way to the FBI headquarters. The muscle machine was light but hugged the lines of each curve and barely lifted a millimeter on the hilltops as he felt the exhilarating G forces. For a few moments the worries of the night before and of what lay ahead disappeared in the rapture of each valley that was tamed under the Pirelli tires and the V4 engine. Stamos smoothly brought the bike down into the garage at the Hoover building, with the deep whine of each rev of the engine announcing his entrance like a mission bell.

As he walked into the office, his mind was racing with thoughts of all they would discover in the next few weeks with their surveillance. He walked toward Chelsvig's office with the determination of the warrior he used to be in his early days with the counterintelligence teams and the anticipation of great new beginnings. He was envisioning the next hour sitting down for planning meetings. What he did not expect was Chelsvig already walking out the door, in a rush.

"Meeting right now! SCIF room. We need you there." That was a welcome wake-up call to the senses and snapped Stamos out of his daydream.

The SCIF meeting and operations room for the counterintelligence division was a quick 30-second walk and it seemed like they made it in 5 seconds flat. The only comment from Chelsvig on the way there was, "This is the biggest breakthrough since the communication between the Russians and the candidate 1, we have less than a week to break on this!"

As they walked into the anteroom, the guards confiscated their devices as usual, but the search and scanning were even greater and reminiscent of higher-level meetings like those for counterintelligence drone strikes and extremely classified meetings. As they entered the room there were fewer participants than at other operations meetings and it was immediately apparent why. Around the table were the Director of the CIA, the lead computer specialist on the team, and two people he last saw at CIA headquarters years ago at a Russia section meeting.

They were upper-level Russia and Eastern Europe section assistant directors who carried significant clout with the CIA director. Conspicuously missing were any of the directors or assistant directors from the FBI and DNI and no lower-level operations. This was a need-to-know meeting only and the less political appointees the better. It seemed everyone in leadership of intelligence and federal law enforcement these days was replaced by a political appointee. The CIA so far had been less touched by this replacement but with this operation, even that could soon change.

As they began to sit down at the table, Stamos attempted to decipher the information on the monitors as it was obvious something earth-shattering was surfacing from simple surveil-

140

lance already. The two far left monitors, however, were displaying something he had not seen so far. Each had the names of Chernov Bank and Bayerngeld Bank and seemed to be a ticker of information scrolling slowly, line by line. It looked like a stock market ticker.

Chelsvig started, "Okay so this is how the game has changed forever. I had a conversation with our friend Steven Point last night. He showed me some of what they are doing at the SEC now with ARTI, which is just our old Guardian fashioned to analyze financial data. They just went live this week and they can input any financial parameter, and ARTI will analyze that data. By IP address he can localize each of these banks and we can access all trades emanating from these banks in real time. He input some information into ARTI and what we are receiving you can see on the monitors. What you are witnessing right now is mirror trading in real-time, people! None of this is known by anybody outside of Point's team."

"Wow! That guy is dangerous with a capital D. I knew he was going to blow the doors off that place! Remember how he single-handedly discovered the Russians' operation in 2016 with Guardian?" Stamos exclaimed. "So now we can add this to our surveillance. Can we bring Point in on this case right now, to even better analyze this or add further information?"

"As a matter of fact, we are video conferencing with him in a few minutes to do just that. I briefed him on all of our surveillance. We are going to input our surveillance into Guardian, and he is going to bring an input from Guardian into ARTI which should bring even more information to bear. With that small introduction, I want to congratulate all of those present in the room. You have been on-boarded to a new joint task force that is the culmination of our previous work with German Bank and now includes Chernov Bank and Bayerngeld Bank along with Steven Point's work. Here is the Director to explain more."

Just then, on a monitor to their right, the connection started with a security feed, and then the face of Steven Point, flanked by two other men in black suits came on the line. The director of the CIA began, "Good morning, officers. This is the beginning of the joint task force Manchurian Market. This joint operation of the SEC, FBI, DNI, and CIA will be Top Secret and compartmentalized. The jurisdiction is now with the CIA and FBI with the CIA as the lead agency. No one outside of our team, even those with top-secret clearance will know about this until further notice. That means nobody who is outside these two rooms including superiors and directors."

All in attendance in the SCIF sat forward in their chairs, eyes wide open, hearts beating, and their palms beginning to sweat. Mirror-trading, live, full-stop. This was a game-changer. They were catching criminals as they were laundering money. Could they intercept the trades?

"With that, I will turn it over to Steven Point, of the SEC, formerly with the DNI and FBI."

"Thank you, Mr. Director. What we have seen, gentlemen, and this may be just the tip of the iceberg, is the largest, most coordinated trading scheme that we have ever seen or could ever imagine, for that matter. So far, we have detected, or I should say ARTI, has detected and brought immediately to our attention, this pattern of trades going on from these two banks. So far, the AI has detected more than a hundred other IP addresses not associated with these banks that are participating. We are tasking this team to investigate these IP addresses and add them to our surveillance. The trades and the income of this scheme are in the range of a few hundred billion dollars in the 24 hours we have monitored it."

The details of what was known thus far about the banks and their connections to the Russian underworld were already known. What was not known was how sophisticated these connections were. Without any imagination necessary, everyone in the room recognized that the events of the next several weeks would reveal the real reason Russian oligarchs, expats, and sympathizers were becoming multi-billionaires overnight.

The director ended the meeting with, "So Chelsvig, you and your team will continue surveillance along with our CIA teams in place in Germany and Kyiv. We also need your team to coordinate with Point's team to investigate these IP addresses and who these operators are. The first IP address we have ascertained to be spoofed but we are interrogating the VPN that it is hiding behind, which is located in Russia. It appears to be a hedge fund out of London controlled by offshore interests. It is mostly controlled by the Russians and a family out of St Petersburg. We will find out more. This carries the utmost national security interest."

As Stamos and Chelsvig prepared to leave the SCIF, Stamos remarked to the team, "Alright, so we need to be sure not to tip off the VPN to our queries. The VPN is probably an in-house VPN with monitoring capabilities. We will need to spoof our IP addresses to appear to come from within their network. Let's get to Munich, like yesterday."

Few words were spoken, for each participant was too busy wrapping their heads around the enormity of it all. They each realized the impact their work would have on the fairness of the markets and the repercussions of what could happen if this trading continued or if it collapsed on itself.

Chelsvig simply stared at the monitor for a full minute, watching the scrolling trades march down the screen, reiterating for a third time, "Wow!" He turned to Stamos, and they followed the director toward the exit, pure adrenaline flowing freely through their veins.

That day they set to work in their situation room analyzing all the IP addresses and toiled all night to bring to light the true location and identity of the 150 different perpetrators. The key would be to ascertain the origin of all the communications so they could identify the head of the criminal organization involved. Once they identified all of the locations, on-site surveillance would be requisite. Stamos had a feeling it would all lead to Kyiv and ultimately to Russia from there.

~

CHAPTER 18: IDA

~

By the time CAT and ARTI were up and running late last week, Natalia's AI had already been working for a week searching the data from not only the US stock exchanges but also the Chinese, Japanese, Korean, and European exchanges. Jignesh and Sebastian were working on the cryptocurrency and IP address connections. Initially, her editor allowed her the latitude of this project as a means to hone her uncanny predictions and prognostications, because his notion was that they were developing this program to determine the patterns of trading among the different stock exchanges. Little did he know that it would bring to light an entire network of Russian dark trading that would attempt to decimate the Western world.

Natalia had just finished her workout and Monday morning run through Central Park. It was now 8:00 am and she needed to indulge herself with much-needed coffee to continue the endorphin surge into the day. She stopped at her usual java stop on the way to the Journal building and sat on a small park bench for a few minutes to get a moment to talk with Chip since it was afternoon in London. Natalia had agreed to only talk and text via encrypted formats and via a VPN thus providing two layers of protection from spying.

"Hi, Chip. Yes, oh my God, we are rolling! This week will be the coup de grâce as we input the IP address tracing. The full identity of every trader will be public knowledge," Natalia began the conversation with her endorphin-fueled superlative, purposefully piquing Chip's interest.

"That will be the dagger. You will have blown the lid off this scheme but also all illegal trading schemes for that matter. I can't wait to see it in person." Chip was genuinely inspired by her comments.

She let him know more about their progress and it was great to get some motivation and encouragement from him about the project. She had hoped to beat CAT and the SEC at developing and utilizing this AI to analyze market trading. While she wouldn't have as much data as CAT, she would be close and had the potential to access more data from other sources not available to CAT. She informed him about the crash and the possible coordinated trading that they had found.

As she was getting off the phone with him, Chip gave his characteristic inspirational quote that always kept her moving forward. "You know you wouldn't have gotten to where you are with the second-best financial news outlet in the world if you weren't the best financial genius in the world. You should come back to London, and you can be my boss."

It was the kind of compliment that was also kind of self-serving, but it would work for today. She knew she was on the verge of the ultimate success that until now remained just beyond her grasp. She felt the same as when she was an underclassman at Oxford winning races in practice, yet she hadn't won it all. That grit and drive led her to Gold at the Olympics and now was going to bring a great analytical tool to the world of trading.

As she loftily walked into the Journal offices, she thought what she didn't know yet was how she would use this information. Would the culmination of her labor solely be to augment law enforcement or for market research? It seemed preordained by her AI and the massive amount of information

146

they would be uncovering, to be, at least in the beginning, the former. She thought of the two companies that Stamos had asked her to investigate. She could look at those as a starting case to monitor. When she walked into the computer lab, she gave the names of the companies to her interns.

"Run these through the AI to see what we come up with for analysis. Let's start with that and then let's turn on the full analysis," she figured she couldn't go wrong with a small test. As it turned out, it was this first small test that primed her AI to set up a pattern recognition around trading at Chernov Bank and Bayerngeld Bank. This would spark its interest in the patterns that on her end would uncover the same coordinated trading schemes that Steven Point had found.

As world-changing as it turned out in the end, the initial findings were actually drab and dull. These two companies were not engaged in any untoward trading activities that the AI could discern. Both were rather small in terms of trading volume and scope. That did not deter Sebastian from searching further. He did a manual search of all trades for the past year from both trading firms and still nothing. So much for their first targeted research. As such, they were discouraged at the outset.

What seemed like a waste of a few hours would turn into some unpredictable results. They all assembled at the central conference table to regroup.

"Well, that turned out to be a nothing sandwich," Sebastian mused, proud of his use of a popular colloquialism.

"Let's return to the primary objective. This is not about these two companies," Natalia said with renewed enthusiasm.

"Agreed, let's play ball!" Jignesh was getting in on the American slang now too.

Sebastian had a question, "But wait, what should we call her?"

Natalia knew exactly what he meant. How could they have created this intelligence without naming her? And it WAS a her. At least for Natalia anyway.

"Well, probably not something cheesy, like HAL or anything like that," she said, referring to the decades-old robot.

"I was thinking Deep Green," Sebastian retorted, playing off IBM's first attempt at Artificial Intelligence.

"I already have a few ideas," Jignesh blurted out. "What about Intelligent Detection of Algorithms or IDA? Or we could call her Patterns and Algorithm Recognition Unmasking Language, or PARUL." He liked the Indian female name of one of his college crushes.

"IDA is simple and short but sweet. She could probably name herself. Why don't you ask her?" Natalia didn't want to dwell too long on this matter, because there was a lot of work to do. She was sure that IDA had already detected the algorithms and trades she was looking for, she just needed to teach IDA to start learning for herself.

Sebastian took the name and ran with it in all directions. "Okay, we can perform the test run on IDA today and begin with the full analysis later. Will let you know when I am finished. Incidentally, we are getting some intrusion alerts from our firewall detection systems on the servers. So far, they have not penetrated. I have beefed up the security in the firewall with IP and geographic exclusions and multiple other fail-safes. We should all change our passwords today to ultra-strong passwords and only from the main server. Do not log in remotely until I figure out the source. I will disable all remote logins." Sebastian, just like Natalia, was a stickler for security.

It wouldn't be the last attempted incursion on their systems. Everyone would have to watch their back from now on. Natalia and the interns had agreed that all emails would be scrutinized, no phones were ever allowed into the server room, and as usual, the coding computers in this lab were isolated network-wise to prevent any outside monitoring. The Journal prided itself on having a network and building that would be difficult for even state-level espionage, including the US government, let alone the Russians.

That very afternoon, as it would turn out, IDA had already begun to parse the data and was uncovering massive amounts of data and trading patterns, some of which were innocent, and some of which were not. Some of these were nefarious in a small local market manipulation way, but similar to ARTI's findings, there was a definite pattern to multiple market manipulation schemes. Would its discovery ever reach the light of day?

~

CHAPTER 19:
MEANWHILE, THE SURVEILLANCE

~

Meanwhile, with each passing minute, ARTI continued to amass more and more information that would change the world. For what was now the underworld would cease to be. Point could now envision that they were finally bringing this dark world into the light. The hacked information from the cryptocurrency trading was breaking this wide open. But now they required more of the specific identification of the entities involved, which would demand more inputs that were not readily available from the main feed from the cryptocurrency exchanges. The as-yet-to-be-revealed IP addresses and the identification of the actors promised to advance their analysis several steps further.

Now more than ever, he knew if there was one person in this world who could identify the perpetrators with surveillance, it would definitely be Stamos. He was the same agent that identified, with hard-nosed espionage, the Russians and Americans behind the election fiasco that was 2016. And almost none of that information had reached the public yet due to the protection of classified information. Point was determined that it would be different this time. His GAI found out the whole truth and only those with the highest security clearances knew what really happened and who directed it. This time, even if they were Americans or people in positions of power, they would be identified.

First, they would need to find out the location of documents and then proceed with electronic and physical surveillance. With the amount of money involved, hundreds of billions of dollars stolen from everyday Main Street investors, he was sure this would be tougher and deadlier than 2016. He trusted Stamos would be ready for the challenge, for Point fully understood this kind of fieldwork was his specialty.

The rest of the potential coordinated trading ARTI was spitting out would have been deemed useful to investigators in the past, but peanuts compared to this network they were discovering in Operation Manchurian Market. For the next year, ARTI would keep the SEC busy with new tips on insider trading and coordinated trading now that it could analyze the whole market. The public would not find out about the existence of ARTI and its ongoing analyses for another year. Though in the underworld of dark trading, its potential to disrupt their operations would be known soon enough.

That morning Point's security team was also busy fending off attacks on their networks. Moreover, a few of the connections on the broker side that existed before were being shut down. This was proof that the other side knew they were discovered. The connections from Bayerngeld and Chernov banks were still live but probably not much longer. It was too late to hide the dark trading activity though, as Point and his men already knew the IP addresses and broker identifications and could monitor from the trading platforms of the DOW and NASDAQ. It would become necessary to add other foreign markets and cryptocurrencies to the analysis in the next few days to stay ahead of the game.

Now it was up to the surveillance units in Munich and Kyiv to bring home the coveted information on who was behind this scheme. Stamos and Chelsvig would be on their way to Munich any minute to crack the case wide open. The clandestine team would not be in touch with Point for hours. The intelligence that GAI was bringing in from Bayerngeld Bank was helping immensely as they were bringing in additional data, but most of the data the program was gleaning was in the form of IP addresses in Kyiv. Kyiv was the key to unlocking the mystery of who was behind this. For now, those involved could rest easily hiding behind their VPN, and the central commanders must be emanating from one entity in one location. Was it going to be in Kyiv or elsewhere? Point's guess was it would ultimately be necessary to infiltrate a location in St. Petersburg.

Simultaneously, the team in New York was working on the VPN and the IP addresses in the US that were hiding behind that same VPN. The IP addresses seemed to be multiplying like rabbits. At last count, there were over a thousand possible actors with half of them in the US. Decoding this maze was going to take some time. But did they have time, and could they collect the evidence quickly enough to get to a FISA court?

CHAPTER 20: MUNICH

So, it was decided then. Chelsvig and Stamos had one more meeting that evening in the SCIF with the CIA director. These three had become thorns in the side of criminal enterprises across the world as the FBI director was aggressive in the use of CIA and DNI resources to investigate money laundering and other financial crimes from foreign organized crime. And with this new intelligence, this would be the most aggressive, wide-ranging investigation in history. Everyone knew the time constraints they were under. There was evidence that these enterprises were already initiating attempts to hide their tracks. The perpetrators already operated under several layers of protection due to offshore trusts and other entities, and Stamos would need to act quickly to assemble a team for investigation and surveillance.

First, they needed to track the real owners of the capital being traded and who was behind it. To set up this intricate and extensive operation would need to have powerful state backing, Russia, China, or North Korea were the most likely, with the former almost certainly the lead actor. The first place to start was with these two most linked banks. They knew other banks would ultimately be discovered, and it also appeared multiple brokerages were involved. For this, the investigators would bring the initial discoveries to the FISA court for sealed subpoenas for information on banking clients, disguising them as vaguely looking for fraud involving a few small-time actors. Second, they would need electronic and physical surveillance to get more evidence to point them in the best direction for these subpoenas. Now with ARTI, they could subpoena the trading platforms that were performing the mirror trades.

What made ARTI most effective was that nobody, not even their leaders, was cognizant that it was operational. The longer that was the case the better. Stamos thought to himself, Maybe it wasn't so bad that the Zorin administration kept delaying the official launch date. Keep delaying it for all we care.

They received one breakthrough just in the past twenty-four hours with regard to a communication interception. After the information on this communication broke at the meeting this morning, the Russian and Eastern European section directors recently set up their own electronic surveillance on Bayerngeld Bank and Chernov Bank. The Eastern European Section of the CIA set up this surveillance and had several offices rented in the adjacent buildings in both Munich and Kyiv. Modern surveillance would now be utilized to monitor the outputs from individual computers with the best de-encryption methods.

However, in the case of both banks, this was the first time the computer surveillance technicians already in place had ever seen this program the bank employees were using. And it was encrypted well - better than any surreptitious bank communications they had seen before. If they were going to obtain this information, they would need to get inside this bank with some video capture malware and keystroke malware programs. Keystroke malware would allow the CIA to capture the messaging these employees were sending in real-time, and the video capture would capture the incoming messages to be recorded.

After hearing this information, Stamos finally admitted to

himself what this mission would require of him. He needed to get into those buildings, and it would once again require disguise and subterfuge to accomplish the necessary physical surveillance. If there was one thing the last several years of modern surveillance told him, it was that these criminals were always one step ahead of the good guys as far as covering their tracks with the newest technology, but sometimes good old-fashioned physical espionage beat technology.

"What legitimate investigations do we already have ongoing with anyone with accounts at those banks. We need to find out where these directions are coming from and where they are forwarding them to. I need a cover to get inside these banks, starting with Munich. That will be the easiest. Then on to Kyiv." Stamos had entered battle mode, intent on establishing his alibi from the outset.

"We have several. These two banks are well-known for being heavily interconnected with banks in Crete and the Caymans for money laundering," Chelsvig answered, secretly worried about the stakes involved with Stamos going undercover again.

Stamos impatiently interrupted, "Which ones are still in the subpoena process? It should be outside the financial system, no money laundering, and no Russians. We don't want any Russians questioning why the FBI is in Munich before we even get to Kyiv."

One of the CIA section chiefs spoke up, "One step ahead of you. Here's what we dug up this morning already. We have an investigation of the furniture king of New Jersey. That guy has bank accounts everywhere including Germany, Crete, London, and the Caymans. And his investigation is not one of money laundering. He is mafia and, while he has cultivated some Russian connections, his crimes are more tax evasion and RICO-related. There is also a German accountant who maintains an office above the Bayerngeld Bank for whom we can arrange a subpoena. That will get you physically inside the bank building, the rest is up to you and your incursion team."

Perfect, that would be the entry point, Stamos thought. "OK, Let's ready the subpoenas on this guy and his organization. Can we get the subpoenas by tomorrow morning? Keep them under seal and we can fly to Munich tonight." Stamos would direct the FBI lawyers to subpoena both banks for his accounts, then he would be part of the team of lawyers presenting them to Bayerngeld and Chernov banks. The next few hours came and went in a flash, and he and Chelsvig readied the team for the surveillance.

There was no time for complete mockups of the banks for operational integrity, but they also would need real-time reconnaissance to know where to plant the devices for the video monitoring. That would have to be carried out once they arrived on-site and the procedure plotted on the fly.

This meant the planned surveillance was all the more critical. The Munich and Kyiv missions would be wheels-up tonight. A few planning meetings were all that stood between him and the real action. The planes would meet them in Quantico, so Stamos needed to exit the SCIF to begin making preparations there as well. Once again, he straddled the Superleggera and was soon flying down the Virginia highway toward home with DC finally in the rearview mirror. He hoped the mission would be as well tuned as this lean, mean, road machine that he trusted more than even his 911.

As they departed Quantico that evening under cloak of darkness, the unmarked plane made a swift ascent through the clouds as Stamos and Chelsvig nervously walked through the process, the equipment they would be planting, and how to make the incursion into the bank offices. If they couldn't penetrate the offices they needed to access during the day, they surmised the operation may require them to perform a night break-in through the roof. Similar to past operations in Germany they would land near Munich to avoid public airports. To bypass busy and more visible international airports, the CIA and FBI frequently used military landing fields to evade detection in friendly countries like Germany. Their transponders would be turned off, flying absent tail numbers, remaining over the ocean to avoid radar, and filing no flight plans. Once on the ground outside Munich, Chelsvig would remain with the planes to provide communications and backup. After the
158

last mission, he was in no shape for fieldwork.

As they touched down at the now too familiar Fursten-feldbruck Air Base, the first thing Stamos spotted while taxing down the runway at the antiquated airfield was the old World War II bunkers and barracks that had survived allied bomb-ings. This was the training center for the Luftwaffe during the 1940's and was not usually used for missions until late in the war so it mostly escaped the scrutiny of our B17s and Russian ground assaults until later in 1945. There were few, mostly military planes on the tarmac as this airfield was still mostly used for minor operations and training. The ironic history of eight decades ago when Russia and the United States worked together against tyranny was not lost on him. Only a few years later, Russia descended into its own tyranny from which even today it had not escaped.

The FBI and CIA exploited military agreements with the German government to fly into this airport from the Middle East when they wanted to avoid detection as most Russian surveillance targeted the NATO air base in Frankfurt. The US operated a small but heavily guarded hangar under the guise of a shipping company. The plane quickly taxied off the runway and into the open hangar door to avoid scrutiny. It wasn't just government surveillance they worried about, as now there were airplane enthusiasts who would photograph tail numbers and airplanes and publish these on the internet. Every once in a while, an international incident would occur after one of these aviation paparazzi revealed possible CIA or Air Force flights carrying terrorists or prisoners.

As the door to the hangar started to close, Stamos and his team waited at the top of the steps until it was completely closed, then stepped down off the plane into the dimly lit hangar and the awaiting black suburban. The required secrecy prevented Stamos from using his trademark dismount from deployed stairs while the plane was still moving. Despite this, the clandestine arrival increased his basal adrenaline levels enough to heighten his awareness of his surroundings as the operation commenced in earnest. As he studied the interior of this seldom used building, in the corner of the hangar behind a makeshift wall, he took notice of two marines with M27s at the top of a stairwell and an iron door. What they were guarding, he presumed, was not something he ever wanted to know anything about, and he looked away, taking precautions not to make eye contact with the guards.

It took only a few minutes for the team to load the equipment they were carrying into the back, and they were off. Stamos sat staring at the passing scenic German countryside as they neared beautiful downtown Munich. It reminded him of the suburbs of Virginia where he had lived most of his adult life. Between his training for the FBI and CIA, and now working in this capacity he came to appreciate the serene, wooded environment of the areas around Quantico. The ride through these areas in Virginia gave him the peace he needed on his way home each evening, and this similar landscape in Germany gave him an odd calmness now as they prepared for a tense week.

As they arrived at the surveillance offices, the Suburbans were parked in the underground parking garage. The agents exited the SUVs and entered through a side door into a private elevator to the 6th floor of the office building. This was the command center of the multi-agency operation. It was 3 pm local time, and they had better serve the subpoenas soon. The team in place already was holding the German process server on standby. Later in the day was better, after some of the early departing employees had left the bank.

They collected their devices, placed them into hollowed-out cell phones, and proceeded back out to the SUVs. They would take a circuitous route back across the river and by Parliament House to pick up the junior FBI attorneys at Munich International Airport and return to downtown Munich. They arrived at the bank thirty minutes later and met the process server outside the front door. As they entered the bank lobby, they met the security guard and asked for the manager on duty. The svelte young woman with a thick Ukrainian-Russian accent met them in the lobby and graciously received the subpoena. It was served with the German process and Stamos asked the woman if he could see where they kept

160

their accounts and signature cards.

"Yes, you can come this way," she answered in English with an inviting smile.

The objective was to make it to the fifth floor which was the top floor of the bank offices. There was an elevator near the lobby and a grand stairwell that led to the second floor overlooking the lobby. Stamos pretended to be looking at his phone and typing a message of something of importance.

"Do you have any private offices in the bank?" one of the junior attorneys asked.

"We do. They are on the fourth floor. Why do you ask?"

"This second subpoena lists an accountant that has offices at the same address. Do you know where this accountant is at the moment?" He asked, showing her the name of an accountant on the fourth floor.

"His offices are on the fourth floor. I can direct you once we return to the lobby. You take that elevator on the right," she reported.

That would be convenient. The ruse subpoena provided them with a reason to access the elevator. Just hit the wrong button and they were in. As they went through to the back offices, they asked if there was a signature card for either of these accounts on the subpoena to see if they could get any immediate information. Within minutes, with her attention diverted, one device was easily deployed on what looked like a server in these main offices. Now to get to the fifth floor.

"Thank you, you have been most helpful. What did you say your name was again?" the young FBI attorney tried his best flirting glances toward the manager, unaware of the intentions of his superiors who were with him that day.

He's doing a great job, without even knowing it, Stamos thought as he readied himself for the hard part. He would make it a point to reward this attorney if the mission was successful, but only if he performed well on the fifth floor. Utilizing unsuspecting FBI attorneys was a necessary evil, but carried with it risks that the uncontrolled variable might catch on to the ruse and not play along.

"Yes, you are welcome. It is Svetlana," she responded

with renewed interest in her guests. She flipped her hair and adjusted her dress for the benefit of the Americans, who might be entertaining.

"Let's move on to see if the accountant is in," Stamos wanted to get the main surveillance in place, which was the computer located on the fifth floor.

As they made it to the elevator, as luck would command, the manager did not ride along with them. So far so good. Stamos made sure to be at the controls and hid them so the young attorney who was not involved in the operation would not see him hit the number 5. As the elevator stopped, Stamos hurried the attorney out the door so he would not realize the contrived mistake.

They made their way down the hall to the office. The computer was alone in the correct location. There were a few people in offices down the hall. Stamos quickly ducked into the room, and before the server or the attorney could notice, placed the device on the side of the computer and placed the camera, which was smaller than a computer chip on a file cabinet across from the monitor. Success!

Just as they exited, he could hear someone getting up from a desk down the hall. Stamos quickly walked toward the noise.

"Hello, can you help us find this office?" Stamos asked in English.

The stout young man that exited the door, spoke in broken English, "Which building?"

Stamos turned to the process server for assistance.

"Welches arbeitsplatz ist das?" he asked, pointing to the subpoena.

They spoke in German, which Stamos could understand but feigned indifference to their error. The man pointed back down the hall at the elevator. The camera that was recording from Stamos' lapel continued to capture good footage of the interior rooms as they walked down the hall. He made sure to point himself toward each open doorway to get a concept of the layout of the computers on this floor.

He asked the process server, "Where is it?" continuing to pretend he was looking for the correct office on this floor.

162

"It's one floor down, we are on the wrong floor," he said.

"Oh," Stamos said and, as he leaned down to tie his shoe while they were waiting for the elevator, he placed one more camera on the floor next to the elevator against the wall. They only lasted a few weeks and were read via remote reading of the hard drive. No transmitter was required, but it only worked in locations that did not have electromagnetic interference or blocking.

They served the subpoena on the accountant and prepared for the boring part, but at least now the dangerous part was accomplished without incident. He didn't feel secure until they were in the Suburban several blocks away from the bank. They crossed the river towards the airport to drop off the naive attorney for his long flight home. Now that was smoother than the last mission, he thought as they directed the junior attorney to his airline.

It took another few days but with the intelligence they were gathering it was readily apparent who the ringleaders were. The connection pinged to Chernov Bank and also a computer in a museum in St Petersburg, Russia. Far away from what would have been the Russian GRU. Stamos was expecting it would be Moscow, but St Petersburg? What was in St Petersburg? The museum was a local art and family museum regarding a dynasty of tsars of Russia that had long passed. Then he suddenly remembered Natalia's family was from St. Petersburg. A building in that city might be an easier target for the CIA to get their hands on the identity of the perpetrators, than any location in Moscow.

Now, the next and most difficult phase of the surveillance shifted east to Kyiv. It was a long drive along German and Polish highways to reach the Ukrainian border, but a necessary one, as they were unable to land a transport plane in Kyiv. Almost all the agents would travel by land, and the Polish border with Ukraine was the easiest to pass through without suspicion being raised. Chelsvig would rush with two of the unmarked Gulfstreams to the Antonov International Airport for backup and extraction purposes. One of the junior agents would disembark from there as they feigned some business connections there.

Chernov Bank was going to be a more formidable fortress from which to extract the intelligence they required. First, it was located near the bustling Independence Square and there was heightened security this summer with Russian separatists engaging in terrorist activities in the capital. In addition, according to the CIA, there was a clandestine Russian presence in the area, spying on the former Soviet country's government and any Ukrainians who were not pro-Russian. There was a treasure trove of intelligence emanating from Kyiv these days that was important to multiple governments as well as other bad actors in the world.

There was also the incidental but real danger of being caught up in criminal activity as this capital city had its fair share of Eastern European mafia and traffickers to be concerned about. However, the plus side of this location was the hectic tourist traffic on foot overflowing from the square into the rest of this area of downtown Kyiv that would provide perfect cover if they required urgent egress.

~

CHAPTER 21: READY

~

The afternoon before the full launch day, her day filled with monotonous article editing tweaks, Natalia received an unusual phone call from Katya. She was in a crisis again. She had caught her boyfriend cheating on her and was in the throes of self-pity. Once more, as it always worked out, Natalia was head of the rescue crew, which meant moments later, a knock on the door and Katya walked into the apartment with a box of tissues and Swiss chocolate coffee gelato in tow. Somehow Natalia always managed to avoid saying I told you so.

There could not be another woman who was more unlucky at love. Natalia predicted this event weeks ago, as Katya was famous for looking for love in the wrong places. The rich or famous party scene in New York was not the right place, of that Natalia was certain. The pair were sprawled out on the sitting couch with the view of Central Park in the background. Luckily for Natalia, this episode of transitions from crying, then self-pity, to anger only took less than an hour. Anyway, she needed a break from planning the rest of the week and another editorial that she was writing.

At that point, Katya turned to eating her gelato and since

there was not much to catch up on over the past week, the conversation once again turned to the Russia Day party and whether Natalia was going to meet her in Cannes before they returned to St. Petersburg. Truth be told, Natalia's defenses were already up, and her tone with Katya was beginning to mimic her attitude with her uncle. It seemed she was showing up at odd times and really just appearing to parrot her uncle's same tired dialogue.

Hence Natalia's next response was vague and non-committal, and she began to search for an excuse to make leave from this tired old friend who might be one of her uncle's information sources. "I will let you know. But we will definitely have to catch up in St. Petersburg. You should stay at the summer villa with me for a week or two. Do you think there are any new restaurants in St. Petersburg that would be worth looking into?"

Katya agreed, "Yes, that would be fun! I've heard the nightlife has really turned around in the past few years!"

Natalia could sense this crisis was nearly over and really needed to get back to work. "Alright, Katya, if you want to finish your gelato, I am going to continue to work on my article. I'll be right in the next room."

"That's okay, I'll head down to my place. Let's grab sushi later this week." Katya did eventually leave, however only after several minutes and close to a dozen goodbyes.

The call came to her just before 5 pm that day. Which was after 1 am in St Petersburg. Her uncle was a night owl but usually called in the morning New York time. Natalia glanced up from her phone to the afternoon sky, "Why can't you leave me alone?" she asked aloud before answering as if looking to the heavens above for help. And she was knee-deep in programming and oh-so-close to completion. She felt guilty but let it go to voicemail. She could read it or listen to it later. It didn't matter, she knew what it was.

There was a certain nervousness in the voice message. He had invited her to attend the Volkov Operations Committee video conference meeting that was tomorrow. It would probably last the whole morning, starting very early Eastern

Standard Time. Which would mean she would have to forego the launch that day and delay it until the next day.

She came up with a plan though. She could say she didn't see the voicemail. Then delay until this evening, when she would surely receive another phone call. Then she would put her foot down and say she had a meeting to attend with her boss. Otherwise, this behavior would continue until she acquiesced and returned to Russia. At this rate she was not coming back at all, maybe even running away and going into hiding, she thought irrationally. This was too important to back down now.

She had had enough of the delays from her family. She had grown suspicious of her uncle's intentions as he had already caused postponements to their launch by a couple of weeks. Honestly, she could not remember a time when he and her whole family were more overbearing.

She decided to head to the office and see how Jignesh and Sebastian were coming along with the testing. She reached for her phone and decided to video chat with them first to see if she could be of any help there. She needed to complete just a few more items on her checklist of editing. She had a good chat with her two interns on the encrypted app and they said everything was ready to go. She quickly grabbed her keys and descended the elevator to complete what she wanted to accomplish today.

In the server room and computer lab, the three of them would work well into the night. There was a sense of euphoria that they were not just uncovering something criminal but perhaps permanently changing the world. Natalia perfected the final touches on the AI programming, Sebastian was almost ready with the IP and cryptocurrency plug-ins, and soon they could really get to work.

"Well, shall we get to work in the morning after you complete your portion? I'm tired and we need to be fresh for tomorrow." Natalia was exhausted from the past week's activities.

"Ok, the process shouldn't take more than one more hour on this plug-in. I can finish everything up tonight. We can start in on the final testing in the morning," Sebastian said.

Jignesh was standing there, watching over Sebastian's shoulders, his mind in a fog. "I'm exhausted too. I'm going to take a nap while you complete the IP plug-in." He settled himself into his gaming chair, which often served as a bed on long nights.

"Alright, so I will meet you guys back here at 730am to get this show on the road!" Natalia was on cloud 9 anticipating tomorrow's historic occasion.

As she left the server room and ascended to the real-world streets of New York, she realized that she never received the phone call she was expecting from her uncle. She thought that was a relief, maybe he was going to respect her wishes for him to leave her alone, for once in her life.

~

CHAPTER 22: TAKE CARE OF IT

~

President Zorin took this last-minute meeting with Senator Speransky without hesitation. As Chairman of the Senate Finance Committee, he would be useful in the next cycle to obtain financial assistance in the right places for his re-election, sustain the profitability of their business allies around the world, and continue their access to capital and property in the US. There was no doubt that influential investors in the US (both foreign and domestic) had helped him win the last election and they would also be the lynchpin to his success in this year's election. It was already the first of July, and he needed a boost, for he was still barely behind in the polls. Speransky owed him an update anyway on his cousin's operations.

It was late in the evening, but the White House was all abuzz with preparations for the G7 meetings. Already the staff of every agency had been prepped to include Russia in the conversations, and some were directed to start to float the term G7+, so that they could ease Russia back in. The State Department would set aside a block of hotel rooms to change the ease into a surprise elevation if their allies would not come to an agreement on G8. That should be pleasing to the Senator and Prokachev, the President thought.

President Zorin met him at the entrance to the Oval Office, more official than their usual location, and shook his hand with a smile. Jack Speransky took his handshake with a solid arm grab and thanked him for seeing him on such short notice. Jack entered the room looking downward, conjuring up some thoughts, and turned when he reached the sitting area. He glanced toward the two people already in the sitting area and found it necessary to redirect his thoughts.

"Mr. President, I have heard some concerning news about the economy, the state of our financial system, and how it relates to some of our allies," he started.

"Jack, do tell. We definitely will be needing these allies to be as strong as possible in the next 6 months if we are going to continue our good work for them."

As his assistant closed the door behind the Senator, it was just the two of them and the Treasury Secretary Stanton and the President's chief of staff, Mark Salgado, who were both close allies of both men. Tom stood to shake the Senator's hand, while the chief of staff remained sitting. A few pleasantries were exchanged among the group of powerful men and Jack remained facing the President. An awkward minute of silence ensued, during which time President Zorin's mind escaped briefly to a poll he had just heard about a few hours ago. As Jack's spear-like stare penetrated through his thoughts of the election, President Zorin could tell that this would require an even more personal and privileged conversation.

"Tom and Mark, can you leave Jack and me for a few minutes to talk about this? I would like to solicit his unfettered advice." Tom was probably privileged to hear this conversation, but he didn't want to involve Mark, who was a stick in the mud and was not part of the financial advisor network. It was best to have them both leave for a moment. If there was one lesson learned in his storied past, it was not to have witnesses to any important conversations, especially ones this critical.

As the smooth, curved door closed behind the two exiting the room, Jack turned toward President Zorin with a con-

170

cerned look on his face. "Our European allies have begun to detect some monitoring of their networks. We are not sure where it is coming from, but they are investigating."

"That is not good, Jack. We can't have anyone meddling in what is a perfect economy. Is it one of our own agencies? If that is the case, I can put a stop to it swiftly. It could be anyone with investigative capabilities. FBI, CIA, DIA, SEC, Secret Service, the Europeans, Chinese? Could be anyone. Journalists? They have been a hindrance since the beginning." President Zorin walked around the Resolute Desk to distance himself from this threat, but Jack Speransky followed him to keep the pressure on.

Jack unrelentingly put his hand on the President's shoulder and obtrusively blocked the President from sitting down at the desk, then almost shouting, asserted, "I think you need to put some pressure on the agency heads to root this out. If the meddling is coming from outside the government, we also need the FBI to help with the investigation. Can you get Director Thomas to accomplish this?"

The President felt trapped but had no choice but to acquiesce, "Definitely, this needs to be priority one right now. We only have a few months to go to cement my legacy on the economy. If we can get through this election, then we can weather any storms after that. Our network can only assure us of this record-breaking economy if we support them."

"Peter, it appears the network feels that this is not just a concern about being discovered. I think they are starting to perceive that there is a possibility of disruption of the entire network. They are getting nervous."

"That could spell some kind of doom for us. The buy-backs could also stop. Do we have a plan B?" he asked.

Jack took a few steps away toward the sitting area with his back toward the President. He then turned half-way around with his hand stroking a stubbled chin. "There is no plan B, Peter. This is it. Our network has saved us from our own undoing in the past and even showed us how it cannot save us if we stray from the plan."

"I will get the Director involved and will also ask Tom to

assist. He has some of the most loyal troops to our cause in the Secret Service. We can stop this in its tracks." This President demanded loyalty from all of the top lieutenants, and they in turn recruited their loyal troops for their objective, which was to continue the prosperity of those devoted to the cause.

As they left the Oval Office, Jack Speransky expressed his relief but couldn't help but feel that extra defenses were necessary to combat this intrusion. President Zorin commanded his secretary to call in the Director of the FBI immediately. Tom Stanton, who was in the hallway just outside the secretary's office, walked in just then, and the President called him into the Oval. Thankfully, the chief of staff was already back in his offices down the hall.

"Tom, this is serious," he said as they walked toward the light-yellow couches that were steeped in history. "We need some protection for our network."

"What is it?" the Secretary was confused.

"It seems someone is trying to discover and then disrupt the network, and it has our allies spooked. They are looking to go to war over this. They want us to snuff this out," he paused for effect, "and quickly."

"I have some people on standby for just this occasion," Tom reassured the President. "There is no way this will meet the light of day."

"Remember what I said before, we need all the agencies involved in protecting this network. Do you have all of your ducks in a row at Treasury? You need to make sure the director of the SEC is on board with protecting our economy." Indeed, this meant war for the President too and he was going to raise a stink until he found out who in the executive branch was against him.

"Our trading network is secure. It would take espionage that even the FBI and CIA don't have the capability of yet, to break through the network." Stanton's confidence beamed from his wry smile.

"So, who else do we need to involve at this stage? I have the Director of the FBI coming in. Should we involve the CIA or DNI? They are not as privy to our network."

172

"Let's let my agents deal with this. They will have direct communication with the network security personnel and then we can direct our focus on who the targets are. The FBI would be helpful for some backup so let's talk with him." The Secretary of the Treasury commanded a very ardent and faithful set of agents that in general were more loyal to him than anyone, but if convinced with the right incentives they would go along with anything he said.

The President was grasping for straws, but sensed Tom's willingness to do anything, "You know the network security personnel are already actively engaging in surveillance and pursuit now, so give them all the assistance they need. You know, you can use your Secret Service security details to arrest these actors based on federal law for disrupting stock market trade security."

"Agreed. But it would be bad optics. The network should be able to operate in relative obscurity. If necessary, we can plant some espionage or treason evidence on whoever they tag this on."

"This is everything," the President warned. "I don't want to hear another thing about this. I want this threat extinguished now. I want you here when I meet with the FBI director?"

"Yes, sir. Consider it taken care of," Tom uttered obediently as he stealthily exited through the curved door.

∫

~

CHAPTER 23: COORDINATED TRADES

~

With her head spinning from the excitement, Natalia headed straight home from the office on this peaceful, warm, Manhattan night. For a brief moment of relaxation, she was able to watch a few snippets of a 24-hour business television talk show. What an enigma this economy was, with pundits only able to hazard a guess as to what would happen next. She could only stand watching a few minutes of the drivel emerging from the screen. She disgustedly turned off the TV and for a few fleeting minutes in the dark, stared out into the peacefulness of the lights and foliage of Central Park. She practiced a few breathing exercises to placate her fears, releasing the negativity, which in her life consisted solely of her family. Now that was relaxing, she thought. It was well after midnight when her head hit the pillow, and her breathing allowed her to sleep, but she undoubtedly would have chaotic dreams due to the excitement of what the next 24 hours would bring.

After all the delays, it was time for the real work to begin. It was also time for this AI she and her interns developed to do its work. Her sleep was restless that night, but she awoke again with the endorphins flowing through her veins. She went to the gym and, after escaping the older hedge fund manager's gaze, exited the Plaza at 6 am at the edge of Central Park and headed straight to her caffeine fix. It was warm and the sky was clear which meant it would be a nice day in Manhattan for a change. Summer was in full swing, there was no doubt about it.

She took her time at the Java Cave with her coffee and began the short walk to the Journal where she would finally be allowed to test her years-long project. The usual morning ritual of tens of thousands of people was beginning on the streets of New York as delivery people, workers, finance bros, etc. were all scurrying about. A myriad of birds were starting their day also, flitting about their perches on trees, lampposts, and traffic lights. There was something surreal about the magic of life in the summer for those who could be aware of all the nuances that sprouted out of the spring. She walked the few blocks, but really she could have run for all she knew since it only seemed to take a few seconds.

Her interns were already there, and Natalia had a suspicion they had slept overnight there again. As a matter of fact, Natalia thought this most nights. They spent the majority of their time in the computer lab they had set up. There were some mornings that she forced them to go to the company gym to take a shower in the interest of maintaining cleanliness, the server room was a clean room after all.

This morning, however, when she arrived, both Jignesh and Sebastian were relatively well dressed and showered. It seemed as though they were teenagers ready for the science fair to begin. Their hair was even combed like it was combed by their mothers, and they were nervous and jittery like high school boys. It appeared to Natalia like a scene out of the Big Bang Theory TV show, whose stars reminded her of these two nerdy college interns.

"Guess what we have been doing?" Jignesh blurted out with a giddy crack in his voice.

"Up to no good? Getting into trouble? Found two girlfriends online?" Natalia joked.

"While you were dreaming with your head on your pillow, we launched the AI with your tweaks, and it has been more deeply analyzing the data for the past 10 years. It's going to take a while, but we already have details about exactly who and what caused the 2018 crash." Sebastian could hardly contain himself.

"That quickly? How much do we know about who they are?"

"Well, the IP addresses of a majority of the shorts on that day all come from one type of VPN setup. It is a VPN that is used by the Russian GRU but appears to be based in St. Petersburg, Russia. We can't say for sure, but it seems that is the answer. The IP says that it comes from various US addresses, but they are spoofed. Many of these IP addresses actually do originate in the US but they all have the same VPN signature. This is how all of these filthy Russian billionaires are making their money," Sebastian responded, his speech pressured like someone who had just witnessed a heinous crime.

This was hitting VERY close to home, Natalia thought, as her mind turned to her uncle and his financial activities. It HAD to be. It COULDN"T be. Could it? What was he doing in 2008? Back then he had only just begun his foray into investing.

"The only way to know who it really is would be to hack these IP addresses and hack the VPN," Jignesh added.

"Let's not do that yet," Natalia needed to backtrack to make sure they would not be discovered by whoever was behind this. "But here is what we need to do. Let it analyze the whole data set. Then plug in these IP addresses and let's look for a pattern of their trades. What I want to know is how often they are trading, how often they are shorting the market, and how much volume is it? And these spoofed servers and re-routing servers - where are they?"

"Okay, it will take about a week to analyze the data set fully. Then it will take a few hours for it to parse out a hundred or so IP addresses," Jignesh predicted. "Maybe it could be finished in only 4 or 5 days."

"Do you guys know the implications of this? I wonder how much volume or total assets they have control of. If these trades are all being commanded by one entity, this is absolutely shocking. And criminal! We need to get this information to the FBI before we do any more investigation. And guys, we cannot tell anyone anything we know. If this is coordinated by my countrymen, they won't play nice."

She knew personally what would happen in Russia if you crossed the paths of the elite oligarchs. One of her friends when she was 12 years old at the École Suisse Élite in Geneva was a girl named Katrina who was a few years younger. Her family had crossed the wrong family with better connections and the whole family just ceased to exist. First, the news of her parents' death spread, and within a few days, she never saw Katrina again. That was the kind of thing that happened in her world. She had seen it many times over, it was just part of life.

"Please, whatever you do, be careful, watch your back, secure the servers, and make backups of the data. You two cannot fathom the lengths these people will go to keep their income stream uninterrupted. Do not hack the IP addresses yet."

"Agreed, multiple backups of the data. We will do daily changes of passwords and secure authentications. Nothing to do but let IDA do her work. She can defeat these thugs with one hand tied behind her back. Jignesh and I have been thinking. Do you think IDA will take over the world?"

"Okay, you guys, keep it serious. We need to focus."

But Natalia was still reeling from the shock of realizing that her family could be involved in what would be the largest criminal enterprise ever. Not just involved, they would have to be orchestrating the scheme. There was no one else in St. Petersburg who commanded the type of money that this would require. And all these meetings with managers, what did it all mean? What was her uncle up to now, if he was part of a stock market crash more than a dozen years ago? According to his own words, it was about meting out victory over the West. Something more than a small crash, it would seem.

As luck would have it, it would only take a matter of hours for IDA to analyze the data which Jignesh thought would take days. It was about 6 pm when Sebastian strolled into Natalia's office to make the announcement.

178

"You'll never guess," Sebastian started.

"What is it?" Natalia couldn't even hazard a guess. There were so many sticks in the fire, from IP addresses to VPNs.

"IDA has already analyzed the whole data set and has live input right now and it is giving me suggestions. It is highlighting a set of traders that it thinks are coordinating. It looks like there could be many traders, actually, maybe a thousand. They are all executing the same or similar trades within less than a minute of each other. And they are all in the fringe of the market, using the best offer trades to drive the market up, then turning around and selling. Driving the market down, then buying."

"How much is the capital?" asked Natalia.

"A lot, like a trillion dollars on each of these. It is gargantuan compared to anything I have ever seen. And nobody has noticed these. Amazing!" Sebastian's eyes seemed to be popping out of his face with incredulity. "I can try to locate them all, but it looks to be the same as the 2018 anomaly."

"And is it the same network, same VPN, same location in St. Petersburg?" Natalia knew the answer already.

"The IP addresses look and act the same. Can we hack them now?" Sebastian so wanted the answer to be yes and wished it to be right now.

"Soon. Let it keep analyzing. We will get down to that soon enough. I don't want to tip them off just yet," Natalia explained as she was beginning to envision the colossal size of the organization that would be capable of pulling this off. To have this much capital would require the resources of more than the entire economy of Russia. Whoever or whatever government was involved in this scheme was slowly increasing their capital by coordinated trading over the course of years or even decades.

"Was there an endgame?" she thought to herself as her uncle's words echoed in her mind.

～

CHAPTER 24: JIGNESH

～

Natalia was so elated yet devasted about her findings that she had to share them with Chip. It was after one o'clock in the morning in London, so she texted him in a hurry that day as she uploaded her data on the 2018 crash to a secure cloud server so that she would have access to it outside of her own servers at the Journal. She was extremely careful with the data and security. She hadn't even shared the news with her editor yet. She would do that in person after she received advice on her next moves from Chip. And she had a dinner date with her old friend Katya tonight that she was certain to be late for so she would have only a short time to relay this data to Chip and then to her editor. She swore her interns to secrecy before she left. They had already signed extensive nondisclosure contracts, but she knew how computer hackers were with sensitive information.

Just to make sure, as they all left the computer lab that afternoon, she disabled almost all of their abilities to edit or download the data. If there was one thing she learned in all of her dealings with fellow computer science majors at Oxford and ever since it was that she didn't trust anyone. Except for

Chip of course. There were only three people she trusted in this world. Her father, Katya, and Chip had always been the trio of reliable constants in her sphere. Now only Chip remained. Tonight, for certain, she would skip dinner with her old friend.

If her data was correct, the amount of manipulation of the markets outside of the view of the SEC and Treasury monitoring was immense, and this manipulation could make hundreds of billions per day for whoever was using it. And if her calculations were correct, her family's network was manipulating on a daily basis. The AI pointed to hundreds of points of entry, but they seemed coordinated and when added up, they amounted to 25% of the whole market trading on some days. They could short the market with 75% of the money and with the other 25% drive the price down, thus making double the investment in one fell swoop.

Could this be why there was such resistance to implementing the CAT monitoring program to begin with? Could that network prevent it from becoming operational? Because once it was operational, the gig would be over. To add to that, it seemed likely the Zorin administration was about to delay it again from all reports. Natalia was sure there would be intense lobbying by all involved to accomplish just that.

This kind of manipulation would be able to prop up the market at will but also could be used to tank the market if whoever was in control decided to do so. It seemed coordinated but from where? Was it her family in St. Petersburg or was it the GRU? If only they could find out which command was the first, maybe they could hack that IP address and find out what communications they were receiving. Sebastian was up to the task, and he could easily spoof a Russian IP address, so if the perpetrators discovered the hack, they would think it was coming from inside Russia.

Before they attempted that, she had to run this by Chip. She wanted the data in the hands of others she trusted before they tipped the criminal enterprise off to their knowledge. Who else should she get it to so the data would be safeguarded?

She quickly texted, "Chip, very important. Call me."

She wanted to send an encrypted email and an invite to the document. But even that was unsafe. She needed to directly connect with him.

As she left the Journal offices, she glided down Fifth Avenue swiftly and, as she rounded the corner near The Plaza, she felt her phone buzzing. It was Chip already, she thought as she reached into her back pocket to answer. As she looked at the caller ID, she noticed it was her friend Katya. Dinner tonight! She forgot again. She would have to talk to her later. She dropped the phone back in her bag and within a few minutes was at the back entrance to her condo building.

As she was dropping her keys on the foyer side table, her phone buzzed again. This time it was Chip, "Hello, Chip! I need you to download a dataset. Can you connect with me on a secure call? On second thought let me get somewhere safer." She suddenly decided, and wisely so, that her condo was not as secure as she thought it was.

"Yes, I can. What do you have for me? If it is bigger than your last revelation, this should be good!" Chip and Sam were in Cowes, preparing to leave for New York already. They were pacing the galley of his enclave making security preparations. Natalia made her way down to the lounge area in the central terrace patio. It was a public-facing network, but she would use the new VPN that Sebastian had prepared for her just today. She then called him again on the secure line.

"Absolutely earth-shattering, Chip! Okay, now let's connect."

She connected with him from the computer on a VPN encrypted call and continued, "This has been going on for at least a dozen years. Someone is making billions if not trillions of dollars on this. I am direct-transferring this file to you. I am telling you I have uncovered the crime of the century!"

"Trillions? Seems impossible!" Chip exclaimed as he almost fell out of his chair and dropped the papers he held in his hands all over the floor. He bent down, out of view of the camera, and Natalia laughed but continued.

"We have determined that someone is manipulating the markets with up to 25% of the market cap. And it seems to be a centralized command, and it may be in Russia, specifically St. Petersburg. Chip, my family may be involved. My uncle has made a lot of money diversifying Volkov into securities in the past decade."

"That would have been inconceivable prior to your last revelations. There are supposed to be safeguards for this. But I guess not if they are fringe trades. Are you sure it's not just computerized trading algorithms?"

"We are one hundred ten percent sure, Chip!"

"Okay, let me see what you have," Chip studied the data for a bit before letting out a sigh, "I'll look at it more closely but it doesn't seem to fit any other scenario and definitely seems coordinated in time and securities traded.

"What do you think I should do? I need to get this to law enforcement before anyone knows we have this information. I recently met an FBI attorney asking about our programs. He was working on some financial crimes. I'll call him tomorrow. Can you safeguard the data on your end?"

"Definitely," Chip assured Natalia. "Who was the FBI attorney?"

"That guy from Cambridge, Sean Stamos. Do you remember him?"

"Okay, our chief Torey is on the other line. He knows him. I seem to have a recollection of one of the rowers on their team named Stamos. Anyway, let's get your data secured physically also. We will want security beefed up on your server lab and your condominium. Can the Journal help you with the security of your data? When you talk to your editor, have them put a security detail on your floor. We also have some people who can work on this. They are also there to help you if you need them too. They are already there in New York near your condo."

"Okay. I have to go to dinner with Katya, then I will get back to the lab and get the Journal to provide more security."

"Are you sure you want to do that?" Chip questioned. "If your uncle is involved, Katya's family is also involved."

"I have to. I changed my mind about that. I have to look like everything is normal." She hadn't completely analyzed or

184

explicated the possibility of Katya herself being involved. She did seem to be a parrot for her uncle lately.

"Well, Sam and I are moving our operations to New York, we will be there by morning. I will send you information on how to get in touch with our security chief in New York. His name is Torey. Don't go anywhere without him with you."

There was not enough time to contact Torey prior to dinner, but this encounter with Katya went surprisingly smoothly. She endured the usual, exhausting questions about their impending return to Russia and the holiday celebration in France. Afterward, Natalia had the sudden feeling she needed to check on her interns. She headed to the Journal to increase security on that basement floor and to assess the security that Sebastian and Jignesh had implemented to prevent the hacking attempts that would be almost continuous over the next few weeks.

As they walked home, Natalia feigned the usual excuse about forgetting something at the office and dispatched Katya at the corner across the street from the Plaza. As she turned to walk in the opposite direction, she spied Katya out of the corner of her eye, looking at her surprisingly. And she was reaching into her purse. Natalia knew immediately. In that frenzied few seconds, she wondered where Torey was.

She would call to arrange for the extra security at the Journal. As she walked the few blocks, she called with the encrypted app the number Chip had given her.

"Torey? It's Natalia. Oh, I'm sorry!" she exclaimed as she nearly ran into a nun walking the other way on the busy sidewalk. "Torey. I just bumped into someone on the sidewalk. Chip wanted me to call you for assistance with security here in New York. He said you were nearby?"

"Yes, I'm very nearby. Don't be alarmed but our team has been outside your condo. We saw your exit just now from the restaurant. No need to be afraid. We are here for your protection. Are you headed to the Journal? I will send the team ahead."

"Okay, I understand. I just want to check on the servers and my interns to make sure everything is buttoned up for the night."

"Agreed, but after this, we don't need any unnecessary exposure. From now on you travel in our transport but let's try not to let it be known we are transporting you. I am one block behind you across the street. Don't turn around again. Your friend just turned toward the Plaza. She is on the phone."

"Alright, this is bringing back flashbacks of old Russia. This time they won't be fighting on their own soil." Natalia had been shielded from most of the turbulence of old Russia and knew it really had not been any better lately, but it seemed scarier back then when she personally witnessed friends and even whole families disappear. Her family had always been granted tight security and there were times in the distant past when they had to watch their backs even more so than now. "I'm almost there. I will call you when I am inside."

As she strolled into the front entrance of the Journal's New York Headquarters there was some commotion in the lobby with security crawling all over the place. She did not notice the several police squad cars and SWAT team that were around the corner from the main entrance. As she made it to the security clearance desk, she was greeted by her editor and the chief of security.

"There has been quite a commotion here. There have been disruptions all afternoon here. We've had bomb threats, you name it, we've had it. Where have you been?" for the first time her editor was grasping the gravity of her discoveries.

"I've been at the Plaza, uploading some of the data. Is the lab secure?"

"Yes, it should be. There is nobody except essential Journal employees getting in or out right now. Everyone else is working from home. And now the FBI and Secret Service are here!"

For a split second, Natalia was relieved. Then, the noises were barely perceptible, but she could tell from where they emanated. They were coming from the stairwell to the left of the bank of elevators, which led directly to her lab. Security officers ran toward the stairwell, which began to fill with smoke, and upon opening the door, the smoke bellowed out into the

186

lobby at Natalia's feet.

At that moment, in a flash, she grabbed the director of security and yelled over the commotion, "Come with me, we need to get to the lab!".

As they reached the opposite stairwell, and yanked open the door, two men in black suits walked swiftly by, flashing their badges, guns drawn. Natalia sprinted down the stairs to her lab, and as she exited the stairwell, with the dark, dank scent of smoke filling the air, she covered her nose and mouth with her shirt. She could barely see the outline of Sebastian, stumbling toward her. There was blood soaking his shirt over his chest and his shoulder, and it was briskly running down his arm.

"Sebastian!" she screamed as she ran toward him. "What happened?"

"We need to get to Jignesh! We protected the data.... The servers are intact! He's in your office!" He then collapsed.

"Stop the bleeding with your shirt," Natalia ordered the security chief, who immediately followed the command. She scrambled into her office to find Jignesh on the floor, and there was so much blood surrounding his body that she knew it was not going to be good. "Oh, no, no, no..." she muttered as she knelt at his side, cupped his head into her lap, and felt for a pulse. He was not breathing.

Just then, the paramedics burst into the lab and took over tending to Sebastian, and two of them knelt beside Natalia, also checking pulses and breathing. There was not much they could do for Jignesh at that point, but Sebastian appeared to be semi-conscious and breathing.

The paramedics quickly wheeled Sebastian to the stairwell, avoiding the elevator. "Where are you taking him?" Natalia asked.

"Closest hospital is Memorial," they yelled from the hall.

After several minutes, Natalia rose to her feet, with a steel resolve. She had to protect herself and her data. She had a gun in her office desk buried in the bottom drawer with a magazine in the opposite drawer. As she pulled them out, she finally thought to call Torey, who was probably outside watching this scene unfold.

"Torey, are you outside? One of my interns is dead, there were explosions all over the basement near my lab!"

"I think I heard that. Yes," Torey explained, "we can extract you if you need it."

"It looks like we may need some assistance getting out of here. There were two guys in black suits that came out of my lab. They looked official, like FBI or something."

"I don't think they were FBI. I just saw two Secret Service guys leaving. Not sure why they were here. I will have my guys watch their movements. Can you have someone allow us in? With guns?"

Natalia turned toward the Journal security chief, "I need you to let a security team in the front door and down this stairwell. And can you alert your men that the two official-looking men we met in the stairwell may have been involved in this!"

"We can do better than that. There is a side door into the garage down this hallway."

"Did you hear that Torey? Enter the garage and head down one level. There is an emergency exit door there. We will let you in."

As they walked toward the security exit, covering their mouths with cloths to avoid the smoke, they could barely see their way. At the same time, they knew their way instinctively. Feeling their way along the walls, they came to the door with the red emergency exit bar. The security chief fumbled with the myriad of keys on his key chain, and finally inserted the right key, unlocking the door. As they peered out into the garage, they could see the outline of two men coming toward them.

"What's your name and who sent you?" Natalia asked.

"Torey and it was Sam and Chip," he answered correctly.

"Thank God, we need to secure the lab!" Natalia exclaimed.

Torey noticed she had a tight grip on her firearm, which was an older MP-443. "Loosen your grip on that. Don't want it to discharge accidentally."

She lowered the gun and relaxed her arm at her side, still with the gun at ready. She seemed at home carrying a pistol, with the finger outstretched on the barrel, just as her father had taught her at the firing range when she was a teenager.

"I think we need more help here than just our team, to be honest. We can't provide security for a whole city block basement with just the three of us," Torey surmised aloud to Natalia and the security chief that there would be more attempts to disrupt her servers. "There is chatter about some heavy hitters in the area."

"Well, we have a few more options to call in," the security chief relayed, informing them that in reality the options were thin.

Natalia hoped there would be an army of options, for her servers' sake.

"Not to worry, I have plenty more options, we have three teams on their way," Torey sounded comforting in his confidence. He reassured her, taking her under his wing, guiding them back to the server room.

∾

CHAPTER 25: DOUBLED

∾

Earlier that day, before Stamos' team finally crossed the border into Ukraine along the Polish border, they placed diplomatic license plates from the Polish government on all of the G63s that they were driving. These G63 vehicles possessed one-of-a-kind armor from head to toe but were designed to look like they were authentic European vehicles. Some entered close to Lviv, and others crossed the border near Kovel. Their drivers were well-spoken in Polish, Ukrainian, and Russian. It is not an overstatement to say that linguists were the most important asset to espionage. The entries went smoothly, and they were soon entering the outskirts of the old European charm that is Kiev.

There wouldn't be much time to waste when they arrived in the city center. Similar to Bayerngeld, this bank was located in the heart of the bustling business and tourist district. In most instances, this would work to their benefit, as any escape route would lead anyone pursuing them through the crowds. They planned their entrance to be late afternoon to blend with the crowd, and followed a narrow alleyway, through a small tunnel to a small parking area behind a grand ornate office building. There was one building between them and Chernov Bank, but the offices that they occupied protruded posteriorly and offered a great vantage point that proved useful during their surveillance. Stamos was disappointed this parking area offered only one egress by car if the situation demanded a sudden departure.

"Our egress routes need to be changed immediately. Can you bring in extra cars? I didn't know this was going to be so tight," Stamos commanded his driver. "Place them in the crowded areas around us."

"Yes, sir. We will have to borrow some armored cars from the embassy. We can make it look like we are providing drivers for some of the young diplomats."

"That works," Stamos agreed while closely studying the skyline of the Chernov Bank. One thing Stamos loved about these ancient European cities was the ornate buildings and their scalability. Gargoyles and large ledges made for great handholds. Even better, the rear and sides of this bank retained their old drop-down ladders. How convenient he thought as he also scanned the roof lines of all of the edifices that surrounded this small courtyard-like area. "Alright, let's commence with the real surveillance!"

Just as the team set foot in the building, two of the CIA agents were walking down the stairs near the elevator. These were the advance troops who had already been in place for the past week. Having worked with them before in Germany a few years ago would help dispense with the formalities. Without verbally acknowledging them, Stamos signaled for them to return to the offices. They all jumped in the elevator and headed up to the top floor. From the minute he stepped into the lobby area on their floor, Stamos could see how their offices provided the perfect surveillance perspective. The top floor of this office building was one story above the roof next door. Sean could practically walk over to the top floor of the Chernov Bank and knock on the window. The gargoyles above seemed to be beckoning for him to climb them.

As they shut the metal cage at the door to the interior offices, the agents signaled it was ok to talk. Sean started, "Hey,

Tyler, Stan, can you catch up to speed on what you're finding and what assets you have in place?"

One of the men rolled out a schematic of the Chernov Bank onto the table and began to point out the locations of offices and servers of interest. There were two computer monitors on the credenza behind them and momentarily some surveillance video began playing, along with a real-time data stream, showing active pinging or communication from an unknown location into these server rooms. The advance team was able to discover the encrypted communication, but not the contents or the source. That would require similar techniques that they utilized in Munich.

If only this operation ran as smoothly as that one, Stamos thought. "What do you guys think makes sense to get into these offices?"

"Well, at night there is only one guard at the lobby area, but the building is very secure. There are no outside entity offices within. We have already sent agents to set up accounts there to check out their security systems. They are pretty tight on security. There is no real guise or subterfuge to gain entry to the upper floors. I think we will have to do this at night and break in."

"When do the last employees leave? If we are caught, we will need egress and we will need it to be early enough for there to still be foot traffic in the plaza area. Do you think we could gain entry at 8:00 pm? It would be nice if we could wait for a Saturday night, but we don't have time to waste." If Stamos was right, they would need to act quickly before the leads went cold.

"Yes, sir, almost all of the employees are out by 5, with everyone except the security guard exiting by 7," one of the other agents said with a slightly pressured speech.

Stamos asked pointedly, "Do you have roof satellite imagery and the infrared surveillance ready to go so we don't have any surprises on the other end? I think we can climb to the roof pretty easily. It's just a matter of how quickly we can break in without being noticed. Let's not have a repeat of 2016, shall we? Also, get me the schematics of the fire exit doors so we can reroute the door alarm."

Answers were provided to his satisfaction as he stepped back to appraise the men and the situation. It was good to have familiar CIA agents that he could trust, but at least two of these agents were present during the deadly 2016 incursion. If memory served him right, they also received medals of service for their heroics that night.

As night began to close in on the city center, Stamos was pacing the make-shift operations room, watching the surveillance monitors, waiting for the building to empty. The infrared cameras were in place but a few areas of the building were not penetrable. They surmised these were rooms with vaults. Seventy-five people had come into the building that day and seventy-three had left. "Time to go home people, we have work to do. There's always one workaholic in the business," Stamos muttered under his breath.

As they watched the last worker stand up from his desk and stretch, Stamos' men began to ready the tools of their trade. The only other man in the building was a security guard at his post on the first floor. Intensely scrutinizing the monitor showing the employee walking toward the elevator, Stamos began to think this mission could go off without a hitch.

It was barely seven o'clock in the evening and the team could use the cover of darkness to easily scale the single floor to the roof. It would be an hour before they began their mission, but they rehearsed their entrance more than four times during that span. All contingencies were planned for. If discovered, they would descend either the front or the rear of the buildings and all would scatter to one of ten exit vehicles pre-staged among the streets below.

Stamos again thought back to the last failure several years ago and his closest confrontation with death ever. The schematics were exactly the same, but the overall atmosphere was different, as the country of Ukraine was much more friendly to Western powers than it had been in 2016. Among the present team, these two other surviving members of that mission, the two CIA officers who were the backbone of the surveillance, had performed admirably that night. He didn't have time to reminisce. It was now time for action, the mission's triumph was at hand.

A few minutes later Stamos found himself one grasp-hold from the top of the building. As he lifted himself up to the roof, he identified the target rooftop door. As he neared the outline of it, he could discern that the alarm system was just as advertised. Two other younger agents arrived just behind him with some of the equipment he required to mirror the trigger switch. As it was deployed, they keyed the lock, and in a flash, they were inside the narrow stairwell descending with infrared headgear in place.

As they gained an entryway to the top floor, which was essentially one large room, with what appeared to be a vault in the corner with a trove of wiring exiting the top. This was where they hid the server room, but the door was ajar. That didn't seem right. One of the men was busy planting a few surveillance devices on computers nearby and Stamos headed toward the vault. Just then the silence was broken, and a bright blinding light flooded his infra-red sight. The door of the vault swung open and there was gunfire that immediately struck the other agents. There was nowhere to escape except behind a filing cabinet in the middle of the room. Stamos clutched his chest where he had been shot. The armor had done its job, but Stamos still struggled to breathe. He checked his hands for blood

The backup agents on the rooftop descended the stairwell and returned fire through the doorway. There were at least six of them, an ambush. How did they know? Stamos could barely think through the fog and pain. From his view, he could see his men in the doorway returning fire, when one of them was struck. Stamos unholstered his only handgun but regained enough strength to reciprocate a salvo to the side of the filing cabinet. His M4 remained in his duffle if needed which had luckily fallen only a few feet away at his feet. He rearmed his weapon from his belt-mount and returned another round. Other than the vault, their adversary had no cover to protect themselves. They were gaining the upper hand it seemed as he observed at least four bodies strewn on the floor between him and the vault. The gunfire stopped suddenly, and he could hear the final man drop. The team required an immediate extraction before more of the adversary showed up.

He struggled to get to his feet and ran in a crouched position toward the stairwell. Along the way, he could see the now obviously deceased young CIA agents. There was one heavily armed backup left in the stairwell, who helped Stamos up the steps. As they reached the roof, they needed to assess the egress routes, front, back, or sides. The front of the building was more lit up from the city lights. As they peered over the edge of the rear of the building two black vans pulled up to the bank building and the building they occupied. Those were not their vehicles. Their only choice was to descend the other side of the building, rappelling down to a neighboring building. They set their hook, and both descended in one swift motion, that actually seemed an eternity to both men. As they reached the ground, fortunately, the alley on the other side of that building had not been compromised as yet.

Both shed their gear except for their handguns and their duffles. "You go to extract point ten, I will go to four," Stamos semi-whispered. As they reached the front of the alley, the two men parted ways, left and right. Stamos briskly walked toward the busy plaza as the street they were on was not busy enough to blend in yet. As he reached the crowd, his senses detected more danger ahead. On the plaza, there were multiple non-tourist young men either sitting at benches or standing around. As they started to turn toward Stamos, he began to sprint to the opposite side of the fountains just as they started to erupt in blue-colored spouts of water. The extraction point was less than a block on the other side of the fountains.

This was just like 2016 with the Russians, he thought as he sought to muster all of his speed through the park. What if there was a mole? The extraction point could be compromised. As he neared the black diplomatic car, he could see more than one man at the car as police were questioning the driver. He ducked down an alley to the right and gained a hiding place in the triangular courtyard of a set of buildings. He brought out his phone and immediately dialed Chelsvig.

"We've been compromised. You need to take off immediately."

Chelsvig replied, "Roger that." There were some unintelligible words spoken in the background. "Are you safe? Can you reach the Canadian safe house? It is right beside the embassy."

"Got it. I can get there. I can hide out there until you get me a secure extraction. I think all of the present extraction points are compromised. Call it in and text me the code. This is just like the last time we almost got our asses handed to us, Bret! Only go through DNI channels, don't use the CIA, I think one or both of those two same agents who worked with us last time are doubled." Stamos rarely used Chelsvig's first name and only used it for dramatic emphasis.

"We have your location, and we have an extraction coming in one hour at the safe house. Coordinates sent to your phone. We will have to debrief this one in a bad way. See you soon. Godspeed."

Stamos waited only a few minutes before exiting the courtyard on the opposite side and made his way to the embassy area, having to cross the crowded plaza again, this time a block north of where he originally traversed it. Luckily, the men who were there previously had vanished. Once he was close to the embassy he walked an extra four blocks, north and doubled back to ensure he wasn't being followed. He entered the encrypted code with his phone and unlocked a back gate into another courtyard where he felt more secure. Being one building away from the Canadian embassy meant he possessed a failsafe escape mechanism since he would then have diplomatic cover.

Within an hour he was secure within the confines of the unmarked jet as the wheels retracted, ascending into the misty clouds of the Ukrainian sky. More casualties and no more information gleaned from this portion of the mission. Nonetheless, he had the utmost confidence that Point would uncover the identities of those involved.

"Well, that was an utter failure, and I think we had at least one mole. Do we know the locations of the two other agents?"

Stamos asked.

"No, we don't. We have the entire Eastern European section on it. Top priority. It does not appear they were killed in the ambush. Surveillance shows they exited the building and did not show up at extraction." In his mind, Chelsvig had already started to run down the activities of those two agents during the last mission and since, and what information they had access to. This included the identities of clandestine personnel that were compromised, including that of his star protégé, Sean Stamos.

"Well, let's let the CIA deal with that. We have bigger fish to fry," Stamos led, "If we can't get the information we need this way, we can get it through other means. You know this may mean that Bayerngeld is compromised also. Regardless, let's get back stateside."

~

CHAPTER 26: FIGHT AND FLIGHT

~

In the ensuing panic, Natalia made the call to Stamos, really out of desperation because Chip wouldn't arrive in New York for over 8 hours, and she needed help now. She had thought about calling her father, but he would probably just suggest she fly to St Petersburg. While the jet was still in Teterboro and could perhaps fly her to safety, she instinctively knew this was no longer an option. The information she possessed could implicate her uncle, so Dimiitri was also not an appropriate plan. She loved her father, but she trusted her instincts and her instincts told her that Stamos and Chip were now her only friends. She knew that Merlin Commerce provided first-rate corporate security, probably better than her own family's security, and could defend against most countries' armies.

Torey slowly informed her that Chip had already mobilized his entire security team in the US to rendezvous in New York. As part of the sprawling shipping and port security company, Merlin Shipping also employed a division that specialized in executive security at the highest level, which meant in New York, D.C., Chicago, Seattle, San Francisco, Los Angeles, and Miami he had access to security specialists and armored cars. Torey had been in New York all week monitoring the situation, ready to be called up at any time. He was staying a block away from the Plaza and had even watched Natalia from afar when she was jogging. He knew of her early workouts and the team was positioned outside the Plaza each day between 5 and 7 am to be ready for her jog and also were aware of her stops at the Java Cafe.

"So, you've been there the whole time and I didn't even notice you? And I thought I was aware of my surroundings." She vaguely remembered meditating about presence and awareness when she was stretching just yesterday.

"Yes, ma'am. You've had other followers also. Probably from your family. You will need to leave your domicile," Torey instructed her. "We may be able to extract some belongings from there after our teams secure your servers."

"Well, at least I don't have to return to St. Petersburg this summer," she quipped.

As Chip and Sam made the trip to the airport to fly to Teterboro, Sam found that there was an influx of flights into Teterboro that day from Eastern Europe. After the events of last night, he knew there could be more than the usual security issues. He had all the respect in the world for Torey, who was a former Army Ranger and now retired FBI agent who led personal protection teams in some of the most dangerous areas of the world. This was the guy he would want on his side in battle anywhere in the world. He already had three armored teams in place in Teterboro, Long Island, and Manhattan, and more on the way.

As Chip made his way back as quickly as he could to America, Stamos, also many time zones away, saw the incoming call and immediately answered. "Hello, Natalia. I understand you are getting somewhere with your program." Stamos and Chelsvig were still several hours away from the States, having just taken off themselves, after their chilling escape.

"Stamos, I am afraid some of the information I have is rattling some cages," she said, matter-of-factly.

Stamos tensed. "I am sure it has. This appears to be a wide-ranging syndicate that has operated undetected for years.

They won't go quietly. "

"I need help. We have uncovered more than just money laundering. This is market manipulation on a giant scale. A fourth of the market cap is involved. I think they are onto us. One of my interns who developed my AI is now dead and the other is in the hospital! Now I am afraid they are coming after me!"

"Wow, now that is concerning to the nth degree! Where are you? I can get you more protection." Stamos was offering assistance that he could furnish through the FBI, but he also had some private security contractors that were retired agents and Marines and would work alongside the FBI. Otherwise, he felt powerless as he was still more than a few hours from landing in Quantico.

"What is the situation?" Chelsvig asked.

Holding the phone so she couldn't hear, Stamos answered, "Natalia Volkov sounds like she is in danger like we suspected.

"Is she in Manhattan? Let's reroute to New York." Chelsvig was already on his way up to the cockpit. "After the last 48 hours of near-death experiences why not another adventure?" He also directed his communications agent to reach the FBI Counterintelligence Office in Manhattan for a conference call.

"Okay we are sending someone to help, and we are rerouting to New York now. I will call you back soon with instructions. By the way, where are you and where is your data?"

"My data is at the Journal computer lab on the basement floor. I have also uploaded part of it to my cloud account. I am at the Journal at my lab right now with Torey, one of Chip's security chiefs in New York."

As Chelsvig returned to the main cabin, Stamos had a request, "Let's send someone to safeguard her program and data at the Journal. Do you think we should have Steven Point involved? He could help with safeguarding the data and also with interpretation and investigation of what they have uncovered."

"Yes. Get Steven Point on the line. And what about her intern who is still alive? We may need him to decipher this data." Chelsvig realized this situation fell within both the

Counterintelligence and the SEC jurisdictions.

"Stamos, be careful about the Secret Service, Torey thought he recognized some of the men coming out of my lab as Secret Service."

"Secret Service? Our own guys? Hey, Natalia? Before I let you go, what hospital is your intern at? We need to send a protection unit for him also. And if the Secret Service is involved, we need to keep this team we assemble as close to the belt of Counterintelligence. Maybe even they can't be trusted. I know some people. We will arrange it from here. By the way, is that Torey Severin? I heard he left for private work a while ago."

"Yes, and my intern is at New York Memorial," she answered, relieved that Stamos was thinking of these details. She spent the next minute explaining to Stamos that Chip also had security details on the ground in New York.

Torey interrupted, "Once our team arrives, which should be in just a few minutes, let's get you to your apartment so we can assemble our team there for egress out of the city. That building is a fortress. We need to get out of this trap and this city is just one big trap. There are too many variables here."

Just then, Stamos' phone rang. "Look at that. It's Steven. Hello?"

Stamos put it on the speaker for Chelsvig to hear. "Stamos. I think we are running into some trouble here. Two of my top guys were just gunned down in Brooklyn last night. Security footage shows two white SUV's driving by. I've put stricter security measures in place for our team, but I think you had better increase the protection of your team as well. They may be Russian."

Chelsvig replied, "Yes, we definitely will. Steven, we have a situation on our end as well. Remember that Journal investigator we had spoken about, Natalia Volkov? Remember how I told you she had an AI that rivaled ARTI and your program? Well, as I told you, she is related to some really bad actors in Russia, and she is running into the same problems as your top lieutenants. She had both of her IT and computer programming specialists attacked. One is dead and the other is in the hospital."

"Wow, this is getting to be a coordinated attack on anyone who could find out about this trading."

"Steven, can someone from your team get to Natalia's Journal lab at some point today to, first, preserve and protect the data and second, help decipher what information they have and compare it to our own? I will send an outside security unit to your location to accompany you."

"Yes, I have two guys. Ok send the protection unit to the SEC building and we will go over to her lab with them. Where is Ms. Volkov? Do you want her to help us with this?" Point was getting restless, anticipating the danger his team was putting itself in.

"Yes, we are working on protecting her too. She is heading to the Plaza next to Central Park not far from the Journal offices. And Point? Don't trust anyone, not even FBI or CIA until we speak again."

As Chelsvig hung up the phone, Stamos recognized the look on his face from every other time they were up against the wall. That signature look, which Stamos had copied himself time and time again, meant it was "Go-Time" and no prisoners would be taken.

$$\sim$$

CHAPTER 27: ROAD RAGE

$$\sim$$

Chip had not yet told Natalia, but she would soon learn that the mobilization of his security firm in New York, Washington, DC, London, and other areas of the world was well underway. Once they all assembled in Manhattan, the most logical plan would be to meet the security team at his Long Island home to regroup. From the information Natalia had given Chip and Sam, they immediately recognized this had all the call signs of a Russian operation and, if so, even her father would not be able to protect her. Her father was a big player in Russia but not THAT big, but her uncle was more powerful. To Chip, the thought crossed his mind that her father could even be involved in this attempt on his daughter's life. If the operation implicated any of the big players in Russia, then it would require her uncle's approval to proceed.

During the short helicopter ride from Cowes to London, they opened a communication line with Natalia to give her some direction regarding Torey. "Hello, Natalia, it's Chip!" Chip didn't have to raise his voice, but he felt like he had to in the helicopter as it was old habit. "I hear you have already met Torey!"

"Yes, I have, Chip," she yelled, over the din of the still blaring emergency evacuation recordings. "It is reassuring, to say the least. We are leaving here soon to meet two other teams at my condo."

"Not a good idea. Change of plans, you are to meet us at our Long Island home, but be careful! Don't trust anyone in your former sphere, including Katya," Chip cautioned.

"Agreed. I was wondering where her loyalties lie earlier this week. She was parroting my uncle to a T." With each passing hour, Natalia became more and more convinced that Katya could have been a plant all along.

"Once you guys regroup, the waterfront at my home will be easier to defend. We will be there in about 7 hours. Natalia, you will be safe at my home, we have three tactical units that will be guarding you - with armored cars." Despite his reassurances, Chip wondered if it would be enough.

"Okay, that is a relief. We will be there soon. Torey is here and we are about to leave the Journal. And Chip, thank you for being there for me."

"You mean more to me than you know. It is only reciprocating all that you do for me, my dear," Chip revealed reassuringly.

Sam added from the seat next to Chip, "This is Sam, Natalia. Don't you worry, Torey will guide you to safety. The tactical units are the best at what they do, Natalia. Torey, let me know if you require further backups. More are on the way."

"We have to go, Sam. Our extraction has arrived. Let's go," Torey commanded. Within minutes, Natalia was spirited through the same exit door that Torey had entered, and they climbed into one of the three armored cars.

From the confines of the vehicle speeding through the parking garage, Natalia fought back tears realizing her family was trying to crush her whole world, "You have to know that the people that we will be up against are likely Russian and it could even be my family," her mind kept returning to this probability.

"Okay, it doesn't matter who it is. They are not going to touch us!" Again, Torey's confidence was comforting.

Tactically the best option was to egress immediately to the Queensboro Bridge to Long Island. Any plan involving a tunnel was not a viable option.

"Are you going to give me a gun?" Natalia asked forcefully.

"Yes, instructions needed?" he asked.

"Not if it is any usual standard issue M9 or Glock. They teach you these things in the Swiss Alps to defend yourself."

"Here you go, M9 standard. Don't bring anything along that could have a tracking device. No purse or jewelry, lose it out the window now if you have any," Torey gave her his second firearm from his tactical gear pack side holster. Natalia checked the magazine and safety and clipped the holster to her pants.

As Sam and Chip got out of their helicopter at Gatwick Airport south of London, the blades had not yet stopped so it was a bit difficult to hear each other as they jogged toward the oversized hangar that held the Airbus ACJ380 that was the flagship for Merlin Corporate Security. It could carry 100 passengers comfortably with four staterooms and had a garage that held four armored utility vehicles. The security team of 20 was standing with their gear ready in the hangar. This was only the second time Chip had flown in her, as she was usually reserved for Saudi Princes and heads of state. Her corporate codename was Guinevere of Camelot.

They swiftly ascended the stairs, and, as they were settling into the main cabin, Chip and Sam addressed the men to apprise them of the situation. They would meet one of Torey's units at their hangar at Teterboro airport, heading directly from there to Long Island. These men were very familiar with the US operation as many of them knew Torey personally and had been involved with him in security operations around the world.

Once they completed boarding, the men stowed their gear in the main seating areas. Chip and Sam headed directly to the conference room where the encrypted communication gear allowed for uninterrupted contact with the teams. They would wait until they were airborne to make the call to Natalia so they could use the satellite capabilities. It was a long flight over the Atlantic, but they were assured that so far Natalia was safely heading to Long Island.

"Sam, let's bring additional firepower to bear. Can we bring the Miami and DC teams up to Long Island? We can stage them at East Hampton Airport for an extraction if we need it." As they were lifting off, they set up the satellite conferencing lines with the three teams and planned for the logistics once they landed in Teterboro to make it all the way to Sag Harbor. The problem was at present, they didn't know where Natalia would be when they got there. By that time, she and Torey could have managed to make it anywhere from Manhattan to the Hamptons.

"Yes, let's do that," Sam responded. "I will conference them in next. Let's also get the tactical helicopter in the air now before we even get there. It could help Torey in case he is outmanned or gets pinned down on the road."

Across the Atlantic Ocean, Torey and his men had already cased the streets and sidewalks above the parking garage, and, as they passed the exit gate so far, the egress path was clear. The rest of the team planned to pull up to the side exit within a minute prior to the extraction so as not to tip their hand too early. As they reached the first stoplight, one of the men on the street growled into Torey's ear that there were two suspicious men on the street corner that they would have to account for. "Roger that, stay between them and the door."

As the team turned the corner, it was immediately obvious which men he was talking about, as Torey immediately locked eyes with them. Keeping Natalia ducked down in the back seat, they were around the corner in a flash, being covered by the team across the street. The extraction was going well so far, but given the look on the faces of the two Russians and their obvious Russian Army Spetsnaz appearance, it would not be the last they would see of these two. He was surprised to see they were wearing their blue berets in public in the US.

Now motoring through traffic in the SUV, the team was relatively safe as long as they didn't get stuck in side road traffic. "Okay, go, go. They know we are on the move. The longer lead we get on them the better. Assuming they don't have any listening devices, they may not know where we are going, but we need to plan for that possibility."

As they crossed the Queensboro bridge, they encountered unusually smooth traffic, but on the other side of the East River, the gridlock required some tactical weaving around the commuters. If they were delayed by any amount of time, it could allow the pursuing vehicles to catch up to them.

Just then, in the rearview mirror, Torey's driver spied the two white SUVs gaining ground on the tail vehicle. There was just enough traffic for the driver of the tail vehicle to slow the advancement but either way, they would likely encounter these guys sooner or later. Just as they were passing Flushing Meadows and were almost in the clear of traffic, there was a bottleneck caused by a car accident.

"No, no, no. Okay, be ready for an encounter here. Hopefully, they can stall them back there. GPS says this will be a short impasse. The only way they can stop us is if they ram us. Don't let that happen, John." Just then the tail car appeared to spin out of control as they were rammed by one of the white SUV's. There were enough cars between them though, and hopefully, they wouldn't ram all of them.

Suddenly a call came into Torey's headset. It was Sam telling Torey they had a helicopter on the way. They were conferenced in with the pilot. No sooner had he said the words, than from the North came a welcome sight. In this traffic, though, it would be risky to engage these guys. As the helicopter came over the horizon and drew closer, Natalia looked back at the white SUVs. "They're getting out of the trucks and moving toward us, Sam." Torey drew his weapon and released the safety.

A few of the Russian men indeed dared to bring AK-47 rifles with them as the deadlocked traffic allowed them to walk unimpeded toward Natalia and Torey. The Russians both noticed the helicopter too late as the rotor wash suddenly over-came them. One of them managed to shoot one or two rounds blindly toward the helicopter, but the team overhead engaged both of them. With the helicopter snipers having the tactical advantage, the men in blue berets were sitting ducks. The next targets were the white SUV which were not armored, and the tires were effortlessly punctured with a few rounds. Meanwhile, miraculously the traffic opened up as Torey's remaining two SUVs hightailed it toward the end of Long Island, with the helicopter guarding it from above.

"Well, they now know where we are going," Torey surmised to Sam over the comm.

"Don't worry once we get there, we will be safer. And I have some extraction contingency plans," Sam said convincingly.

It seemed like forever even at the speed they were hurtling down the 495, but as they reached the backroads of the Hamptons, they knew for now that they were alone. There was an SUV at the gate with multiple armed men, and they were motioned through with the gate closing behind them. As they pulled up the drive, the helicopter descended behind the main residence.

Both teams tactically entered the main foyer, while some of the men set up on both sides of the stately mansion. As they collectively breathed a sigh of relief, they observed there were now not one, but two helicopters on the lawn. Torey took notice also of three boats now perched on the beach of the estate with several men with binoculars setting up for sentinel observation. The teams seemed to be reaching garrison proportions and Torey and Natalia were starting to feel safer in this location.

Another call from Sam came over Torey's comm, "They want to speak with you, use this earpiece," he said, handing Natalia one of the earpieces

Natalia took it and placed it in her ear where she could clearly hear airplane sounds from the other end. Without waiting for their introduction, she remarked, "Chip, it seems we have an army here."

"You should be safe at the rendezvous point until we get there," Sam's voice reassured her.

Natalia hadn't told anyone yet. "Chip, I have some bad news. The men who were in the lobby and now chasing us... They were my uncle's security team. That speaks volumes.

They were looking to kidnap me at best and possibly kill me. My family is most certainly in the mix of this market manipulation."

"How many men do you think your uncle's security team might be?" Sam asked.

"I'm not sure, I think he has a team of twelve or so guys that are regulars, but I think they could triple that easily."

Just then another familiar voice came over the comm. It was Stamos. "Hey, Natalia, It's Stamos. I'm on this comm too. Glad to see you are alright. We have the FBI guarding your intern and your servers. Your intern is now out of the hospital."

"That is so great to hear," Natalia sighed with relief. "How are the servers?

"We have the architect of CAT and ARTI at your servers right now. His name is Steven Point from the SEC and Secret Service, he is on the line, and he is with your intern, Sebastian."

"Okay, that is great news! Sebastian is going to be ok! And maybe they can get some further information about the attacks?" She turned to look at Torey, but Torey's look didn't flash approval.

"Hi, Natalia! This is Steven Point. Can you unlock the servers so we can do some analysis?"

"Can I talk to Sebastian? He can accomplish that for you."

"Yes, Natalia, I am alright! I wasn't sure if it was okay to give them access." Sebastian's voice was trembling and sounded a little weak. She gave him the full operational passcodes but not the admin passcodes to protect the data.

"Natalia, this is Steven again. Based on CAT and ARTI and what your friend Chip sent us, we think there is an imminent attack on the US markets. The IP address trading patterns that Sebastian explained always match a certain pattern. First, they buy certain stocks in patterns that are buy-high trades that aren't detected. That sets the stage for a high market. Then anywhere from a few minutes to a few days later, they short the market and sell at the same time, this time with buy-low trades. They do this a few times a month on a smaller scale, but this time it appears to be on a larger scale like in 2018. We are attempting to pinpoint a better estimate of their operation timeline."

"I understand. We need to figure out a way to stop this. This is why my uncle wanted me out of the country this summer. I kept avoiding it. I think the fact Zorin could lose the election has them exacting revenge on the US for voting him out. Maybe they will wait until after the election." Natalia thought that was wishful thinking. Maybe Zorin had crossed them.

Natalia giving the operational passcodes to Steven and Sebastian was a necessary risk, she reasoned. At least they could not change or delete any data. The amount of money on the other side was enormous and almost impossible to prevent. It appeared the only way to prevent the attack would be to shut down the markets and halt all trading or get the SEC to prohibit short trading. Or they could freeze all of these assets, but how could they derail all of the assets these adversaries had under their control? While anything was possible, either of these options might rattle the markets just as badly as the original plot.

Stamos' voice came over the comm again. "We are on our way to you. Let's get you guys safely in the hands of career FB agents. I have a few offline assets that we can garner in case the FBI is tainted. You said the Secret Service may be involved. The same could be said of the FBI. We will land at East Hampton, and I will have a few bureau choppers waiting to take us where we need to go."

~

CHAPTER 28: SAFE

~

As soon as Guinevere reached US airspace, Chip and Sam predicted that bigger issues would arise than one small security team to handle. Sam's advance team on the ground called when they were only an hour out to tell him that there were several jets landing at Teterboro from Eastern Europe. It was not unusual to have several private jets landing at Teterboro each day as this was one of the main airports for those wanting to avoid the press and scrutiny at the larger airports of New York City. However, several Russian and Ukrainian flights in one day were unusual.

As they landed, they were greeted by a customs agent and two tall ex-marines in green polos with the Merlin logo. They each had sidearm holsters that were, for the time being, empty. They also had two uniformed, armed airport security personnel waiting next to two patrol cars positioned between them and the hangar.

"A lot of activity here today, and this is my first time seeing this type of jet that is not arriving from the Middle East," the customs agent queried Sam.

Sam responded, "We are Merlin Commerce, Security

Division, this is our CEO Chip Merlin. I had filed an emergency import license for these armored vehicles. They are American-made and titled. Our men all have business visas."

"Don't worry, we will get it processed. In the meantime, unload the vehicles in your hangar and we will inspect them," the customs agent assured them.

Sam reacted quickly, "Can we get a few of the men processed?" He wanted to get one of the divisions on the road with the vehicles that were pre-positioned at Teterboro.

Sam and Chip took four men who cleared customs and immigration quickly to the awaiting SUVs and as they climbed into the back seat, Sam remarked to Chip, "I think this is going to be a wild ride your friend is about to get us into."

Chip just nodded his head. "What gear and ammunition do we have in the back here?"

The driver barked out like military orders, "Sir, we were told there was the possibility of Russian contractors. We have every option covered. Got your Glock G21, Tavor rifles, and Several RPGs that are in the hidden compartment in the back, sir. What do you need at this time, sir?"

"Ammunition?" Sam asked.

"Sir, there are multiple clips for the handguns and the rifles in each of your doors and in the seat pockets in front of you. Also, you will notice some Kevlar vests hanging in the back, put those on. They have adjustable straps."

The time was after midnight by the time they pulled up next to the gatehouse of Chip's estate and were waved through. So far, no nefarious activity appeared to be anywhere nearby.

Most trips to the US commenced at this estate, and neither Chip nor Sam had witnessed this much activity here in all their years. It was a surreal sight to behold, all the vehicles and men milling around, yet the night was eerily silent, with the sounds of crickets and frogs in the background. The pair rounded the corner of the driveway with their security team to enter the main house, which was lit up like a shopping mall.

As Chip entered the great room, Natalia rushed to him and hugged him firmly. Natalia wasn't the kind of girl to fall into a man's arms like a weak human being but always hugged

214

with self-confidence even in these circumstances. She had always felt strong even when in dire straits. Even in the present situation, pitted against her own family, now more than ever, she felt determined to do the right thing and defeat those who would think she couldn't or shouldn't stand on her own two feet.

"I think I have a plan. To alert the SEC to block funds, or trades, or shorts would probably cause just as catastrophic a slide as the shorts themselves," Natalia announced to a surprised, yet receptive audience.

She continued, "What if we installed commensurate countermeasures in place? In other words, buy high when their sell-low trades go in, with the same amount of capital. That would counteract the slide and stabilize the market. Then the shorts would still be outstanding, the perpetrators wouldn't have the capital to shore up their losses, and then they would lose their shirts. Their sell-low would lose 10% and their shorts would lose their entire value as long as we could keep the specific stocks or funds high. We would have to match their trading in real-time. They would be powerless then to do anything."

Chip affirmed, "That could work. But how do we get that much capital? Natalia, did you say that they had assets of 9 trillion dollars? That is between ten and twenty-five percent of the market. Commensurate might mean we could require 25-50% of the market. Even whole countries don't have that kind of market cap."

"Let's run this by Stamos and his boss. They should be here soon," Natalia hoped. This was going to be a long night and would take a lot more than a gunfight to win in the long run. Luck was on their side so far.

Coincidentally, just then, Torey received a call on his comm that Chelsvig and Stamos would arrive momentarily with both a convoy of vehicles and two helicopters. "Here comes the cavalry," he announced, "this place is going to be even more crowded. How much landing space do you have on your lawns? He asked Sam.

"I think we could fit six helicopters, easily," Sam pointed

out. "Two more will be fine. We may want to keep two of our helos in the air. These perps obviously know we are here. They may start to try to come for us."

"Better to be on offense than defense, I always say," quipped Chip to lighten the mood, which received little to no laughter.

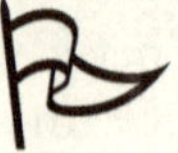

CHAPTER 29: THE PLAN

It was beginning to sink in for both Natalia and Chip that her uncle's diabolical plan was to weaken the United States if their efforts to help re-elect President Zorin and Jack Speransky failed or to prop up the economy with manipulations if their relationship remained a supportive one. The Russians had someone in Zorin whom they could control, and he was helping them spread the Russian ideology of autocratic rule around the world. And it was working in many countries including Syria, Georgia, Serbia, England, Spain, Italy, Poland, Africa, South America, India, Malaysia, and almost everywhere else that mattered. In their eyes and those of President Zorin, traditional right-wing conservatism had not worked over the past 50 years because there was too much balance of power wielded by those interested in freedom and democracy.

For Russian President Mikhail Prokachev his plans couldn't have been executed more flawlessly and with such tremendous results. For over 30 years they had invested heavily in stocks in several countries, concentrating on the US. He and his predecessors had leveraged their natural gas and oil reserves to control the management arms of hedge funds, brokerage houses, insurance companies, and even pension funds around the world. For good measure, even several stockpiles of gold were under their control. They now controlled 25% of the world's liquid capital wealth and it would take a miracle to block their scheme. Thirty years of suppressing their citizens' upward mobility was finally paying off.

However, now that their syndicate was on the verge of being exposed, they would accelerate that blueprint for disaster of the Western markets. The anonymity of all those involved in the trading would make it impossible to prevent the inevitable collapse of Prokachev's archenemies. Each of these hedge funds and pension plans had managers who were completely complicit Russian ex-pats and would follow orders to the end. Exposing all the actors in this plot and then stopping them would prove beyond difficult.

In the distance, Chip, Natalia, and Torey slowly began to hear the faint hum and vibration of rotors as they estimated the damage that could be done to the world economy as a result of this conspiracy of epic proportions. Natalia opined, "There would have to be a whole network of people in our country and our government that were at least aware of this plot. You can't just amass a fourth of the world's wealth in a concerted, controlled fashion without people in high places being involved in this."

There was continued discussion regarding who in the world would be able to command another 25% of the market capital to combat this sinister plan. In order to assemble the funds and coordinate the trading, they would certainly tip their hand at some point if they attempted to recruit someone on the other side of the coin. Heretofore, the conversations were being held around a massive kitchen island that overlooked the lawn behind the great house and Sag Harbor Bay. At that point, they spotted Stamos and Chelsvig walking up the stone walkway from the expansive lawn that now had four helicopters parked, with the blades of two of them still spinning slowly.

Torey and the other men opened the large sliding glass door to let them in. It certainly was a sight to behold as Stamos, decked out in a bomber jacket and black T-shirt, sauntered

218

in from the black night, with city lights reflecting off the water behind him, like a World War II movie star. He quickly appraised the present company before positioning himself at the center of attention. Chelsvig had relinquished operational control to him for the delicate cooperation between the FBI and the Merlin teams since he was more familiar with all the players involved.

"Hello, gentlemen... Natalia," he tipped a proverbial cap at the mention of her name. "I have been on the phone with Steven Point and your intern for the past hour and it seems that with this scheme, the Russians have been propping up the markets for the past two years at least. Every time there is a negative news or earnings event, the market drops some 0.5% or more, and then they kick in some buying and slowly over the course of a week or two, sell the proceeds. They must have a cash reserve to effectuate this. I am not sure why they are propping up the US markets in bad times. But also, for some time, possibly twenty years, they have been engaging in coordinated trading to make their profits."

Natalia spoke up. "The issue is, unless we have access to every name of every individual involved, it would be impossible to arrest them all before they execute their planned assault. If we were able to match their capital, we could combat their trades in real-time. That could mean more than 25% of the market cap would be required. And the Russians already have 25%. Who could we recruit that would not tip our hand as to our intentions?"

"The Chinese would have a lot of capital. Do you think they are in cahoots with the Russians?" Stamos asked, knowing fully well the futility of that plan. He realized that they needed Steven to be in on this discussion.

"It's possible. Let's think of that as a last resort," Natalia added.

Chip chimed in, "What about Ben Longley? He has more money than all of us combined and maybe more than God." He was talking about the tech guru whose online cloud data systems and other software systems were the basis for every cloud computing system in the world. And he was not a fan of

President Zorin, and President Zorin had made it well known, he was not a fan of Longley.

"He is probably in California. Difficult to get an in-person meeting at this time." Natalia surmised. However, in her previous forays into developing markets, she had met him, and she thought of him as a genuinely honest man, despite his ruthless business dealings. "Maybe we could teleconference him in if we can get him to return our call."

"I think we need to act quickly to prevent catastrophic failure of our way of life. This action could take place at any time," Stamos conveyed the urgency to the group as he took a seat at the kitchen island beside Chip.

As Stamos settled into his chair, Natalia rose to her feet to address the long mathematical odds standing before them, "How many hundred-billionaires would it take to make nine trillion dollars? And there are only three hundred-billionaires in the world. What we need is a large fund company that is not cozy with the President or any of those around him. We can surmise that any hedge fund or exchange-traded fund manager who is cozy with the President is involved. And our own Treasury Department is certainly not an option. What about one of our allies?

She paused for a few seconds, moving to a position behind Chip, then continued, "Spatial Cap Investments is the largest fund manager in the world, and they have assets of around six trillion. And then High Voyage Investments has the next most at over five trillion. If we can get 4 or 5 of these companies to put in a trillion dollars each, then we will be close. None of these top companies is close to the President, Tom Stanton, or the Russians. Almost all of the big banks have been very intimate with the President since he was elected. There is one bank that has not though, and that is Lexvale Bank. I am not sure of their assets, but they are one of the top five banks."

Chip provided another option, "Then we would need about 4 or 5 countries to chip in another trillion each. Germany, France, Canada, and South Korea have not been fans of the President and have knocked heads with him in more than one way, including trade wars. We would need to be able to bend the ear of each of their Secretaries of Treasury and probably Presidents. And without our own President finding out."

Chip had an epiphany. "All we need is one President or Secretary to bite and to bring the others on board. The German Minister of Finance went to Oxford with Natalia and me, and we knew him well. That is where we will start. Anyone else have any contacts?"

"Through the Journal, I can bring my editor on board, and we can reach out to Spatial Cap. Then we can use their CEO as a springboard to the other fund companies." Natalia's connections in the US financial sphere were increasing, but, on a whole another level of connection, her financial editor had previously been the vice president of Spatial Capital.

Chelsvig, who was quietly listening in the background then added, "That is a great start. Chip, if you need any help with Germany, I have the personal phone number of the head of the Federal Intelligence Service."

Chip, phone already in hand with his thumbs scrolling through contacts, responded, "That would help if we have trouble getting through to him. The fortunate thing for us right now is that it is early morning in Germany. I have a cell phone number that is pretty outdated. Let's see if it works."

As Chip was dialing their friend in Germany, Natalia was already on the phone with her editor, who was a night owl, but was obviously asleep when she called. Fortuitously, having independent wealth from his banking days, he lived on Long Island and was probably only about fifteen minutes away. She swore him to secrecy for now but needed him to join them right away. He was already aware of the FBI's commandeering of the computer lab, so Natalia did not need to explain the urgency of their plight. She dropped Chip's name also just to add to the credibility of the late-night soiree.

As Chip tapped the hang-up button on his phone, he started with the good news, "Alright, so far, I only told him it was a global financial emergency, but he said he had a meeting with the German Chancellor in less than an hour. He was heading directly to the Chancellery and would return my call as soon as he arrived. The Russians may have some active surveillance there in Germany, so I was directed to call through a secure line at the SCIF at the Chancellery."

Stamos had a warning for the group, "I know myself and Chelsvig and Torey have encrypted phones, but even those are not foolproof. We need to get to our own SCIF for this plan to succeed without detection."

Chelsvig added, "Yes and it's not just the Russians that may be listening to our conversations. Our own government may be listening. I haven't told the entire group, but the director of the FBI has tried to call me twice already since we landed in the US. He wants to know why we landed on Long Island and commandeered two helicopters. To know that information, he would have had to track us at this time of night, which is suspicious. Now the real issue is getting to a SCIF with secure communications that we can access without our government finding out. The second either Stamos or I swipe our FBI badges at a facility, someone is going to know about it."

"What about our plane, Sam? Do you think its comms are an adequate defense against the US government?" Chip asked.

Sam proudly responded, "Its situation room is as secure as any SCIF. It is certified by most governments as a SCIF. We have heads of state who travel with us. We have to wipe it clean after every flight, and we have security officers who monitor the encryption. But the plane is in Teterboro right now. It can't land or take off at East Hampton. Should we fly to it?"

Stamos could envision the plan taking shape in his mind and nodded his head, adding, "We can take the helicopters. From the lawn outside, I see we have room for all of us in these helicopters. The rest of the tactical teams will drive to Teterboro and to Manhattan. The FBI issue and our tactical helicopters all have defensive capabilities. We maintain air silence except to file plans last minute with Teterboro. We can probably make it there in 45 minutes. Get the pilots to start the rotors now."

Natalia rejoined the group just in time to add, "Everyone, I know this country and the world owe you all a debt of gratitude for what you are about to sacrifice in the name of the greater good. Godspeed and good luck." She was sure she was quoting some wartime movie, but the message was genuine just the same. They would need strength beyond their numbers. She turned to the window behind her and gazed out the window as Chip came up behind her and touched her shoulders. She drew a deep breath in with the force of her steely will and exhaled any negative thoughts she might have about the uphill battle they faced. We will win, she thought, at the end of it to cement calm intention into her psyche. As with all adversity she had faced in the past, she would overcome it.

A small flurry of activity started as a few of the pilots headed out to the vast waterfront terraces. Natalia's editor walked in, escorted by the agents guarding the front gate. Natalia quickly filled him in on the urgency at hand, as by this time all in attendance began to scurry about so there was not much time for fine details. However, it was the details that would matter in the end, for nothing in this plan would leave a fraction of an inch for error.

"I am concerned about the risk we are taking with flying. Any attacks they could plan, Bret?" Stamos asked his trusted mentor, Chelsvig, as the two gathered their gear for the next leg of the adventure.

His answer was not reassuring. "Surface to Air, I think that is possible. Could they have their own helicopters with offensive capabilities? I would say that would be a definite. I think at this point they are still scrambling to figure out where we are on Long Island."

"We are about to find out," Sam pointed out. "Our helicopters have some limited offensive and defensive capabilities but are not a match for surface-to-air. We just need to have a coordinated take-off to Teterboro at top speed and top ceiling so if they are waiting for us, we won't be easy targets. Once at the airport, we can board the plane and should be safe there. Let's maintain a unit outside the airport in the flight path, just in case. Anywhere within striking distance of that plane outside security."

Stamos, Chelsvig, Sam, Chip, and Natalia followed the pilots and other team members out into the dark of night to confront the unknown.

CHAPTER 30: GUINEVERE

By now, with the reality of the impending attack on the financial system sinking in and the reality of multiple witnesses being eliminated, Stamos and Chelsvig found themselves once again in crisis mode, which meant they were in their element. They knew that decisive action and attention to detail were the critical elements through which battles were won, and that required having the right warriors on the field at the right time in history. As they and the pilots scanned the horizon for any sign of hostile fire or boats in the water to their right, the chill of the night air was barely noticeable. When the four helicopters departed Sag Harbor, they made a rapid ascent and then hugged the coastline of Long Island Sound. They wanted to avoid the highways of Long Island and the airports to the South.

They would circle in toward Teterboro from the North where their flight path would not be expected. The critical turn would be entering the runway approach. The route would be expected and predictable but could not be avoided. To mitigate the risk, they would send their protection units still on standby to the streets near the end of the assigned runway. At that point, they would send one helicopter in as a sentinel to flush out any would-be attackers.

The pilot turned toward Sam and Chip to relay news from the tower, "We will be approaching from the north then circling all the way around the runway and finally entering from the south. We intend to swing around along the west side of the airport and bring it in on a tight bank at the airport border. That is a heavily traveled highway there and should be safe. It is right at the south end of the runway that there are a bunch of warehouses. That is where we will need our protection."

"Our plane should be at the southern end of that runway. Do a fast descent bank too so that we are higher in the air than normal coming across that border. I will send our protection teams to that area and also to the warehouse areas to the west. Then they will converge on the airport and air support hangar areas once we land," Sam answered, while simultaneously calling Torey on his commlink, relaying the same information to him. Next on the list to call was Stamos.

Stamos, from his jumpseat in the hold of the speeding helicopter, shifted his gaze toward the three other ones flying in a distant formation. Turning his comms on as he received an encrypted call, he answered, "Hello, Sam. Where do you want our men?"

Sam replied, "We don't have much time, we will be there in 15 minutes. Send them to the warehouse areas to the south and west of the south end of the runway. I will send two units there also. Then once we have all 4 choppers landed, converge toward the air support hangars on the service road. That will be the one weak link after we are landed where they could fight their way in or launch a strike."

Both Sam and Stamos radioed their respective instructions to their units with explicit warnings of an imminent attack. Shoot-to-kill orders were given by both men, knowing full well the ramifications of the Russians' earlier lethal posture.

Unbeknownst to the small Merlin army approaching, there was another ominous set of stocky Ukrainian mercenaries that had been setting up a makeshift command post at

226

the exact points that were already outlined by Sam. The protection teams, if they were not prepared for a firefight, would have a shocking surprise. Any team loss would mean a chink in the armor whereas a few unfortunately missed RPGs due to that loss would be devastating.

With the lights of Newark in the background, the airport was slowly coming into view as they circled to the North. What they couldn't yet witness was what was painfully happening on the ground. As the security team arrived at their position, they exited their G63s and began to set up their command posts. From the shadows behind them emerged several men, some with blue berets, but all were clad in black and heavily armed with drawn AK-47s in attack formation.

As the first shot rang out, and the first of the team members flew to the ground, contorted with the power of the strike, the men scrambled for cover. As luck or good preparation would have it, the team had already erected the mobile Kevlar barricades at the rear of their vehicles. A barrage of gunfire ricocheted off the surfaces with high-pitched pops followed by the telltale growls of the Kevlar giving its best effort at repelling the impacts of the armor-piercing rounds. The echoes from the surrounding warehouses made it sound as if the gunfire was emanating from everywhere. The resulting confusion caught the men off guard initially as they surrounded themselves with the protection by circling the wagon so to speak.

It quickly became apparent there were only two groups of fighters converging on them. At first outmanned, they commenced returning fire, having the advantage now that the barricades afforded. The commander crouched at the barricade and bellowed into his comm, "Position 1 compromised, two bogies, from South and West." They would soon have the advantage of the flank as the Russian and Ukrainian fighters from the West would soon be caught between the two Merlin teams, not to mention the FBI strike team soon circling in from the South.

Though they were pinned down, the present firefight situation resulted in the intended consequence, as the Russians were unable to set up any position to target the helicopters as they approached the runway. Without warning, the second team rolled in with guns blazing and immediately dispatched with one of the opposition teams. For the Russians, it was a complete flanking surprise, and they promptly found themselves lying in a bloodbath, decimated, to say the least.

As the flock of helicopters performed their high bank to the south and west of the runway, Sam detected the flashes in the darkness below. Pointing to the ground, Sam yelled at Natalia over the noise of the rotors, "Did you see that? We would have been sitting ducks flying in here without those men! Look at the RPGs lying on the ground next to them."

Natalia reiterated her thanks for the bravery of these men, followed by, "Wow, that is a textbook can of whoop-ass!" She gave a few more shouts of victory to add to their celebration, then pivoted to scan the horizon to be sure her unadulterated revelry was not premature.

The pilots were ready to deploy their flares if needed, but there would be no rockets propelled toward them at this time. To Sam, it reminded him of the countless protection missions in the Middle East while landing in hostile conditions below. He had definitely experienced worse situations with less cover than they had tonight in the usually safe confines of this dark night in New Jersey. Due to the bravery of his men, their approach so far was unimpeded.

One by one, the helicopters banked and descended sharply, and followed the proscribed flight paths afforded them by the runway lights. As each of them landed next to the Merlin flying fortress that was parked next to the hangar, several of Sam's men began to assemble in a defensive formation surrounding the plane. Before the blades could even start to slow, Chip and Sam jumped to the ground running toward the secure confines of Guinevere, the ACJ380 behemoth. The protective staircase was deployed below the forward landing gear with hanging curtains of Kevlar that Chip had never seen before.

Upon reaching the stairs, Chip exclaimed to Stamos, Sam, and Natalia, "Come on we have some work to do." The four warriors ascended to the relative safety of the fortress Guinevere to prepare for war, soon to be joined by Torey, Point, and the rest of the team.

∾

CHAPTER 31: ROGUE

∾

Jack Speransky could tell that everything he had strived for to bring together the movement in the US was unraveling before his eyes. His backers were becoming increasingly vocal regarding the financial monitoring systems that were about to come online. The ungrateful, jealous cousin he hated as a child had become downright threatening, just like the spoiled four-year-old he remembered. Nonetheless, their demands were not so unreasonable to the Senator, and he reassured them that he would speak candidly with the President again to prod him to publicly announce a delay in the connection of CAT. Surely, this would reassure their investors.

Coincidentally, Jack Speransky joined President Zorin as they were scheduled to attend a Rose Garden ceremonial meeting with the President of Ukraine. As he sat across from the President in the Oval Office, the mood was a somber one. The most powerful man in the world stood anxiously behind the resolute desk while Jack stood facing him with his hands leaning on the back of one of the dark antique chairs beside the desk. Both were impeccably dressed for what should have been a joyous occasion, the election of an ally of the movement in Ukraine.

"Peter, apparently, we have heard there is someone in our government not to mention some reporters who are digging into the financial safeguards that have kept our network of supporters in control of this recovery. These patriots have risked their financial livelihood to keep the markets heading in a positive direction each and every day. The checks and balances against market volatility and global fluctuations cannot be uncovered. Our followers have ensured the financial backing of the movement."

"I understand. You know as well as I do, that I have tried to break down the traditional supervision of the markets. I have delayed CAT for 3 years now. I don't see any reason that we couldn't delay it further," the President reassured him, taking a piece of candy from the secret stash in the side drawer.

"The fly in the ointment here is there must be a few in the FBI and the SEC that apparently Secretary Stanton and the FBI director do not have complete control over. They are rogue actors who are continuing to advance this CAT program. We must stop them before it is too late."

"Okay, Jack. Let's get Secretary Stanton in here now. I will shorten this photo-op with Ukraine. The assistance they agreed to for the movement will happen regardless of our backing anyway."

The President lifted up the phone to his secretary. "Sally, can you get Secretary Stanton here urgently? If he can't arrive soon, tell him we want to teleconference him in to the Oval."

After a few minutes, she buzzed in, "He will be here in 10 minutes. He was meeting with the Ukrainian delegation."

Jack hesitated, but then just came out with it, "You know, Peter, they are threatening to pull out of the whole deal. And that could have disastrous consequences for our markets. And so close to the election. We need to get on top of this right away." He said, wanting to even better portray the urgency of the matter. "They were already wavering and outright threatening because of our hesitation to go along with the G7 changes that they wanted. I know that they have been a pain in our side for a while now, but our economy is in great shape in no small

232

part due to their efforts."

"I agree. Let's get Tom to put some pressure on. I take it your contacts probably already have their own security measures to keep this from happening? I understand there has been a flurry of activity to stop this nonsense."

A few minutes later, Tom Stanton walked through the door, having been let in by the Secret Service.

The President started, dispensing with any hint of small talk, "Hello, Tom. We have a grave matter before us. Jack here has been telling me that this CAT program that we were supposed to be putting off, has been moving forward."

"I am unaware that it has moved forward. It is on hold as far as I know. Many of the connections that were mandated by law are in place but there is no data back and forth and no analysis. It is all at a secure facility in New York under the watchful eye of our SEC director. They have a new guy, Steven Point in charge." Tom moved forward; he had two good men who assured him they had disabled the persons in charge of the Journal computer lab. He would add the rest of the SS protection unit to the case.

"Maybe he is the rogue link. I want you to make sure that this is not going operational. It is now a national security risk. They are threatening to tank the stock market if we don't stop it. Get your guys to New York to make certain we have control over this."

"Understood, Mr. President. I will increase the manpower to handle the situation." Tom paced the floor on the Presidential Seal carpet beside Jack Speransky.

Jack spoke up, shaking his finger in the air, "Let's get my cousin on the line to discuss our strategy. They need reassurances."

"Okay, set it up through my assistant. I can assure them we are on top of this." The President recognized the need to control this situation before it got out of hand. His personal word should carry the necessary clout.

It was less than a minute later the phone was ringing through to the large digital phone on the Resolute desk. After a few greetings from everyone, the tone became serious on the other end.

"Listen, we have a lot riding on this investment that we have in your markets and decades of planning and building up the method to not only fund our activities but to assure stability to all of our work. If," the voice on the other end began but there was an ominous, long deafening silence for what seemed like a minute. "If," and another shorter hesitation, "If we can't assure the security of our systems, we cannot assure your financial security or your election."

All three men glanced around the room at each other with incredulous expressions. The President was the first to utter a word. He cleared his throat first, nervously. This self-made man was never nervous or at least never showed it. He learned long ago to command respect from his loyal employees, and showing any sign of weakness just never occurred. The seriousness of the statement and the weight that it carried in the President's election-obsessed mindset changed everything. "We agree, we have all of our resources on this. There will be no disruption."

"Good! We are on the same page," boomed the voice on the other line, "If you cannot assure this thing, the security, we must dump some of our investments. And you know what happened the last time we were not on the same page."

Tom looked at the President. The atomic bomb of what at first seemed to be an off-handed threat suddenly went off in his mind, with a cataclysmic effect. While he and everyone in his network knew this was possible, it seemed to not affect the other two as much. All at once, for the first time, he knew there was information to which he was not privy. Until now, to him, the network only existed to further the cause. At that moment, the existence of some outside force with its own goals was becoming all too apparent.

Jack and President Zorin searched Tom's face for signs of agreement that this was priority number one.

As the conversation ended the President gave his orders. Bring this under control or the network could be compromised. As they were leaving, they were all three sworn to loyalty in the name of the movement in not-so-pleasant terms.

234

The President attended the visit with the President of Ukraine, shaking hands ever-so-briefly, then retreated to the private residence in the White House.

The unraveling had begun, and he just needed to marshal all available assets to halt it. That's what he would do.

CHAPTER 32: RECORD HIGHS

The glorious stock market had continued its upward climb all through the spring and early summer despite multiple indicators of manufacturing slumps and softening of the real estate market. More than forty percent of American companies were posting losses, while big banks and investment companies were about the only sectors posting profits. While there were occasional warnings and dire predictions from talk show guests, most of the mainstream hosts continued to be the cheering section from the bleachers watching record high after record high go down in the books.

As the Dow happily marched to another milestone and subsequently blew right past it, those same pundits privately wondered if this was sustainable. They looked on in amazement as the Shiller price-to-earnings ratio remained above 25 and sometimes 30 for the longest time in history. But not very many were sounding warnings about what a continued presence above this price-to-earnings ratio meant. In the past, it had always meant an imminent crash. But during the past three years, the markets had defied gravity, so why wouldn't the exuberance continue? When the first few small dips occurred, a few had sounded alarms, but the markets rebounded. Secretary Tom Stanton held conversations with those few who had publicly worried about a coming recession and soon not a single choir boy was singing sad songs.

While the Shiller PE ratio was climbing, companies were privately expanding their operations, because money was free, as interest rates were at or near zero percent. Hence corporate debt was at an all-time high even in China where the lending spree was out of control. Even the most cautious investors did not heed the maxim of going home when the price-to-earnings ratio reached 30. It was this kind of hubris and overconfidence that was pumping the market. Everyone was treating it like the office Christmas party and throwing caution to the wind.

There was something magical about these times, most were observing. Everyone was high on the hog, traveling, vacationing, gambling, buying up companies, buying homes. There wasn't much that capitalism couldn't accomplish when there was free money available. All who wanted a job had one, albeit for low pay, and for those who didn't want a job, there were opportunities for investing. Those who were stashing their money in the markets, whether stocks or digital currency, couldn't lose. It was like an eternal payout at the slot machine, it just kept on spewing out returns.

Yet no one seemed to notice that some in the market were doubling those returns at the expense of those who were not shorting the dips. What was noticed was the sudden appearance of multiple billionaires around the world due to these markets, and everyone wanted to be like those guys. Yet the lucky few were not letting anyone in on their secret investment strategies.

Everyone knew but ignored the inherent risk; if any small event perturbed the market, it could spell doom. What were they going to do when there was no more free money and interest rates rose? Could the corporations pay off their debt? The governments of most countries were buying corporate bonds at a rate that essentially made money cost less than zero percent interest. This was like the historic printing of money of the 1980s but on steroids.

The present administration was no different, the US Federal Reserve was busy buying corporate bonds, but only those of the network's allies. The non-loyal were not invited to the party. There was no scrutiny and no accountability for which bonds were purchased. The network also had advanced knowledge of which bonds were acquired and when. Keeping it in the family, the assistant Treasury Secretary in charge of the purchasing was none other than a cousin of Jack Speransky.

The meetings of the G7+, as the name was finally settled on, came and went with much fanfare for the inclusion of Russia in the talks. They were welcomed back to the world stage with open arms by Tom Stanton and the rest of the administration to the chagrin of many Eastern European countries. Unfortunately, it was also on that stage that Russia continued to threaten the peace of Europe and the Middle East with its destabilizing influence. To say the oil-rich country was happy with its investments would be an understatement, however, those investments would not be able to sustain themselves if they were discovered by meddling bureaucrats or journalists.

With that happiness presently assured, the market marched upwards, past another record high and climbing. Almost a certain lock for re-election now, President Zorin had seen his poll numbers soaring. So confident was he in his chances, that he was holding back on his campaign spending at the moment. His campaign was buying stocks with much of its campaign contributions. After the telephone conversation in the Oval Office, his confidence took a sudden turn for the worse. A simple phone call to his corporate financial officer would hedge his bets.

These allies were a fickle bunch, and he certainly was not going to be the one caught with no chair when the music stopped.

CHAPTER 33: ACE IN THE HOLE

This was just the luck he needed after the past two weeks of getting shot at and chased all over the world. Now in the relative safety of the Guinevere private jumbo jet, Stamos, Natalia, Chip, and the rest of the team had set upon arranging the procurement of assets. Some of the groups were busy in the conference room and the rest were in the nearby offices that surrounded it. All of the rooms functioned as secure compartments, with encrypted conference phones and anti-espionage tactics. The lucky call came to Stamos through Chelsvig and they conferenced in an anonymous tipster who had an ally who could help. Unusual, but as these were not ordinary times, this tip came through the CIA. Normally this would not be the proper channel, but this was no ordinary tipster according to their contact at the agency.

They set a meeting for that day at the private air terminal in Teterboro and they promised to meet in the secure meeting room on Guinevere. He informed Stamos that he would be flying in from DC on a private plane, so conveniently he would not need to leave the airport. Stamos and Chelsvig discussed whether the new meeting could be a trap, or if it might only provide information that they already knew. At this point, they were running out of answers as to a foolproof way to stop this catastrophe from happening.

The teams working the phones already had the top two mutual fund companies on board and Germany was working on their end to bring the French treasury on board. They were nowhere close to having the 9 trillion they needed for the countermeasures to work. As Stamos, Chelsvig, Natalia, the Journal editor, Chip, and Sam sat in the secure conference room aboard the most sophisticated airplane in the world, they now needed an operational plan. How would they coordinate all of these trades to counteract the Russian plot to destroy Western markets? On the video conference monitor in the command room were both Steven Point and Sebastian, who were still holed up in the Journal server lab.

Sebastian had an idea and piped up, "We could copy exactly what they are doing. We have our own VPN that could be used here at the lab, and as we monitor their trades from that VPN, at the same time we can send the opposite trade requests to each of our partners who would do their own trading on their own platform. The only communication will be the stock market symbol and the buy and sell price. Each trade would have to be actuated within less than a minute, if not more like seconds, of the Russian trades."

"Can you set that up?" Stamos asked.

"Definitely. It will be pretty easy. We just need to get our partners to upload our VPN and IP address, and they will be online with us."

Stamos then turned toward Natalia. "Natalia, how is your work with Longley going?"

"Funny you should ask. He just texted me to call him. Let's get him on the secure line." Natalia's adrenaline shot up like a rocket, yet she remained calm, utilizing her breathing techniques.

Point turned toward Sebastian and gave him some marching orders, "Okay, Sebastian, we will let you get to work. Be ready to bring everyone online to your system. Set up a download site for your VPN. And set a secure key that cannot be duplicated."

Stamos wanted to make sure Point remained with them during this all-important call. He swiftly interjected, "Stay on the call, Steven. We will get on the board next."

As soon as Sebastian was off the call, Steven Point brought up some disheartening news that he had not brought up so far this morning, "Now that we are alone on this call, guys, I have been waiting to tell you this. I heard from the SEC director today. They are bringing heat down from above to stop our monitoring and shut ARTI down, so it is of utmost importance that we have Natalia and Sebastian's systems operational. Do you think we should send additional protection teams here? And how many more teams do we have at our disposal without involving the FBI director? CIA? Is anyone uncompromised that we can trust anywhere within our government?

Stamos, standing up from the conference room table, expressed his displeasure at the notion that the mechanics of the federal government were being used against them. He turned back toward the video monitor to show his support for Point, fully agreeing, "You are right, but I think there are a few we can trust in the Agency. Maybe before we get video conferenced in with Ben Longley, we need to get CIA involved for extra protection. We are maxed out on our in-house protection. And each of our fund partners also needs a team. Can you get the director on board for that?" he asked Chelsvig.

Chelsvig replied in agreement as well, "Yes, but let's go through section chiefs instead to get a few levels away from political appointees. They can get some of the heat off of us and they are off the board. They should probably be onsite here also. I will call them now. Remember what happened in Ukraine? I think there is a large amount of compromise in-house at the CIA also, so we need to tread lightly and involve as few people as we can."

They turned their attention to the video board as Chelsvig was dialing on the teleconference device sitting in the middle of the table. Steven Point offered his best assessment of the situation, "Even with these well-placed patsies, I would imagine that the Russians' support in our government will tank the moment they try to crash our market." It didn't take long for Chelsvig to shore up a few teams of protection from his most trusted allies in the CIA. As he hung up, Point sensed a new level of despair from Chelsvig, "What's the matter?" he asked.

Chelsvig replied in an earnest tone, "The Russian section chief confirmed, there are directives to shut down the SEC and the FBI investigations, and the CIA chief was just summoned to the White House. But we got our protection teams."

Natalia wasn't surprised in the least, "We knew this wasn't going to be easy with our government against us." She leaned over the table to reach the dialer and confidently and purposefully punched the buttons as though she was dialing a friend and not the world's richest man.

Typically, the most upbeat personality as the person closest to being a trillionaire in existence, Ben Longley had a somber, stern look in this picture on the screen as it became less pixelated.

"Natalia and Chip, it looks like we have a difficult and almost impossible situation. It's good to see we have the brightest minds working on this, though. How can I help?"

Natalia began, "Well Ben, it seems we need a lot of money to counteract what is happening. We have a group of Russian actors who have what we think is more than 9 trillion dollars of market cap at their disposal to do coordinated trading and then also to potentially crash the market. Now, we know that you do not have anywhere near that capital, but we have potentially others who are putting in a trillion dollars each. We are hoping to get 8-10 partners. And it seems the present US administration may be either involved or complicit in this so we cannot bring anyone on board that may be involved in any way with President Zorin's operations or allies. Any ideas?"

"Indeed, that is a tall order. As you know, I probably only have about 50-100 billion dollars of liquidity, but I think I could get a few people on board to contribute close to a trillion dollars of liquidity in the form of cash. My company could get close to 200 billion within a few days and I know three other people who could amass more than that each. I will coordinate it. What would we do with the equivalent of the US economy if we amassed it."

"The idea is to counteract each of these trades in real-time so that they cannot short the market. In the end, they will lose their shorts, and it will give us time to seize the appropriate capital. We don't even have our own treasury on board so it is not like we can seize it currently. We now think our own treasury may be involved or complicit." Natalia turned toward her editor and Chip. They were nodding in agreement.

"That is a risky undertaking. How do we do our own coordinated trading as this would be?" Ben had a point.

"Exactly. It is a risk, but the only way to avoid certain catastrophe. We are going to set up a VPN and our own coordinated trading, just like you say. You will need to download a VPN from our Journal site. And you need to do this on a completely secure system."

Just then, Torey knocked on the door and entered. "Our visitor has arrived; it appears it is a Secret Service plane."

En masse, the whole team walked out the conference room door to peer out one of the few windows of the plane. He was right, it was a Secret Service Gulfstream jet, and it was pulling up alongside the Airbus. There was no tail number and no markings except in small letters by the door. Perhaps their tipster was more important than they thought.

"I thought it was just an aide in the Treasury Department," Chelsvig mused.

As the door opened to the G6 and the stairs dropped, they could see the Secret Service agents emerging. Natalia, knowing that Secret Service agents may have been involved in Jignesh's killing, stepped back, but then did a double take. Appearing in the doorway was someone they did not recognize, but he was decked out in a blue baseball cap, sunglasses, and a jacket with the lapel close to his clean-shaven face with his head down. He was young, in his twenties perhaps. Even if he was Brad Pitt, he would be difficult to recognize with all the disguises. He began to descend the stairs and kept his face lowered, looking at the ground.

"Deploy the secure stairway!" Sam commanded the pilots

who were sitting in the fore of the plane. The Airbus had a secret loading entrance below the front of the plane that looked like a spiral staircase in a palace. The kevlar curtains remained in place and the security teams were at their posts.

As soon as the rotary hatch was opened, two agents and their mystery guest boarded the plane.

"We didn't know our clandestine visitor would be arriving so officially," Chelsvig stepped forward and gave the official greeting.

"Well, I am not the only one arriving. My name is James Stanton, I am the son of Tom Stanton and his assistant deputy secretary. My dad is on the plane, we just wanted to ascertain the security situation. There is a lot at stake here. We heard you are the cavalry and the only opposing game in town."

"I guess we are. But we thought..." Natalia began.

Their tipster was indeed more important than they thought. "All clear." The Secret Service agent announced into his hidden earpiece.

Tom Stanton emerged from the plane and strode down the stairway in a dark blue jacket, hat, and sunglasses, mimicking the way his son had just stealthily sauntered down the steps. Two more secret service agents appeared behind him and followed him toward Guinevere.

"Greetings everyone," their new guest belted out as he alighted the top step and reached out to shake Natalia's hand first. "So, you are the one setting fire to the world's underbelly. Good for you, this world needs some heat where it hasn't been felt in a long time. What can I do to help you? I, for one, am not going to sit by and let them put the fire out. This network at first was seen as the means to stability, but I now know it is not meant for stability at all but for revenge against our good country."

Stamos fired a welcome greeting and a handshake, "Well, let's get to work. We need a few trillion more dollars. Let's get into the secure command room so we can explain our plans." They spent less than a minute explaining to Stanton in simple terms who was involved to counteract the Russians' plans.

As they entered the conference room, Stanton com-

246

mented, "As you know, we have a lot of powerful people against us, including the President, Speransky, all of Russia, and a large contingent of the financial infrastructure in the form of sham hedge fund managers. What is your plan?"

Chip chimed in, "We definitely have our work cut out for us. I think with our newfound team member, we have that much more of a shot. Natalia, take it away."

He let Natalia explain the plan in more detail since most of it was her baby. At this point, they were still all standing around the conference room, silently, as they awaited the approval from their official guest.

Stanton let out a heavy sigh, sank into one of the chairs, and suddenly the sour look on his face turned to a nodding smile. As the rest of the men and women observed his change in demeanor, they also sat down at the conference room table, ready for whatever assistance they might receive from the lone government ally. Stanton started the conversation with a caveat, "Okay, so I don't have 9 trillion dollars at my disposal, but I do have a good portion of that in the form of held corporate bonds that we bought. Probably 1 trillion of that is with three companies that are not part of the network. I will bring them on board. In addition, I have another 500 billion in relief package money that has already been earmarked by Congress that I could spend on purchasing company stock in a crisis."

The team thoroughly explained to the Secretary the logistics of making stock purchases and sales through the VPN that by now had already been created by Sebastian and Steven Point at the Journal offices. He was a little taken aback by how advanced the plan was to combat the Russians.

"Wow, this is far more advanced than I thought. I knew the plan was going to be a shade better than your average day trader or even Robin Hood, but this has a real chance of working. Can I set up my operations from here?"

"Yes, that would be best, to do it from here, so we can be involved. No offense," Chip commented.

"You can set up from the command room on this system," Sam showed him the controls to the side monitor. With that, they could very well be in possession of enough capital to buy

SEAN STAMOS
most countries.

~

CHAPTER 34: MASSACRE

~

It was less than two weeks until the election and to Peter Zorin, his whole Presidency was falling apart at the seams like a circus tent with runaway elephants that suddenly found itself without poles to support it. And there were rogue elements of his administration that were conspiring against him. He was going to demand action to ensure nothing like this could happen again. Somehow, he always knew that the FBI and the CIA would be the ones to undermine his policies and here they were about to cause the financial meltdown that, if severe enough, would be the nail in the coffin of his four years in office.

"Beatrice! Can you get me the FBI director? Summon him to the Oval Office and make sure the CIA director is on his way now. Also, get me Attorney General Blackmon. I also have some letters for you to type," he commanded. He needed to gain control over this situation. It was for the good of the country, he told himself.

"Right away, sir!" The answer came booming across the intercom.

As he sat alone at the large English Oak desk, he felt some

of the power he had grasped and ripped away from his adversaries four years earlier slip away. They had told him before he ascended to the office there was no way to keep the economy going this strong for another four years. Financial systems were cyclical like the tide they said and could not be controlled, and any attempt to modify the tides would result in a more severe reaction in the opposite direction. Well, he definitely showed them the error in their theories, and he was determined to continue doing so for four more years.

Thirty minutes later, he stood in the center of the room, in front of the resolute desk, while the FBI director, the CIA director, and the attorney general sat on opposite sofas staring at each other sheepishly. One of these accomplished men would not be leaving this room with their current position intact, that seemed certain to them.

"When I brought all of you into this administration this year, I thought we had an understanding regarding our goals for the next four years and one of those goals was to continue our singular message emanating from this administration. It appears there are some rogue actors that do not understand the importance of our strong economy to keep our country leading in the world. I thought by now this national security threat would be stopped. But I hear that it has not. Director Levy, the weight of this failure rests on your shoulders, and I am asking for your resignation."

The director of the FBI, stated unequivocally, "Sir, with all due respect, all of the men in the FBI are patriots fighting for fairness and democracy."

"These men are undoing the American way of life!" the President shouted. "Here is a letter, please sign it and leave it with Beatrice on your way out."

After the similar dismissal of the CIA director, the President slowly walked around the resolute desk with his hand on his chin. After both the FBI and CIA directors left the room, President Zorin sat down in the empty couch across from his attorney general. "What do we need to do to stop the revelations that will cause this group to undermine our democracy."

His attorney general noted with incredulity, "From what

I have heard, and I still only have rumors from the SEC that there is something bigger than either of us afoot here. I tell you honestly that I do not have all of the details as it is a joint operation with CIA leadership now."

"How can I stop these guys? I don't have control over the CIA, and I never have. The only people I seem to have control over now is the Secret Service. The election is a week away and I cannot have this distraction. I am asking for your resignation immediately."

"Sir, I think you are making a big mistake. This is foreign collusion." The attorney general arose from the sofa, took the letter that was the remaining of the three pieces of paper on the table, and exited through the curved door behind him.

"Beatrice, get me the Secret Service detail chief." Charlie was handpicked by President Zorin and was loyal to a fault. This was the answer. What he needed right now was loyalty to the country to save the day.

"Yes, sir." Beatrice's voice cracked as she sensed the gravity of the massacre at hand.

As the detail chief walked into the Oval Office, he observed the President's somber mood and looked back anxiously at the secretary as she closed him inside the room. "You wanted to see me, sir?"

"Chief," the President always called him Chief, though his real name was Charlie. The President paused to give himself more time to think of the right words. He restarted, "Chief, we have a domestic security crisis, and it is coming from within the SEC, FBI, and CIA. There are some rogue actors that are looking to dismantle the financial network that we have created to keep our economy in full recovery. We need to bring these people to justice. I have just fired the FBI and CIA directors, leaving a void of people who can get the job done. Can you assemble a team to investigate and capture these bad guys?"

"God willing, yes!" exclaimed the newly empowered detail chief. Previous to joining the Secret Service, he was an FBI agent in the field of financial crimes. "Do we know the details of who and where?"

"I am told in New York at the SEC and at the offices of the

Journal, and somewhere near Teterboro airport, even possibly on a plane there."

"So, we have three locations to secure. We would be taking quite a lot of men away from detail at the White House, but we do have a lot of firepower here that we can bring to bear. With the Phoenix planes, we can be in New York in under an hour. Do we need to secure you in the bunker?"

"No, I will be fine here. I need to meet with some of the cabinet under-secretaries."

With that, the patriotic agent left the Oval and gathered some men for the short drive to Andrews Air Force base where they would take the clandestine planes used for Presidential transport to Teterboro. He explained to the team there was an FBI agent who was a threat to the President. Their task was to investigate but to expect possible resistance.

Using their motorcade lights, in less than 15 minutes they arrived at Andrews. Chief noticed that one of the planes was missing, which was not unusual as they were used for training flights for Secret Service agents, and it was possible one of the President's children was out of town. It was not important, they still had possession of the other three planes. They would take all three to Teterboro to confront the first danger.

Meanwhile, on the Guinevere, Sam and the men were assembling the trading team. Minutes seemed like hours, but the band of billionaires and fund companies and the few countries were coming together like a rag-tag bunch. Just then, Bret's phone rang. It was Steven Point. Maybe he was having problems with the trading platform.

"Yes, Steven. How goes the work on the VPN?"

Steven's voice cracked a little as he started, "Well, we've hit a stumble on those arrangements. Looks like we have the mother of all hacking attempts against us here at the Journal and at the SEC. They are trying denial of service attacks from every angle on our networks. I'm not sure how they got into the network at the SEC, but they did. We are holding our own here with Sebastian leading the way. This guy should be working for us. So far, our network will hold as long as they don't find a backdoor in. Good thing we are using the Journal lab systems. Probably more secure than our own now that Sebastian is in charge."

"How is your physical security? Do we have enough men to counter an attack?"

"Yes, Bret, we have plenty, I think you sent an army battalion. This place is crawling with spooks."

"Make sure you have our guy in charge and keep track of the men. There could be moles even in these specialized outfits," Chelsvig warned.

The outfits to which he was referring were the specialized units in the CIA who were tasked with protecting valuable witnesses and they were trained in combat and hostage prevention. Luckily the computer lab that Natalia had set up was in the below-grade levels of the Journal building so they were less at risk of outside attack. He had absolute trust in his section chief whom he had known throughout his entire career.

Point proudly announced, "Sebastian and I are right now working on setting up our own Denial of Service attacks on their servers. He is using a different network, so the attack doesn't open up any vulnerabilities."

"Okay," Bret replied, "stay safe and keep that VPN open. It's our only lifeline."

"Tell him to use the research servers at the Post that the Journal sometimes uses to spoof sources," suggested Natalia. The Journal would use this back door to keep any surveillance from knowing where emails and telephone calls were coming from.

"That's a great idea," came the voice of Sebastian, "I was using the Journal's advertising server. I think they are attacking it now!" Each time she heard his voice, she thanked God he was still alive and thought of poor Jignesh.

"One more thing. God, I can't believe I almost forgot to tell you!" Steven exclaimed. "One of the sources of the IP addresses we are tracking? Guess who? Jack Speransky's hedge fund offices in New York. I can't believe they are doing it right from their offices, even if they are hidden behind a firewall and a VPN. We got these sons of bitches. It won't be long until they start the attack. Matter of a few days, I think."

Now all they had to do was wait for the bastards to flinch, Natalia thought as she prepared her mind for battle.

~

CHAPTER 35: ANOTHER ATTACK

~

The next several hours would prove to be the most impassioned and nerve-wracking experience of everyone's lives, including Sean Stamos and Bret Chelsvig. These two, in their storied careers, had lived through, though sometimes barely survived, dozens of deadly, high-stress situations. To survive this one, the crew of financial hackers would need to pull together as a team to create the comradery necessary for the motivation to vanquish their enemies. Already, in this fortress of a jet, pods of personnel were divided to execute trades within seconds of the Russian trade.

For their part, Stanton and his son had set up a command post and, after an hour of finagling, had full access to the capital he needed, filling one of the last gaps. Moments later, a collective sigh of relief occurred after the final piece of the puzzle, the second largest mutual fund company had agreed to the plan after considerable coaxing from the billionaire Ben Longley. It was no secret his data services company supported them to the tune of billions including extensive utilization of their mergers and acquisition division.

Natalia thus far had successfully flipped the tables on her

countrymen to the tune of more than ten trillion dollars with her plan, but she knew she could not have done it without her friends. Ben Longley, still present on the conference call, congratulated her, "Young lady, this is so impressive. Now, for the execution of the plan. Timing is of the essence. All data connections will need to be flawless for this to succeed."

"Yes, and I am sure if they have any inkling about our plan, they will try to disrupt our communications. I will be sure to warn everyone two and three times to protect their data connection at all costs," Natalia concurred. "We will reach out to you soon regarding your VPN credentials."

No sooner had the conference call disconnected when Torey burst into the conference room.

"Sam, you may want to come look at this. Three unmarked planes just taxied up to surround our plane. I don't think they are looking to play nice and I don't think they are Russian. I just commanded our team in the hangar to maintain a defensive posture. We also have teams outside the perimeter of the airport that could assist. I think either of them could reach these planes with an RPG if necessary. But, I think they are armored planes just as much as this one."

"I see that," said Sam, peering out the window. "I don't think they will have the firepower to affect us either. The best they could do is disable us from taking off. Even our power and communications systems are redundant and failsafe."

As Chelsvig made his way to one of the portals, Stanton was doing the same, and immediately called out, "Holy, hell! Those are the Secret Service Phoenix planes. They are indeed armored and armed to the teeth, too. Now there is no doubt the President has it out for us. Make sure to get pictures, somebody. Close the window shades."

Just then all three forward hatches of the sleek jets opened and the airstairs deployed on the opposite side of the planes. More than a dozen men swiftly exited each plane, as they could see their legs alight below the plane. They appeared to be in combat gear judging by the boots and camouflage.

Torey talked into his earpiece, "Ready the armored cars and be prepared to bring them out onto the tarmac. We have trouble brewing and these guys are heavily armed. Can you cover us from the hangar or do you want to advance on their position?" The whole room could hear a few unintelligible words through the earpiece. Then Torey replied, "Copy that. Bring in the outside teams."

"If we exit the plane, where are we going to go? We need to stay at all costs to maintain secure communications," Sam explained the answer to his question.

It was a tense several minutes of suspense as the security team on the plane began to pass around their gear and ammunition. Just then, the sound of gunfire erupted and they could hear the reverberation of shots ricocheting off the Guinevere. The armor was holding for now and the pilots called back, "Everything is holding. Everyone stay down in the hallway."

Sam gathered everyone in the interior hallway and opened a hatch that led down to a safe room. "This will hold everyone if we need it. If it looks like any of the doors are breached, get in there quickly. It has communications gear that we can use and its own oxygen supply. We will stay here in the hallway and keep the hatch open until we need it. From here, we can monitor their movements and counterattack if necessary. They will soon find our plane a bit more formidable than the usual jumbo jet. Even an RPG will not pierce this armor significantly."

As if on cue, Torey kneeled down in the hallway. "Incoming!" The sound of an explosion and a sudden jolt of the aircraft sent a few people against the wall. Natalia looked up from her position, nervously clutching the M9 that was given to her many hours earlier. She lent assistance to one of Torey's soldiers who had fallen against the bulkhead in the melee. Other than surprise, there was no injury to anyone with this salvo. A few more explosions missed their mark and created more noise and vibration than anything.

"Holding!" the pilots shouted.

It took mere seconds for Natalia's journalistic instincts to take over as she obtained evidentiary footage with her phone to chronicle the incident.

They heard another explosion and gunfire that was a

little more distant as the two tactical teams approached their position from the hangar under the cover of the advancing armored SUVs. Stamos crouched at one of the portals and observed a few of the Secret Service men that had been hit. As Torey's teams drew closer, one of the black Suburbans suddenly exploded in a fireball, lifted into the air several feet, and turned over on its side. A few of the men who weren't injured struggled to drag their injured comrades out of the vehicle to safety. Others scrambled to take up a new defensive stance behind one of the other SUVs.

They continued to advance and it appeared they were winning the game of attrition as only a few of Torey's men were hit with the explosion, but the marksmanship of the former Special Ops fighters was overpowering the President's only backing Army.

Suddenly, movement from their adversaries and acceleration noises from the jet engines occurred as all three began to taxi away and several men jumped onto the airstairs of the moving planes. On the fly, with the few remaining men jumping on and struggling to climb into the planes, the airstairs were lifted as they fled the area down the taxiway.

Torey yelled through his comm, "If that's all they got, then let's let them have it! Try to hit their landing gear with the RPG. Aim for the ground 3 feet in front of one of them."

A few seconds later Natalia watched with an aghast expression as one RPG skipped off the ground and into the left rear landing gear, exploding as it skipped. The landing gear buckled a little but did not give way completely. It would be insane to try to take off with that plane now, she thought, as the damaged wheel appeared ready to give way.

Torey's men surrounded the Airbus with the Suburbans and took up positions in case they returned. The three planes taxied down to the far end of the runway, and surprisingly were able to take off, the third plane spewing flame from a rocket device just as it started down the runway and shot almost vertically into the sky. Torey surmised they were not taking any chances on a failed landing gear.

"Well we are safe for now, let's get back to the communications so we can track the trading. Everyone double-check their connections to make sure they are still intact. I think the financial attack will occur any time now," said Chelsvig as he dialed Steven Point on the video conference board. "Steven, what do you have for us? Is everyone ready to deploy our countermeasures? Let's get everyone active on the VPN."

From New York, Steven shot back, almost interrupting his boss, his confident smile radiating from his face, "Yes, the trading system and communications on the VPN are both a go. You should be able to log on now. Let's contact all of our partners to get them on also. I am detecting some coordinated trading already, but it is just small stuff. Let's not tip our hand to these trades. They may be just testing us. Let's wait for the big ones that they will surely lose their shirts on."

Natalia quickly displayed the output from her computer on a video monitor to the left of Point's smiling face. She began working on an application program called a terminal command interface, which was a direct connection to Sebastian's VPN in New York. On the command prompt, the words "Free World VPN>Connected" flashed in red. She laughed and noted sarcastically to Point, knowing Sebastian was busy in the background, "Sebastian, perfect name for our VPN!" She continued typing with a smirk on her face. After a few more entered commands, she nervously hit the enter button one more time, and exclaimed, "We are online and systems are a go!"

"Okay, quickly! Call our team and get them loaded onto this VPN to coordinate our buys. We need to be ready immediately," Chip commanded the team, flashing Natalia a wry smile. As she reciprocated the look, her fingers had already returned to the keyboard, tapping in rhythm with the hum from the plane's electrical espionage suppression systems.

~

CHAPTER 36: THE BIG ONE

~

It would be hours of tireless monitoring of the Russians' activity before any more meaningful trades came in. They slept that night in shifts on the plane, with no imminent physical attacks arising from their adversaries, which surprised Natalia, for she knew more tactical teams had arrived beforehand. Still, Merlin Commerce had deployed more of her own teams surrounding the airport to defend against such attacks. Watchful waiting, cautious determination, and steely resolve would win this game, she surmised, just like she had always done.

"Incoming Trade" read the command prompt on the computer screen in the early morning, just after the opening of trading. The past few hours had been tense as every siren and flashing light was scrutinized to determine the risk of another armed incursion. Every so often, through the night, Steven would announce a few smaller coordinated off-market trades. It would make sense they would wait until morning as off-market trades were not official until trading hours. Now a much larger one appeared on the ticker, followed by another, and another.

"Here we go. This is the big one!" Natalia declared, as the

first of the trades would be broadcast to all of their partners. Each in turn would confirm the dollar amount and number of shares to buy back to all users. Each organization had a three-letter abbreviation to include after their confirmed trade to identify itself. In all, there were 14 organizations, individuals, and countries including the secretive US Treasury operating without the President's knowledge.

In order for the countermeasures to succeed, the trades had to be completed within less than a minute after the trades by the Russians. Equal in amount or more, the trades would counteract the price drop the Russian trades were designed to incur thus stabilizing the price and preventing the accompanying Russian short-trade from making money.

"So far so good," remarked Chip as they watched the ticker price of the targeted stock on another monitor. "Dipped slightly but recovered. Watch for any additional trades on that stock."

"This is financial Star Wars!" exclaimed Steven Point. "Their SCUD missiles are missing their marks due to our Patriot missiles!" He was referencing decades-old American victories in a now-forgotten time, apparently only to his own satisfaction.

Wave after wave of trades came and went that morning. All in all, about a trillion dollars' worth of trades within a few hours. This was an extremely large amount of trading volume and adding to the dollar value of the accompanying trades from Chip's and Natalia's team, the two equaled a doubling of what would be a record daily trading volume. Someone had to notice these trade volumes in the outside world. Why hadn't they noticed them before? Even if outside of the mainstream trading platforms, they were still public knowledge.

The Russian network was bold and, based on the stocks that were chosen, this attack was definitely aimed at the US markets to try to topple them. The targets were quintessentially American companies, many with the words America or American in the name, which meant many were banks and financial companies.

There was a pause in the action, and Natalia, Chip, and

Stamos glanced at each other, then up at the video conferencing monitor at Steven. "What are they planning? It's too quiet. I am sure they aren't finished yet. If they noticed our trades, they probably still think we only have a small, coordinated network," Natalia theorized. "We can match them toe to toe!"

On cue, in what seemed to be less than one second, in came the big ones, plural. Twenty trades in some of the top American companies (including Ben Longley's company) equaling two trillion dollars total arrived all at once. They were gambling all at once twenty-five percent of their remaining capital. They were obviously probing to see how much of a stockpile Chip and Natalia's team had, entirely like a gambler trying to flush out the small fries with a large bet. If they lost two-thirds of their capital on shorts and sold a third of their capital to try to make the shorts successful, then they would still have two-thirds of their capital remaining, but that would assume they didn't triple short or worse. Triple shorting a stock or fund meant that one would gain triple the loss on that stock for that day, but if the stock price increased, the attackers would lose triple the amount of that increase.

"Match it and more," Steven said over the video comm as the trade commands came across the VPN screen. "All of the fourteen partners responded, we are good. Let's load the pricing of these twenty stocks. There we go, all holding steady and... Yes!! An increase in most of them."

All eyes were on the ticker as they watched some of the largest companies in the world take a slight dip and recover almost immediately. The stock price of most of them actually increased. "If they make another one of those trade flurries they are finished. We have them matched dollar for dollar and more," Natalia informed the group, smiling from ear to ear. She allowed herself the luxury of walking over to Chip's desk for a congratulatory high-five. They hugged ever-so-briefly, for even Chip and Natalia had been caught off guard that their plan was working. Back to war, they went.

In both Natalia's command room and at the Journal lab where Steve Point and Sebastian held court, the mood was lifting from a nervous dread to a cautious optimism. However, it was painfully apparent that the battle had not yet been won, thus keeping everyone on edge, perhaps a little too on edge. Without a defined task other than monitoring the surrounding area for physical attacks, Torey took the opportunity to lighten the mood. He nodded toward Steven Point, still on the videoconference monitor, "Hey Steven, why does everyone trust the dollar?" Not waiting for a reply, he answered his own riddle, "Because it just makes cents." Completely ignoring the lightened mood, Chelsvig and Stamos steadily maintained their battle faces.

Stamos leaned back in his chair with his hand on his chin, deep in thought. He snapped out of it quickly. "What will they do next? They have already lost a third of their money so far. Will they go all-in? My bet is yes. I think they are taking some time to analyze our trade volume now to determine the origins of these trades that are opposing them. Without the equivalent of ARTI or IDA, I don't think they will have the means to accomplish that effectively. But if they get wind that entire nations are involved, they may back down."

With a shrug of his broad shoulders, Chelsvig folded his hands behind his head and also leaned back confidently, replying, "I agree. Hopefully, they think the opposing trades are just algorithms or erroneously that their pockets are bigger than ours. They may wait for a short time before draining their piggy bank, so to speak."

Natalia spoke up, "Let's shore up our resources, we don't want to leave anything to chance, and we definitely don't want to be out-traded on this final volley. Everyone, make sure that our partners are fully on board with the final tally. They probably even made some money with the last trades. And we have to believe there could be interference or propaganda being sent their way from any of our opponents."

Steven Point subtly added, "The previous joke notwithstanding, we need to have trust in our dollars. And our networks. Everyone, monitor your networks for intrusions, malware, or denial of service attacks. We will be fine if we are diligent and steadfast!"

Until the last penny had been counted, Natalia approached

this war as one of attrition, which, like a game of poker, would not be won until the last card was turned over on the table.

~

CHAPTER 37: SPIRALING

~

Meanwhile, in the cozy private residence of the President of the United States in the people's White House, President Zorin was sitting in front of the bank of televisions, with his suit jacket and tie casually tossed across the sofa next to him. His Chief of Staff was pacing behind him, and when the call came from his assistant, he knew who it was going to be. "Yes, let him in. Send him upstairs to the residence."

All of the business shows this morning were abuzz with the news of the trading volume and the sudden dip and recovery. There had never been a day like this in the history of the American stock exchanges. The volumes being traded astounded any of the analysts and talking heads who theorized that once again, similar to 2008 and multiple other events since then, there were automatic trading algorithms as the causative market forces.

Just outside the wide archway that entered the sitting room from the hallway, first just a cough and a firm clearing of the throat could be heard. "Mr. President," Jack Speransky began as he rounded the corner. "What on Earth is happening with our network? They are now more than threatening to back out of our deal. We have to do something to reassure them. Did you see the drop in the markets? I think that was another show of force for us to see the power they wield."

"Yes. I see that. Can we get them on the phone again this time? What can we do? This ARTI thing should be shut down by now."

Jack wiped a bead of sweat from his brow, as he had chosen to climb the grand stairway to the residence instead of waiting for an elevator. Other than being tall, he was not a physical specimen and was not accustomed to physical activity. "Precisely, but it is apparent from the network administrators that this journalist program from the New York Journal ha it out for us. She is sadly a relative of mine. Ex-pat. And will remain ex-pat. And hopefully soon ex. But for now, we need to do something about her. A show of force, so to speak."

"I can do anything you wish. Want me to send the FBI to the Journal now? Just say the word, and it's done."

Jack was now also pacing behind the President as his phone suddenly made a chirping noise in his hand. "Well, now, this could be them. It is on an encrypted app and from my cousin." As he paused the conversation to press the answer button, he placed the phone to his ear, "Privyet? Da, Da." He suddenly threw his hand up to his temple. "No, impossible." He paused for a minute, listening intently with a shocked expression, taking what was being told to him with mouth ajar. "No, you must be kidding. Let me put you on speakerphone for the US President. I am in room with him now."

President Zorin shot out of his chair and stood up so awkwardly it seemed he might fall over the antique coffee table in front of him. "What is it?"

With his hand covering the bottom end of the telephone, the Senator, with tears running down his face, stared into President Zorin's eyes and tried to gain his composure. "They are pulling all out, this will cause the largest crash in the stock market ever. This was what they have always threatened to do, but we didn't think they would do it. They are saying there are some Americans and British and Germans that are opposing their work in the network."

268

Pacing across the room, the President interrupted, "The Germans? What on Earth could they possibly do to oppose this network? The network should be all-powerful by now. Nothing can stop us if they just keep going with the buying."

An exasperated Senator Speransky added, his hand still physically muting their conversation, albeit ineffectively, "They think Ben Longley is part of it too, sir. He doesn't have enough money to oppose us, but with the Germans and others combined? Who knows? The network has lost over three trillion dollars on shorts today alone."

That revelation really irked Zorin to no end. And to think he could have ended any government contracts for that good-for-nothing leech long ago. He wished now that he would have put him in his place when he had the chance. "That traitor. I knew we should not have let him get so powerful. He was never part of our network of Patriots. Let me put them on the speaker so we can convince them. For the love of God!" He paused, staring out the window toward the mall and the Washington Monument, standing tall in its majesty, staring down at him. "This will kill our network if they tank the market. Everyone, even our entire campaign budget, our party, our allies, we are all invested one hundred percent. What they lose, we lose."

Jack, in a conciliatory tone, answered, "Alright Peter, let's see if we can get them to hold off a few more days so we can fight these traitors properly." He placed the phone to his ear, "Da? Da?" He looked down at the screen, relaying to Mr. Zorin, "They've hung up. I will dial them again."

As Speransky dialed on his cell phone, President Zorin's entire world spun around wildly inside his head. He couldn't wrap his arms around the proper direction, up, down or sideways. At one moment he seemed to have an entire army of allies and now nobody could save him if the Russians did not play along in this game of cards anymore.

"Da, da. Speransky, Da, da," he began, then hushed as he listened for the better part of an entire eon. Or so it seemed to President Zorin. Speransky could only listen. Then, "Nyet, no Nyet! You can't, we can still save this! Let me put you on speaker for the President. He is here!" He put the phone down as the President could hear that there was no longer anyone on the other line.

The President could only stutter, "They... They... hung up again? What did he say? He's your cousin and he's quitting on us?"

"I'm afraid so. If they go through with it, we're cooked. We can only hope they don't. I don't think Longley has the capital to stop them. He was talking revenge at the end."

"Well, do you think the American part of the network will go along with it?" To Zorin, the question was a valid one, but then Speransky began to shake his head, dashing any hopes the President had for one or two Americans to lead.

"I don't think they will know until it's too late, and most of our American network are Russian and Eastern European ex-pats and sympathizers to ensure the secret arrangement is kept just that, secret."

"So, when do you think it will happen? I need to make some calls to some of my brokers. You keep trying to stop this from your end."

Indeed, his broker was part of the network as it would seem and did not answer the call. The President put the phone down on his desk, less than resolutely.

CHAPTER 38: FAILURE

It was precisely 3 o'clock in the afternoon. There was one hour left in the trading day and already the markets were sizzling with trading. Natalia had just glanced down at her watch and had glanced from there up to Chip with a smile and that usual twinkle in her eye that Chip loved to see. There was an air of confidence not only in her expression but that of everyone on the entire plane. With the battles so far won, and with the preparation for the ultimate battle running smoothly, there were fist bumps going around to keep the pressure on.

"It's going to happen. I can feel it in my bones. Any minute now!" she exclaimed with every muscle in her body tense for the fight. She realized the negative effect the over-stimulation would have on her concentration, drawing in deeply and holding her breath for a count of ten. Then she exhaled for another count of ten while reciting an affirmation of their righteousness. Relaxed, she was now ever more ready for the intellectual fight.

According to the German chancellor, the Russian delegation in Berlin had requested a meeting with their Ministers, but the Russians were told it would have to be the next day. Flash mobs descended upon the Chancellery Building of Germany, with a protest pretexted on personal freedoms in the country. The internet networks at Ben Longley's company and their other partner, the mutual fund company, likewise were being hit with denial-of-service attacks from an unknown location.

Natalia held an urgent teleconference call with all partners, "The Russian network has most certainly discovered the origins of the trades and must have knowledge of all partners. Keep your networks secure. Create a back door connection to the VPN. We are also creating a second instance of the VPN for backup. That connection IP address is listed on the screen above. Do not use that connection unless you get locked out of the other one. Sebastian, is that connection active now?"

Sebastian confirmed the security and duplicity of their plan to all on the call with a promise to correct any issue on the fly.

Thus far all trading partners were holding steady, and their internet security was holding. All of the freedom fighters remained on the video conference and stood ready to repel the next volley of trades. One by one, the Germans, the French, Longley, the mutual fund, and Stanton signed off on the plan and contingencies. At the end of the call, all agreed to combat the internet attacks and to step up if any one partner had to bow out due to connection issues. With the call finished, only Steven Point remained on the line.

After he was sure he was the only one on the line, Steven sternly brought the mood back to battle-ready. "We need to beef up our physical and IT security even more. They are close to blowing us out of the water if they get just one network. If they deny two of our partners, they win! In Europe you know the Russians have a lot more ability to black out entire grids. And our satellites are also vulnerable to them."

Natalia was not sure why she had never thought of it before. "Why don't we get a backup grid from Longley's company? They do cloud hosting and satellite communications. Get him back on the line. Get the entire group back on the line."

It was a matter of just a few seconds before Longley's mug reappeared. "Can you arrange for us a backup satellite channel? We feel vulnerable on our satellite comm system here. And I think every participant in this will need a backup if these guys black out some grid in Germany, France, New York, California... what do you think."

As the rest of the partners also joined, Longley replied, "Great idea, I can have this link and communication system live in five minutes. We do this all the time, and I have my chief engineer in my office now. Just link a backup connection to our satellite if you need to use it. I will send the coordinates."

With that, Natalia, Chip, and Sam felt a little better about the next battle. It would not be long now, and they can't defeat us with our firepower. We hold the high ground in this battle, she thought. Now she began thinking aloud, "If the Russians are going to hit back, it has to be in the next 30 minutes in order to have time to purchase the short trades and then sell the down trades. We also need to make sure our security teams are ready."

Steven joined in, "It has to be within minutes, they are about to load it, I can feel it. I think I see the first of the shorts coming in. These are the trades. Okay, everyone. Battle stations. Send these out on my mark." He paused to verify his calculations and entered the information on the comm. "Now!"

The ticker for 30 stocks to trade scrolled down the screen quickly. The predictably American financial, insurance, and defense industry stocks appeared on the side monitor, all shorted. The trades were entered flawlessly by every partner and confirmed. There was a delay of about thirty seconds, and then the team was surprised to witness a dip in those same stock prices. Then they continued to decline, and then even further. The red numbers appeared like a blood bath.

Good thing they were not watching the live financial shows because all in attendance were in a panic as they watched the same data. The entire market appeared a full 20% lower in just a few minutes and the free-fall persisted into a never-seen-before negative territory. There were halts to the trading that afternoon at a 28% decline of all three indexes. When halts to trading occurred, only selling and shorts were disabled, but the damage had been done. Buying should still occur, shouldn't it? Natalia asked herself, then confirmed with her editor.

"What is going on? Did our trades not go through? There may be a short delay. If it gets to a 30% decline, they may make their triple short a big winner, but it has to stay that way until the end of trading." Natalia's expression passed from shock to anger and then to steel. She typed a few lines. "Steven, what do you think?"

"Give it just a little bit of time. We still have more than 30 minutes before trading is halted. As long as the SEC doesn't halt all trading, we are okay. Just in case, send another salvo. Send these trades." He typed into his comm device into the VPN everyone was sharing.

Their previous countertrade had almost an immediate effect, Natalia thought. Hopefully, this one would not be a dud. Could their network be disconnected from the trading network by the Russians? Could the Russians be disrupting the networks at the exchanges? It didn't seem possible, otherwise, the tickers would have stopped showing trades, and the markets would not be active.

Stanton typed in his trade and from his desk outside the command room, confidently confirmed, "Everything is going through on my end. It appears to be just a small lag, I hope."

Point saw it first, "You see that? Look at BTWZ, it is coming alive. So are the others. God that took forever. Watch it. Okay, coming up nicely. I want to see green, give me green!"

As the ticker symbols for the thirty stocks all turned green, Chip and Natalia were huddling over Natalia's laptop screen, and then Chip chimed in, "If Natalia's calculations are correct, as long as the prices of these equities stay positive, they are out of money. They should have lost everything. And our double investment just sent the prices for these three stocks far into positive territory. They couldn't respond even if they tried."

Natalia wanted blood from her unscrupulous uncle and his henchmen, "We should do more buying on all of these stocks over the next few days to assure a positive outlook and

274

to crush them."

Steven agreed, "They still have a slim chance of winning this battle but highly doubtful. The only thing I could imagine is some worldwide event occurring, and even with that, they might recoup a small portion of their money back, but they had to front so much capital, that it wouldn't exceed five to ten percent. These guys are finished, caput."

Ben Longley, spoke up from the video conference, "My team here is calculating that our network just made about ten percent on average return just during this last counter. Because by the time the trades went through, the market was down at least ten percent. You can't get much better day trading than that. By the way, could this be considered insider trading? We need to put any and all the profits we make back into these companies and not keep them. Just to shore up the prices. And let's hold onto the stocks and some cash for a short time here in case we need any more actions."

All on the video conference nodded their heads in unison, and Steven was the first to speak, "Agreed. This network's entire mission and goal is the counterattack, and all profits from this enterprise shall be null and void unless we need it for further combat. We should meet as an unofficial task force afterward to empower the monitoring that Natalia and Steven have only just begun."

Natalia proffered, "Let's look further to see if there are any smaller networks out there. Just because this was the mother of all demon trade coordinations does not mean there are not smaller ones already doing the same thing on a smaller scale." She paused for a few seconds as she looked at her watch, put her index finger in the air, and then brought it down swiftly to the face of her watch. "Trading is now finished for the day. Wow! I didn't think it was possible twenty-four hours ago. But so far, we have done it. Let's watch the overnight trading and keep a close eye on tomorrow morning's early trades to make sure they have nothing left in the bank, so to speak. Everyone, stay on this line, and we reconvene in the morning."

Steven wasn't finished, "Natalia, let me be the first to say how incredibly brave you are for bringing this to light, even in the face of your own family and countrymen, and against all odds. If it wasn't for your programming AI here, my program probably would have been shut down and none of this would have come to light."

Chip was the first to stand, looking around at the crowd and the green scrolling numbers before them, and he started to clap slowly but in a deep tone. Then, one by one, the others joined the chorus of congratulations to all the combatants.

Natalia began to blush, "Steven, it was as much you as me, and I also want to remember my interns Jignesh and Sebastian. Without them, we could not have had IDA up and running in time. We also want to thank Ben, our German and French partners, and Spatial Cap and High Voyage. Thank you from the bottom of my heart. You are braver than me, for you risked it all."

Behind Steven on the video board, Sebastian stood up from his computer screen and could be seen over Steven's shoulder. There was a tear rolling down his cheek, but the grandest smile on his face. Natalia's tears were already welling up in her eyes, but the sight of Sebastian and his smile, and the thought of Jignesh, caused the dam to burst forth with the salty tears that were held back for the past week by her steel will.

Even the German financial minister could be seen wiping his face as there was not a dry cheek in the bunch. They all started to hug. It would be a long night as they were not going to disembark until they were satisfied the war was won.

If there were any other moments in her life she had considered spiritual, and she had experienced many along this fulfilling journey, this was the most existentially satisfying of all.

CHAPTER 39: REDIRECTION

For the beleaguered Peter Zorin, the nightmare was just beginning, as worldwide headlines were spelling doom for his administration. Even his own party was bailing on any attempts at a defense that his loyalists were presenting, such as the economy was still good, or that he was the one that discovered the plot against the American economy. The entire Senate, with one vote against, agreed to hearings and a special counsel. The election would come and go in a landslide victory for his opponent, who didn't even need to spend the billions on advertising that was usually required to unseat an incumbent. A week later, he became only the second President to resign from office.

Three weeks later, Natalia and Chip escaped the limelight, news media blitz, and paparazzi in their secluded Swiss hideaway. The pair spent the snowy afternoon decompressing with three warm, loving St Bernards by a roaring fire in the chalet after a beautiful morning hike. Chip and Sam were not taking chances and had four advance teams in place in the four bordering villas. Chip by himself had never required this level of protection, and it reminded him of the details Sam put together for the likes of Gates or Elon. Nevertheless, with Russia defeated and reeling, the real danger had lessened, and his only care in the world was making sure Natalia felt secure.

It would still be a few weeks before Natalia would feel safe leaving the mountain compound. They spent their days cooking and reading, completely ignoring what they had just been through, avoiding television news altogether. Was there any comfort in this world, if your own family would kill you or abandon you for the love of money? How important was the wealth that her family had amassed over the past decade, built on shadowy trades and illegal schemes? What were her father's and her brothers' roles in all of this? She might never know, and she would not shake these feelings of betrayal for years to come.

Volkov Shipping was securely in the hands of her father now with her uncle gone, for he had disappeared without a trace. A tear came to her eye as she thought back through the years at how even her friend Katya was just a setup by her uncle to control the family. Her nearly fatal flaw in blindly trusting her family was now cured, but it allowed her to discover who her real family was and who cared for her beyond what money and fortune brought them.

As she basked in the orange glow and the warmth of the shaggy fur of the lads as they lay across her feet on the sofa, she wondered how long the Times would allow her to be on leave. Yet at the same time, she wasn't so sure that she wanted to return to the location of the violent demise of her beloved intern, Jignesh. Somehow, her old love of researching companies, stock offerings, and cryptocurrency now became the last thing she wanted to do. Maybe she would devote herself to philanthropy instead of money and capitalist ideas. Or sailing? The idea brought the faintest glimmer of a smile to her lips.

It was weeks later that the opportunity finally presented itself. With the benefit of time between the tragedy and that snowy December day, Chip and Sam could sense Natalia was becoming less tense about her safety, and it was then that they approached her. She was standing in front of a large window, contently staring out at the snow-capped Alps. Three weeks ago, she would not have stood in front of this window, no matter how bulletproof. The slight smile on her face seemed to evoke a sense of peace within her soul instead of the furrows and tears of a few weeks ago.

The mountains had just received a foot of snow the night before and transportation was becoming more difficult. For convenience and perhaps safety's sake, the globe-trotters needed to seek a better place to recluse, or they could be trapped here for the winter. Now was as good a time as any for Chip to try to peel Natalia away from her beloved chalet deep in the heart of the Swiss Alps. She had just remarked to Chip how she missed the sunshine, having not seen it for a few days during the blizzard.

Chip took the bait and ran with it, for now was the perfect timing. "Do you remember that we have an island in the Virgin Islands? Do you think that may be something you could handle for a month or two? Nothing but beach, windsurfing, and scuba diving. We could send the Merlin Wizard there in advance. How about it?" Chip queried Natalia. He was referring to their 150-foot sailboat that, through its four Kevlar sails, boasted enough power to beat any power boat. Its base of operations was in the Mediterranean, but she was equally as comfortable moored off their private island.

Sam piped up, "It would be even more secure than the mountain. And we have our island dogs, Luke and Molly there to keep us company." Of all the dogs Chip owned, these were the only ones that were not purebred. Rescue dogs from the islands were smarter than any breed he knew of, and he absolutely adored them.

"Yes, I think I could use some warmth from the sun, the turquoise water, and sea breezes. And we haven't seen Luke and Molly for over a year," Natalia sighed. "But what about the Cup? I am thinking that I want to help. Do you think there is room for me on the crew?"

Now that really lightened the mood. How could he have forgotten the Cup? "Oh my God, the Cup!! Let's take at least a few weeks. Then let's think about coming back to England early for the Cup preparations - when you are ready for it.

Send the Wizard, Sam. It can be there in two weeks. Maybe we can do a little training on-island. Our Cup Challenger is presently back in Sardinia for more sea trials. We can join them also if you would like." Chip hoped she would see that as a natural progression to easing back into society.

Sam replied, "Well, actually the Wizard is halfway there now, and we could be there as early as next week. Richard has offered his out-island as a base for one of our security teams."

"You are such a mind reader, Sam." Chip jested, since the two already had this discussion a few weeks ago.

Natalia, through daily meditation, forced her mind to think clearly about her life and the future. Letting go of the past, which included her family who would not let go of the past, was the first step to healing her soul. Changing her focus back to the future, where her career and destiny lay in front of her. That future life she recognized would always include Chip and Sam. She would never want to be without them because, as far as she was concerned, they were her family.

"Let's take a month, I want to get to Sardinia by the end of January to join the team. Can we?" Now that was a short question full of hope and optimism that was great to give witness to. Natalia's natural competitive spirit was infectious, and Chip was in complete agreement.

"You've got it." Chip and Sam smiled at each other as Chip embraced Natalia with a full-force hug for the ages.

Natalia wasn't satisfied with the agreement. "Alright, it's settled then. But we are training starting now, right? No relaxation in the islands. Can you bring the J-boats and the 470s? I want to feel the wind in all its power!"

"Of course, my dear!"

$$\infty$$

~

CHAPTER 40: AMERICA'S CUP

~

The spring winds on the Solent were ripping westward from around the point at Selsey. The northeasterlies were in full swing this week as the America's Cup was underway. The amazing AC75 under the British flag was showing her power in reaches, up-wind, and down-wind. Chip had been named tactician for the Cup challenge and Natalia was on board as well in one of the pits. Both of them had earned their stripes off the coast of Italy that winter in the tactics and skill training that took place under the more-than-breezy Mediterranean sky.

The sleek monohull had a narrow hull with a small crew pit on each aft. Toward the rear of each crew pit was a helm with a steering wheel that was utilized when the wind was coming from that side of the boat, which was the windward side, and therefore the sails were oriented on the opposite side. On the side of the hull was a mechanism to lower foils or wings down into the water. Generally speaking, the foil was the only part of the yacht in the water, decreasing drag and hence, making them extremely fast, slicing through the waves.

From Chip's position behind the skipper, it never ceased to amaze him the strength that the former little girl from Lake Geneva now possessed. She seemed even stronger now than she was at Oxford. Not a minute passed on the deep blue

Mediterranean without a smile on her face. It was now more apparent than ever that the sea was her natural home. Maybe it was in her genes, honed as they were over the many seafaring generations, to ride the waves as her ancestors once did. It seemed the closest branches of her family tree had abandoned the seafaring life in favor of money, yet here was the strongest branch named Natalia thoroughly embracing her maritime roots.

Her favorite position was firmly grinding the winches on the bow position inside the starboard pit. To spectators, the only hint there was a woman grinding was the small amount of ponytail peeking out from the rear of her helmet. Each race that week had come and gone with a few successes for the team, and they were solidly in second place only by a tie-breaker coming into the final day of competition. For six days they had been in close contention with the Kiwis from New Zealand and the score was knotted at six apiece. The winner today, barring unforeseen penalties, would take home the America's Cup and become the defender for the next round.

While she was not the first female crewmember in a Cup race, she would be only one of a few female starting crewmembers in the final challenge. Today, she was determined to be the first female grinder to win the Cup. This was certainly no small feat as most grinders were large men over 200 pounds, but she proved her mettle in the training grounds. Now in the moment, as the boats were staging to the start just outside the port of Portsmouth, Natalia looked back at Chip and out toward the windswept waves and thought of the Bol d'Or Mirabaud and the myriad of challenges she had overcome to get here.

The call came over the headset inside her helmet. It was Go-Time. And just as a few months prior she had risen to the challenge, so now again she must gather all of her will. For the past week, this grueling course had really tested her stamina, and every single muscle in her body was telling her they needed rest. Nevertheless, she persisted, despite all the odds. It was only one more day. Natalia was not one who needed external motivation, for it was all within. The grit to win was already in

282

every fiber of her being.

As she and the other grinders launched into their duties rotating the winches and controlling the sails, so too did this technological masterpiece that was the AC75 class. But launch might even be an understatement for what it felt like to Chip as the boat, which was slowly moving on top of the water, suddenly rocketed up out of the water and onto both foils and with a reach to the start, one foil was lifted so as to only ride on a single foil. That meant there was a mere 12-feet by 1-foot sliver of fiberglass plus the rudder touching the water as they were now in a matter of a few seconds cruising at 45 knots across the water toward the starting line. And they were in perfect position too, having jockeyed for the best angle toward the south to gain the advantage of the greater wind offshore. This was the upwind leg so they would be battling the easterly wind for quite some time as Chip and the Skipper managed the best heading to win.

Natalia and her grinding partner took turns forward grinding the sail in or out depending on direction. The sea spray on the upwind leg splashed over the bow with each wave they encountered, sending a salty spritz onto her face that she relished, screaming, "Yes!" into the air directed toward the maritime gods.

Both yachts were hurtling across 6-foot waves like they were ripples in a carpet. The gamble with the high speed while running on foils was the possibility of the foils losing grip on the water during any of these jumps across each wave. If there was a wind gust that occurred at the same exact time the foil was out of the water, the flying yacht would capsize. Dutiful Sam was keeping a watchful eye from a distance aboard a chase boat with high-powered binoculars. While the responsibility was not daunting to him, with the power couple committing to a partnership, he now had two high-risk targets to protect.

It seemed like only a few minutes later they were rounding the last mark, and the Kiwis had overtaken them by only a hull length. Chip yelled through the entire team's headset, "This is the final downwind leg. This is the final race! Don't leave anything on this water! Take it all home! Grind like you want this Cup!"

Then luck and skill began to turn the tide as Chip made a few crucial tactical decisions. And just like that, having gained on a wind shadow, it seemed like the Kiwis were just sitting still in the water as the British yacht passed by. There would be no further wind shadows that the Kiwis could capitalize on against the Brits as Chip called for a tack across the Kiwi bow. They were well ahead now, as the skipper agreed to the turn. They changed wheels and maneuvered their way across the finish line in front of the defending Team New Zealand.

It was an absolute triumph! There was not a soul on the mainland, the island of Cowes, or on televisions and computers across the globe who could not grasp the significance of this sailing victory in their native waters. The British had been sailing and controlling these waters for centuries, and now Chip and Natalia had a hand in bringing the America's Cup home to this island nation.

As they brought the boat down off the foil and settled down into a mere 15 knots speed, the feeling of satisfaction was a familiar one to these two who had just saved the world from disaster. There were congratulations abound, and the winner and defender headed to the docks in Cowes. Once on the boardwalk, Chip and Natalia finally had a chance to embrace, a strong full-arm squeeze that lasted for several minutes, simultaneously laughing and crying, as the emotions flowed between them. The Yachtsman and the entire boardwalk between it and the Royal Yacht Squadron were reserved for the celebration festivities which would last for days.

Sam joined the two heroes on their way to the bar for the real prize, a frothy Goddard's and shepherd's pie, which were the spoils earned by the victors. Served by his old friend James, accompanied by the entire crew of the British Yacht HMS Solent Surf, Chip and Natalia would become partners in business for the ages.

When the celebration was all over, Chip and Natalia were finally able to enjoy the Wizard sailing yacht with the setting sun behind them. Lounging in the sun-soaked British Virgin Islands, they could look back and remember the long year of heartaches and accomplishments. Overcoming the struggle against the family she thought she had trusted her whole life was the most difficult personal battle she had ever waged and she had, as always, emerged victorious. Now, her best friend in the world had evolved into a true family that would never change.

www.ingramcontent.com/pod-product-compliance
Lightning Source LLC
Chambersburg PA
CBHW032012120726
47902CB00014B/2090